CUTE MUTANTS

VOL 2:
YOUNG, GIFTED & QUEER

SJ WHITBY

ISBN: 978-0-473-53963-4 (paperback)

978-0-473-53964-1 (ePub)

978-0-473-53965-8 (Kindle)

For all the people who believed in the mutants this far

(yes, this includes you)

CHAPTER ONE

So this is my life: I'm in the closet and I'm making out with my girlfriend. That's not a metaphor—we're literally jammed into the tiny storage space off my hallway. It's dark and cramped and I care about none of that because her kisses, and please excuse the flowery language here, are like fucking whoa.

We're in the closet because I'm hiding from my pillow, two entire clocks, and the other sentient objects in my house. They're all way over-invested in my relationship. Yes, this is my bizarre and occasionally useful superpower: I talk to objects and they talk back.

Right now I'm more focused on the fact Dani has a mouth, and that it's objectively the best mouth in the entire world and why *her* mouth of all mouths is so good at doing this kissing thing. The gremlin lurking in my brain disapproves of my dazed contentment. It's the only explanation for why I pull away.

"Do you really like me?" I whisper. My hand is on Dani's cheek, and she turns her face slightly to kiss my palm. It's lucky my body is not entirely made up of water or I'd go sloshing out under the closet door and ruin the carpet.

"Yes, Dilly." I feel every movement of her lips. "I actually really fucking like you."

My inner gremlin has approximately ten trillion questions starting with *why* and *do you only date gremlins exclusively*, but Dani's talking again and somehow I'm smart enough to listen.

"I used to watch you at school." We're sharing breath, like air is in terribly short supply. This *should* be gross, but somehow it's unbearably romantic. "You were like a clenched fist. I wanted you desperately."

"Now you know I'm squishy, are you disappointed?" I touch her mouth with my fingertips and I can feel that she's smiling.

"I dreamed of unclenching you," she says, with a laugh in the back of her throat. She kisses me again and I honestly think I'll expire right here. When they find my body they'll be like *oh no what happened to poor Dylan, she left us so young* and someone will say *she got too many compliments and her heart stopped.*

"The grumpy one who's only soft for me," she continues. "Besides, you're not so soft that you'd shy away from chopping someone's hands off with an axe."

Okay, so that's a true story. In my defense, he was a villain with earthquake superpowers, and even worse, a predatory asshole. It seemed a binary choice between straight up killing the guy vs cutting his hands off so he couldn't use his powers. Now he's handless in some kind of secret jail. I haven't regretted it for a moment and for once I'm not lying to myself.

Possible sentences flood into my mind about softness and how a certain person could touch certain soft things, but I get locked into a weird anxious spiral. Kissing is easier than talking, and more fun too, so I put my mouth back to hers.

This time it's her that pulls away. "You like me too, right?"

I spend so much time in my own head, pulling my words and actions to pieces, that I sometimes forget we're all a bunch of islands. Dani is a confident and ascended form of human, but insecurities still swirl inside that impossibly sexy brain.

"Yes. I like you. I really really like you." My tongue flicks at the corner of her mouth and she makes a noise between startled and satisfied.

"I love when you do that."

My brain informs me that nestled among that sentence were the words I and love and you. It suggests that I say them. I want to strangle my fucking brain, seriously. The words are in my throat, perilously close to spilling from my lips.

A soft flumping sound comes from the door outside.

"Oh Dylan," a breathy voice says. "She's just so dreamy."

Argh. Fucking Pillow, ruining the mood. I bang my hand against the closet door.

"Pillow, get out of here," I growl, and not a sexy growl either.

"Come lay on the bed together," Pillow says. "It will be so comfortable. I promise I'll be quiet. That includes, but is not limited to, sighing or moaning or little happy noises."

"I don't believe you." There is history here. I mean, I love Pillow. She's always been there for me, right from when I first got powers. But she is thirsty as fuck and I don't need encouragement in that direction. I want to convince her to disappear into my room, but right now I'm too distracted to form coherent thoughts.

Dani raps her knuckles hard on the wall. Pillow's yelp disappears into the distance. I get jealous sometimes, because Dani has proper telekinesis and doesn't need to charm objects into doing her bidding. The downside is she has to be in pain to do it.

"Pillow's on your bed." Her hand tangles in the back of my short hair. "Flew her totally blind. Impressed?"

I can hear Pillow grumbling to herself about how she hit the wall, but I'm more interested in Dani's closeness than correcting her Pillow-flying skills. We find a very pleasant interlocking position in the darkness.

Making out is more fun than pondering my other big change. Until recently, the worst day of my life was my eleventh birthday, which came and went without a letter from Hogwarts. I was extremely unhappy about this failure on life's part. It may have triggered my last proper tantrum. I'm not fucking proud of that, but shit gets real sometimes. I got an obviously fake letter the day *after*, which did little to ease the vast existential pain of being a Muggle. These days, I'm more likely to fundraise for Lou to have his top surgery in the Gryffindor common room, but eleven was the good old days.

Now, seven years later, I have an invitation to a secret training school for people with powers. It was delivered by some asshole in a fancy suit, which is a big step down from an owl. Inside the matte black envelope was a single sheet of paper with a crisp fold. It had a lot of waffly language that took ages to get to the point but the gist was this:

Greetings to the insignificant mutant brat Dylan "Chatterbox" Taylor. This is your government speaking via its well-dressed mouthpiece of corporate assholedom. We know what you and your mutant friends have been doing. Here is your choice: come work for us and train as a real life superhero at Corporate Hogwarts, or be shipped off to your new lodgings in Corporate Azkaban.

It's fine. It's totally fine. I am the cartoon dog in the burning building.

I've spent my life dreaming of being invited to Xavier's School for Gifted Youngsters. Turns out irl it has the vibe of a Dark Kermit gif. I just want to stay in the closet kissing my hot girlfriend. Is that too much to fucking ask, universe?

The universe has other plans for me, and our pleasant closet interlude is interrupted by Pear. No, this is a real person, not another object. Weirdly, I don't think fruit is alive in the same way as objects are. I haven't spent a lot of time trying. Maybe I can convince an orange to peel itself? Anyhow, Pear is my parent. It's a pet name, like Mum is short for mother.

"Dilly? Are you home?" I'm pretty sure they know, because my stuff is strewn across the living room floor. Dani's is piled neatly beside the couch because even when we're staggering for the closet, she organises herself. "Dylan? Dani?"

"Back to reality," Dani sighs, and we half-tumble out of the closet together.

Pear smirks. Dani's lips are all pink and swollen and I bet mine are too. If I put my hand up to check, Pear will say something and they are so annoying with their smart-ass fucking comments.

Summers, simultaneously the stupidest and cutest dog in the world, throws himself at us as if we've been gone for hours. We both crouch down beside him to pay homage to his floofy belly.

"Find what you were looking for in there?" Pear grins.

"Yes." Dani winks at me. "It was just like heaven." Which even I know is a Cure song, but the fact that Dani knows it and uses it to have a little in-joke with Pear makes my heart feel stuttery and huge.

Oh why can't I be as effortlessly cool as my girl-friend? (Is there a sentence that isn't made better by adding *my girlfriend* to it, especially when the girlfriend in question is Dani Kim?) I find it hard to stop look-ing at her, as if she's an illusion who'll disappear if I break eye contact. Everything about her is one long, slow swoon. The precise shade of her warm skin, the dark eyes, the glossy swoosh of hair that falls down one side of her face. Even the scar, still visible through the prickly hair that's growing back on the other side of her head. She got it when part of a building fell on her. It's a long story, but it ends with me, an asshole, and an axe.

"We have another mutant party this evening," I say to Pear, who side-eyes me. We are usually the bestest of besties, but things have been strained. I blame the Yaxley Corporation for breaking the news I was a) a mutant and b) a fucking menace to society. To say Pear was unhappy is an understatement. Their biggest problem is that I hid it, because apparently it means I don't trust them and fucking ugh honestly.

They're making a point of being super nice to Dani. I don't know whether it's to provide contrast or because they're a genuinely cool parent.

I lean against the wall and watch the two of them interact as if it's easy.

Dani thinks Pear is badass, and okay the coat is kind of cool, but it is literally the exact same fucking coat as Spike wears in *Buffy*, so that's just jacking his style. Shaving your head and alternating between Joy Division and Nirvana t-shirts does not automatically make you awesome.

They're having a conversation about schoolwork, of all things, and Pear is using it to backdoor into discussing *Dylan's future*, but Dani is somehow making me sound smart and capable. She reaches out and laces her fingers with mine. I lean into her, like she's propping me up. The same insane urge resurfaces to tell her I love her. People don't do that, right? They don't blurt out proclamations of love when things are still Very New.

It'll make me sound crazy, and I'm not *that* crazy.

"My turn to stick something on the playlist." Dani grabs my phone. "I'm about to blow your mind. Pear, you probably know this one."

"This is so fucking embarrassing that my girlfriend shares my parent's music taste," I groan.

"Just listen to this song, Dylan. It's one of my favourites right now."

I get that this is girlfriend duty, to listen to terrible songs your crush likes but I have very low hopes. It sounds like it was recorded in a cardboard box. Someone squawks over the top.

"Is that singing?" I ask, aghast.

"*Listen*," Dani says intently and okay *fine* it's kind of a bop in the weirdest, sloppiest way. Five seconds later we're dancing around the kitchen until it ends and then Dani plays it twice more.

"They're called Neutral Milk Hotel," Dani tells me. "Holland, 1945."

"It's a terrible name."

Pear swoons over Dani's old person taste. "What else do you like?"

"I dunno." Dani feigns shyness. "Like PJ Harvey, Sleater-Kinney. My ultimate absolute favourite is Bikini Kill though. Kathleen Hanna is like..." She turns to me and there's the full delight smile on her face. "It actually makes a lot of sense."

I shake my head. "Really, because you're not making any."

"I'm just figuring out how much I like messy, foul-mouthed brunettes," Dani says.

Pear starts laughing and I don't even get the joke and like ugh okay so I've finally found Dani's flaw and it's so *boring* omg.

"I don't want to know anymore." I cover my ears.

"I'll play you some." Dani beams, but it feels like a threat.

"So this mutant party." Pear returns their attention to me. "This is pizza, right?" There's a glimpse of hope in their eyes, because it means they don't have to cook.

"Yes, pizza, whatever. This Yaxley thing starts *tomorrow*." It's actually fucking terrifying. It felt like a manageable amount of time away at the start, but now it's in my path screaming at me. "Unless you want to make a giant lasagna or something?"

"Very droll. Do you want to talk the plates out of their cupboards or shall I get them the usual way?" They keep doing this, making offhand comments about my powers.

"It doesn't work like that," I say with a sigh.

"You barely talk to me about how it works."

I fail to swallow my irritation. "Shall we do this now in front of Dani, then?"

Dani raises her hands as if she's surrendering.

"No, of course not." Pear slams cupboards open and shut. "I don't understand why you didn't *tell* me, Dylan." I guess we're doing this after all.

"It wasn't just my secret. It was all of us. I thought about telling you a whole bunch of times."

"You did?"

"Yeah, like that night when I talked to you about Lou. I was so close to spilling everything."

They frown at me. "But you didn't. I can't help feeling like I failed. You never had to come out to me about—" They gesture incoherently. "I raised you to love who you love and identify however you felt comfortable. But then you had this, and you kept it a secret from me like—"

"Like I didn't trust you?"

"Yes." They look at me with doubt in their eyes. "Like I'm a parent who won't give their child space to be how they truly are."

"Mutant's different. And I *wanted* to tell you. Of course I did."

"Oh, Dilly." Their voice is rough, tears shading the edges.

"You know I would." I lean into them.

"Wow, you two are so bad at fighting," Dani says. "Teenagers keep things from their parents. It's like an immutable law of the universe, isn't it?"

Pear looks at Dani thoughtfully, but we're saved from parental wisdom by a loud knock on the door.

CHAPTER TWO

"Hey, Dilly." Lou is on the doorstep, dressed in tight jeans and a Golf Wang t-shirt that shows off how muscly he's become. He smiles and fiddles with his spiky bit of fringe. Lou is Glowstick, whose power is emitting light and heat when he's turned on. He's managed to get a handle on it, which sounds dirtier than it is.

The weird thing about our situation is that it's not weird at all. Ever since we broke up, our relationship has fallen into a comfortable pattern that feels so much better than constantly adjusting and propping up something *romantic*.

"Come in," I say, but he's already walking into the house.

"Hi Dani, Ness." Lou gives Dani a side-hug and joins in with tidying up the living room and clearing enough space on the coffee table for pizza.

Emma and Alyse turn up together shortly after-wards. They both hug me. Before the superpower madness began, this was not a thing I did. Friends didn't come over, aside from Lou. I barely looked at a person, let alone hugged them. Now I feel like this group of weirdos is my family. I'd never say this out loud, because I have no desire to die of embarrassment like a Sim, but it's true.

"Pizza party." I spread my arms wide. "It should be delivered soon."

"Panic party!" Alyse corrects me. Her face elongates and her mouth becomes a dark and fluttering cavern. Her limbs drift loosely around her. This is her power, to transform based on mood, hence Moodring.

I ignore this and pat her on the shoulder. "We're the Cute Mutants. We'll crush this." I'm still not the biggest fan of the name, but I'm learning to accept the things I can't change. Maybe Yaxley will give us a proper name? No, we'll probably just have a fucking official sponsor with their logo on our clothes.

"I've been doing some research." Emma brandishes her laptop at me. "About our new corporate overlords." I try not to pull a face, but Emma can see it anyway. "Cheerful expressions only, remember?" Having her as the other paranoid one makes me feel better. She links arms with Dani and they disappear into a corner together. I suppress an urge to join them. I don't want to be that clingy person who can't leave her girlfriend alone.

Thankfully, I'm distracted by the arrival of the pizza and the final Cute Mutant.

"Hello, darlings." Bianca leaps up the stairs and frightens the hell out of the poor pizza delivery girl. She's dressed in a flowing black lacy dress, and has intense purple lips and black-rimmed eyes.

"Hey, Bianca."

"Fear not, my bébés." She helps me carry the pizza into the house. "I am here to set your minds at ease."

"And how are you going to do that?" I open pizza boxes on the table.

"I don't know, it just sounded good." She cracks up laughing, and I can't help but join in. "I've been hoping you or darling Alyse would cheer us all up."

"I am not the ray of sunshine you're looking for."

"Well *someone* better cheer my ass up." She slaps mine and throws herself onto the couch, dragging a box of pizza with her.

The rest of the mutants gather and everyone starts eating, although Emma's distracted by setting up her laptop. "I made a video about Yaxley. I've been doing research and it's super interesting."

"You made a video." Alyse beams at her.

"It's not that hard. It took like half an hour."

"Sure." I push pizza towards Emma as she casts her screen onto the TV. "Let's see it."

"Yaxley Technology Solutions." The deep voice reminds me of someone. "Where did they come from? What do they do?"

"This is you, isn't it?" I stage-whisper to Emma.

"It's a voice changing app. I wanted to sound like the movie trailer guy." She pauses the video and throws cushions at us until we stop laughing. I sit on the floor in front of Dani, leaning against her legs while her hands brush the nape of my neck. I never knew someone touching you like this could make your heart race so fast.

The video runs through a series of short clips showing various Yaxley technologies like police body cameras, combat armour, security software, robotics, and drones.

"Drones." Alyse nudges Emma. "You'll love them."

"I doubt they'll let me play with their drones. I can't entirely see why the government chose this particular company to handle what they call the 'extrahuman situation,' except they can put us in armour or lock us up if we step out of line."

"I should show up on the first day in my ACAB t-shirt," I say.

"Please don't get into trouble right away, child of mine," Pear calls from the kitchen.

"I also did some digging into the *other* company that was bidding for the government contract," Emma says. "They're a little more interesting."

"Jinteki Research Laboratories." It's a cyborg-ass female voice instead of Emma. "Life, reimagined." A logo of a tree in a circle dissolves into a scene of a laboratory. Every surface is either pristine white or glass. A handsome Māori man wanders into frame. He's dressed expensively with tiny-rimmed glasses. "Here at Jinteki, we're interested in guiding the next steps in human evolution. It is not the strongest of the species that survive, nor the most intelligent, but the most responsive to change. Jinteki means human, and we believe it is time for humanity to leave the cradle behind and reach for the next branch."

"Creepy dude." Bianca shudders and reaches for more pizza.

"Sinister dude," I say. Dani nudges my shoulder. It's an X-Men reference to the villain Mr Sinister, who is similarly obsessed with evolution.

"Maybe we dodged a bullet getting Yaxley instead," Dani says.

"Maybe." I lean my head back and Dani runs her fingers through my short hair. "I still feel weird about it all."

Pear wanders through and scoops up a piece of pizza. "I think you have to trust the government. We've got one of the good ones here. They wouldn't have picked Yaxley if there was a history of ethical issues."

"You're such a good citizen, Pear," I smirk.

They fix me with their best unimpressed stare. "Given you have little choice in the matter, you'd better toe the line and do what you're told."

I mutter something rebellious and Pear disappears into the kitchen.

"Are they cool about the whole mutant thing?" Lou asks. "I bet they're cool, aren't they?"

"Relatively," I admit. "Their big problem is I didn't tell them about it. What about yours?"

He snorts. "They're still struggling to accept I'm a boy, let alone a mutant. They signed the secrecy papers, but they've not mentioned it since. Like they're keeping it secret from me too. They've got their heads buried so far in the sand I don't know how they breathe."

"Through their asses." Bianca laughs loudly. "Mum signed the confidential thing and then got mad at me for drawing attention from the government. She's probably forgotten by now, since it doesn't directly affect her life."

"Mine are choosing to treat it as though I've won some kind of award," Emma says. "Like it's an extra bonus for being such a good student, that I get shiny new powers and special training."

Our Yaxley timetable is going to be fairly intense. Every day after school, we'll have two hours of training, then all day Saturday, and Sunday afternoon as well.

"Mine don't actually know yet," Alyse says. "I'm hoping it never comes up. As long as I can keep them and Yaxley apart, it should all be fine, right?"

Dani groans. "*My* mother wants to know everything about how it works. She's upset that it works from pain and wants to know what I did wrong to deserve it."

"Deserve it?" I ask. "What the fuck?"

"She's convinced it's my fault." Dani rolls her eyes. "She doesn't come right out and say it, but I think she blames me being a lesbian. Or else existential angst due to trauma." Her voice wobbles, and I reach out and take her hand. She squeezes really tight.

"I think Pear's kind of jealous," I say, to cover the slightly awkward silence. "They always wanted to be Nightcrawler and here their gremlin child shows up with some lame superpower talking to their pillow."

"Where *is* thirsty-ass Pillow?" Bianca asks. "Bring her out here and I'll give her a kiss she'll remember, as long as she consents."

"Bianca, that is my fucking pillow and I don't want you corrupting her."

"If she says yes, we could have a beautiful time together." Bianca purses her purple lips at me.

"The problem is she would give me a blow-by-blow account of it all, and I am far too innocent for that."

Pear reappears in the doorway with the last fucking thing I wanted.

"You asshole," I say.

"It's my fault." Dani ruffles my hair and leans in to plant a kiss on my cheek. "I thought you'd like it, because it's both cake *and* chocolate! Happy Birthday, Dilly."

Everyone sings while I cover my face and wish this wasn't happening, except I love every second of it too. When they finally subside, I lean back against Dani again.

"Ugh, I feel so old. Eighteen like you."

"Yeah, now you can officially drink. We can join the Army together. Vote. I don't know. What's good about being eighteen?"

"Nothing," I groan. "Except now I'm supposed to be an adult when I'm obviously fucking not."

"Not with that attitude." Pear looks at me fondly. "Blow out the candles and make a wish."

I don't have a wish. All I want is for us to survive this experience. Does that count as a wish? It takes me three puffs to get all the candles.

"You're supposed to do it in one," Bianca says. "It's bad luck otherwise."

"We don't need any more bad luck." I hope I haven't ruined my wish.

Dani slips a little package into my hand, and I unwrap it to find a necklace shaped like a little DNA spiral, except it breaks half way through. Etched along the spiral are the letters A-N-T. She leans over and pulls her top down a little. A similar necklace hangs inside her shirt. She fishes it out and presses it to mine so they fit together to make a smooth uninterrupted spiral that spells *mutant*.

"It's beautiful." My voice has gone all weird.

"I got it custom made. It's not too sappy?"

I shake my head and lean in against her. We hold our spiral together, hands tangled. My heart feels made of blown glass, resting in Dani's cupped palms. It's been prised open and is full of light and heat. How can my fragile body hold all this inside? I rest my cheek against hers, despite the risk of melting her with my intensity.

After finishing the pizza and the cake, as well as rehashing the conversation about ten more times, people want to go home and get an early night before our first day.

Dani spends a long time on the porch saying goodbye, but eventually tears herself away. It's hard to suppress the worry she doesn't like me as much as I like her. I don't know if I could have broken the kiss.

Alyse stays behind, and we end up in my room watching music videos.

"What do you think they'll do?" I ask. "Yaxley, I mean."

"Yes, I know you mean Yaxley because you won't stop saying their name."

"I hate not knowing what to expect." I squeeze Pillow until she groans.

"The downside of stopping kissing Dani." Alyse lies face-down on the bed, dangling one arm off the side. "Now your brain has time to freak out. You've got your head full of nasty X-Men stories where people take advantage of mutants."

"These people came at us full of threats. It's super fucking sketch, Lys."

"Look at it from their point of view. First we beat Tremor up with a baseball bat. Then we flew a car into a building and cut off his hands. We don't sound safe and stable."

"Wow, nice spin." I nudge her with my foot so she half slips off the bed. "We also saved a bunch of hostages and stopped Tremor from hurting more people."

"Yes I know that! But the other stuff is true too, and they're like boring government types who probably don't approve of axes and hand-cutting. Why don't we try getting on with them first? Your Pear is right, and Dani too. We've got good people in charge of the country. It's not like some places. You really think they'd throw us to the wolves?"

"I guess not." I tell her, but I don't really believe it. I think people are afraid of us. People always said X-Men comics wouldn't teach me anything, but it's not true. It's given me a glimpse of how people react to a new species.

"Listen." Alyse sits up so we're knee to knee. "If everything is horrible and you turn out to be right, you know I'm your friend. And your monster." She shifts into something fiercer, shaggy-haired with glowing eyes.

"Yes." My voice is soft but my smile is wide.

"Cute Mutants." Alyse tackles me all furry and wild.

I dream I'm sitting in Alyse's house. I'm obviously not in my own head, because Dani and I are beside me, curled in together like quotation marks. Dream-Dylan turns her face towards Dream-Dani's and I hear the soft sound of their kiss. Dream-me smiles, and there's an intense feeling between fondness and satisfaction, as if a mysterious puzzle has been solved.

Lou sits at the table doodling, while Bianca toys with a Rubik's cube. They pay no attention, lost in their own actions.

Dream-me turns to see Alyse in another chair. She's lit up from some unseen source. Pear has this painting by some old famous guy whose name I can't remember. It's a landscape under grey clouds with a shaft of sunlight slicing through to warm the world. That's how Alyse looks, as if everything is delighted by her presence.

I reach up and touch my hair, adjusting the soft fall of it. There's so much that it spills all over my shoulders. I've never had hair like this before. Alyse looks at me and her smile is incandescent. She opens her mouth to say something and—

I wake to faint grey light filtering through the gap in the curtains. Pillow snoozes faintly underneath me, and my other objects are silent and still. My alarm clock shows five thirty in the morning.

Today we go to Yaxley, gifted youngsters that we are.

I roll over to check my phone. There's a Snapchat notification from late last night. It's Dani sitting in bed, unfiltered and unfairly beautiful, wearing a baggy t-shirt that's slipped off one shoulder. She's blowing me a kiss. I consider sending one back, but the instant I open Snapchat and see my face I swipe it away.

Dani keeps telling me I'm gorgeous. I can't reconcile her words with what I see in the mirror, a plain face with big eyes and messy black hair that is legitimately untameable without an amount of effort I'm not willing to spend. Oh well. If she insists on being delusional, at least it's in my favour.

I get up and change into running clothes. Ever since we started proper training, I've settled into a half-assed exercise routine. Most mornings, Dani and I do a loop down by the river near her house. It's early, but I have restless energy so I jog around the neighbourhood with Summers until I see her doing warm up stretches at the end of her driveway.

When she sees me, she holds out her hand.

"I'm sweaty," I protest, but she pulls me against her and neither of us care.

We cut across the quiet street and jog through the green expanse that runs down by the river. Summers lets out a joyful bark and scampers off after some ducks.

"Dummy," I shout after him, but he doesn't care.

"It's nice to see you," Dani says. "I dreamed I was watching us kiss."

I stop running. "Wait, what?"

She pauses ahead of me and turns back, jogging in place. "Last night. It was cute."

"Super weird, because I dreamed about us kissing too. We were curled on the couch and I turned towards you and we kissed and Lou was—"

"Lou was drawing at the table." Dani tilts her head to the side, frowning. "Bianca had a Rubik's cube. Alyse was there too, with the world's biggest smile on her face."

The sun isn't up, but my shiver's not because of the cold.

"We're having the same dreams?" I reach for my phone to google spontaneous girlfriend dreams when Dani interrupts me.

"We're watching ourselves in the dream, like it's not *our* dream."

I remember all that hair and who wasn't there. "It's like we were dreaming from Emma's point of view or something?"

"Goddess," Dani says thoughtfully. "She created us."

"And now we're having her dreams?" I'm about to protest that it's nonsense, but somehow Emma can unlock mutant abilities in people. It's how we all got our powers, but where she got hers from is a mystery she's always shied away from. I've respected that, but if we're dreaming as her that means—well, fuck. I have no idea.

I grab my phone and text Alyse.

Chatterbox: hope u slept ok

Chatterbox: did u have any weird dreams last night

It takes her about twenty minutes to text back, while we run a slow lap by the river and I drag Summers away from over-enthusiastically sniffing another dog.

Moodring: well kinda i dreamed about u and dani
making out
Moodring: stfu not in a weird way
Moodring: and then i saw me smiling at me
Moodring: that bit was def weird

Dani's reading over my shoulder and she kisses my bare skin almost absent-mindedly, as if we're so comfortable that these touches are accidental. That thought almost makes me vaporise into the morning air. I have to press my lips together so I don't profess anything reckless. Dani originally refused to join the team because I had no regard for rules and regulations. I'm scared she'll remember that one day, but she's seen me chop off a guy's hands and didn't run away. I doubt I'll do that again. Fingers crossed.

"Do we tell Emma?" Dani asks.

"She can't control her dreams. Won't it make her feel weird to know that we're spying on them? I wonder if Lou or Bianca saw it."

"Maybe best to keep quiet." Dani doesn't look happy about it. Emma's her best friend after all. I don't know where I fit into the rankings, but I think girlfriend might be a separate category. "Let's see if it happens again."

We jog back to Dani's and I head home with Summers. There's barely time to shower and change. I have no idea what to wear to superhero training, so I end up in my Cute Mutants outfit. It's yoga pants and a sports bra so I throw a hoodie over the top.

"Good luck today," Pillow says. "You'll be a star."

"It's your time," my alarm clock chimes in.

"Meow." That's all my porcelain cat ever says, but she's trying.

My Bluetooth speaker goes above and beyond to play the *Yuri on Ice* theme as opposed to his usual 90s sad boi music. I appreciate the effort, but it doesn't stop the churning in my guts. I don't want to end up in a cell next to Tremor.

Pear is in the kitchen eating cereal directly out of the box.

"Role model." I walk up beside them and give them an awkward hug. "No wonder I'm a hero."

"Please behave, Dilly."

I don't know how to respond to this, so I kiss Pear on the cheek and head out the door.

Time to be a superhero.

CHAPTER THREE

The entire Cute Mutants team meets at the bus exchange in the middle of town. We're all quiet and awkward. Even Alyse isn't saying much as we walk down to the Yaxley building. Emma snooped it on Google and whatever hacker search engines she has, but the building is anonymous and boring. It's three storeys with an underground carpark. I'm disappointed there's no space for a Danger Room. The windows are reflective glass so you can't see anything inside. The single door has a very obvious camera above it and a button to press for entry.

Before we reach it, the door swings open with a metallic clunk. The interior is dim and quiet, with two people waiting. It's the woman who turned up at my house, along with an older guy. She's got neatly styled blonde hair and his is grey and buzzed close to his scalp. They're wearing pressed slacks and blazers with the circle-Y logo prominent on the breast.

"The Cute Mutants." The woman's voice is low, and she smiles nice and wide to put us at ease. "You all came. I'm relieved."

I'm tempted to be sarcastic here, but I do have *some* sense of self-preservation. Even Wraith is quiet, over-awed by the threat of being thrown into a black site detention facility. We're clustered together really close, except I've been thrust into the front. Lou snaps his fingers, like he always does when he's nervous. It's making *me* edgy. I nudge backwards with one elbow and he stops for about three seconds.

The ground floor is empty aside from an elevator and a door, both of which have keypads.

"We're glad to officially meet you all," the woman says. "You can call me Aurora. I'll be running your day to day training. This is Bancroft, who oversees the programme as a whole."

Bancroft makes the faintest of nods, as if he's too important to give us the full range of head movement.

"Today we'll be introducing you to the programme and performing baseline assessments. First, let's go up to the main training floor." Aurora strides towards the elevator.

Everyone looks at me. I shrug and follow her. The elevator requires both a keycard and a code to work, but I don't get the opportunity to see what she enters.

We're all jammed in together, but travel to the top floor in silence. We exit into a large open space that smells faintly of paint. There's bland grey patterned carpet on the floor and the walls are all white. It doesn't look like it's designed *for* anything—a space waiting for us to come along to fit into it.

There are a bunch of doors off to the side with numbers on them. Dani and Emma look around with interest, like they've just turned up in a new classroom. Alyse looks nervous, washed out and faded. Lou and Bianca look as unsettled as I feel.

"The fit-out is still in progress," Aurora says. "There will be a gymnasium here with training facilities, plus a limited number of sleeping quarters."

"You expect us to live here?" Lou asks skeptically.

"No, but in the future some may want the option."

I have so many questions I'm lightheaded. The building isn't finished, which means this is all new, but they obviously have big plans for the future. One day this might actually be like Xavier's school. Possibilities splinter and blur in my head. I clench my fidgeting hands at my sides.

"Where's everyone else?" I ask.

Aurora looks at me blankly.

"Is this it?" I gesture at the empty room. "No more mutants hiding away behind door number one?"

"Ah." She smiles. "No. This situation is new and very... flexible. You're the first cluster identified in New

Zealand. Experience overseas has shown it's important to assimilate new extrahumans before things become unsustainable. The Tremor situation could have been far worse, believe me."

I catch Emma's eye. *Experience overseas? First cluster identified?* What the fuck is going on here? How is this not massive news?

"Assimilate?" Dani asks.

"We simply mean we wish you to work *with* the government."

My eyes are enormous. "What does working with the government mean?" Do they want to use us as teenage supersoldiers or lab rats or—?

"We'll be starting with assessment and training." Bancroft speaks for the first time. "First we'll divide you into field and support-oriented roles. You can choose your initial assignments, although we reserve the right to overrule. For example, Ms. Hall's ability would not be suited to fieldwork, and she has obvious aptitude for support."

By aptitude, he means Emma is a fucking whiz with computers and apps and drones. I know she's done things that are technically illegal and I hope Yaxley isn't using that as a threat. Then again, we have Corporate Azkaban looming over us all. I try to haul up my sagging spirits, but it works about as well as you'd expect. I am the grumpy one after all.

"Can I be support too?" Lou asks, which doesn't entirely surprise me. He's never been comfortable with the aggressive side of things.

"That sounds perfectly appropriate." Bancroft seems very Zen. I'm struggling to figure out his vibe. Is he headmaster or father or jailer? Charles Xavier was always slightly creepy, especially in the early comics. Fuck, I hope Bancroft can't read my mind.

Can you read my mind, you pasty asshole?

He shows absolutely no reaction.

"We will now proceed to physical and psychological assessments on each of you," Aurora says.

The room is very quiet. Everyone's attentive, the good students they've trained us to be all our lives.

"One final thing," Bancroft says. "If our training programme proves to be unacceptable or unworkable, it will be necessary for you to reside in our off-site facility." He gives a little cough. "For public safety reasons."

"You mean jail," I mutter.

"You would not be incarcerated there, unlike Mr. Firestone. In fact, you would have pleasant accommodations, chef-catered food and many entertainment options. To perhaps stretch a metaphor, we would simply be taking you off the board. We cannot have unrestricted extrahumans—or mutants, if you must, Ms. Taylor—operating on New Zealand soil."

So there's the stick: very fancy jail. The carrot is the opportunity to be a real live X-Man. One working for the government rather than for a mysterious rich psychic, but both are pretty fucking shady if we're being honest. Still, real live X-Men. It's hard not to be excited about that part.

"Anybody?" Aurora looks around the room, all bright eyes and bushy tail, which is a total fucking asshole move given we've just been threatened with super chill jail. Nobody takes her up on this very special offer, and she beams even wider as if she's won something. "Excellent. Now let's proceed into testing."

Assessment starts poorly. A young nurse dude comes in and sticks a big needle in me to fill a test tube with blood. I don't know if fear of needles will get me in trouble, so I sit and sweat.

"Very good," he murmurs, like I passed.

They give me cardio work and some weight training and a whole bunch of written tests. I think they're figuring out if I'm a psychopath. There's probably a red sticker on a file somewhere saying I'm high risk.

I'm distracted by a couple of objects that are aware. One is the pen I've been using to fill out the tests, and the other is the clipboard that Aurora's holding against her chest. Tests annoy me at the best of times, especially stupid ones like this. I sigh and flop around and mutter to the pen, who is thrilled by my rebellious attitude.

Aurora stands in the corner and watches me with an expression that can only be described as *supercilious*. This is a word I just discovered in the vocab test, so let's all give a round of applause for me, the quick learner.

Once I'm finally done being tested, there's an interview about my powers, which Bancroft runs. He has a tablet in his lap, angled so I can't see it.

"Reports of your powers are rather confusing." He blinks at me, disapproving. "Some of what the unfortunate Mr. Firestone says is hard to rationalise."

When we rescued the hostages, they never saw me use my powers. Tremor spent half the time unconscious or under the influence of Bianca's inner demons. Whatever he told them probably sounded like the ramblings of a stoner.

"My power's erratic," I say with a grimace. "It's based on rage. I call it Hulkinesis."

Which is a) a terrible name and b) a lie. This is *my* test to see how much they know. I convinced everyone to stay vague about our powers. Lou lights up. How does that work? I have no idea, sir.

"We'll need a demonstration." Bancroft's still playing the asshole headmaster. "Of this so-called—" He can't even bring himself to say the word. "This rage-powered telekinesis."

"I'm not very angry. It might not work too well."

"Why don't you give it your best attempt?" Bancroft gives me a thin smile. "We'll worry about your failure if necessary."

Okay, maybe he does have a superpower, and it's the ability to piss people off.

"Fucking move then, you dumb thing," I snap at the pen lying on the desk in front of me. I warned him about this beforehand. "Asshole," I scream, letting my voice turn ragged. "Don't you embarrass me, you piece of shit."

The pen giggles because he gets as much of a kick out of this as I do. "Writing is for suckers," he says breathlessly and goes arrowing across the room. He hits the clipboard and bounces off, still laughing, before hurtling towards Bancroft's head. "Come on, Clippy. Join the party. Write your own destiny!"

Bancroft tries to wave the pen away like a fly.

The clipboard writhes in Aurora's arms, rattling against her chest.

"It looks like you're writing 'fuck you' in the air," she says excitedly.

The pen darts in and draws a raggedy-ass F-U light-ning-fast on Bancroft's neck.

The clipboard shoots across and catches Bancroft a massive whack across the back of the head. He lets out this incoherent bellow.

This is where my lie sort of misfires. I don't have much control once these objects get going. They're picking up on my adrenaline, my nervousness, and my natural dislike of Bancroft. I'm not controlling them. I'm enabling them.

"Please stop," I hiss. "You're making it worse for me."

"Fine," the clipboard sulks, and skids onto the floor at Aurora's feet.

The pen takes longer to calm down, writing most of a C on Bancroft's neck and slinking back to lie inno-cently beside my hand.

Aurora's jaw is basically lying on the floor beside the clipboard.

Bancroft's jaw is clenched like it's sprouted little muscles.

"I told you it was erratic." I keep my voice as calm and casual as I can.

"Fascinating." Bancroft rapidly types a bunch of notes. "Very interesting indeed. A petulant display, but noteworthy. Your anger triggered their initial response, but they performed further complex movements with-out encouragement from you."

I know there's this thing called micro-expressions but I don't know what they look like, so I can't hide them from Bancroft's intense gaze. He's a smart motherfucker and it makes me nervous.

"It's rather excellent, Ms. Taylor. From what Mr. Firestone said, you moved a great many objects simultaneously during the hostage intervention. I suspect with training and discipline, you may have a rather effective power indeed." He powers off his tablet and zips up the fancy leather case. "Thank you. Aurora, please reassemble the team."

The rest of the team is already waiting in the main training area. I wonder how they all performed. Nobody looks worried or upset, so that's a good start.

"Well done," Aurora says, a beaming smile plastered back on. "You all tested successfully as expected. From the Firestone Incident reports, it appears you wore a mixture of homemade and store-bought costumes. The advantage of the financial and technological backing we provide is that you have access to something more advanced."

One of the doors opens and out come two people, dressed from head to toe in black. Gloves, boots, masks. I guess we're ninjas now.

"These uniforms are light, flexible and highly robust." Aurora talks like she's presenting us with a prize. "They're like wearing a full-body bulletproof and stab proof vest."

I glance at Dani, who shows no reaction, even though *bulletproof and stab proof* means there's the possibility of danger. It's scary, but exhilarating too.

"You might enjoy the fact they're customisable." Aurora taps a button on her phone and the uniforms light up with patterns. One looks like Captain Marvel and one like Superman. I'm impressed despite my attempt to be jaded. Alyse literally clasps her hands together and I think I see faint heart-shapes in her eyes. Lou is grinning, even though he doesn't want to be a field guy.

"Unstable molecules," Dani murmurs. It's a reference to how Marvel costumes can be worn by people that catch fire or stretch. I wonder how Alyse's will work when she shifts form.

We're sent back into the small rooms to change. This time they're empty, although I bet there are cameras. I change with the least chance of accidentally flashing any Yaxley security staff, but it's super awkward. The mask pulls up over my head like a hood and then down over my face, flexible despite the complex machinery in it.

I can see better than real life through the augmented lenses of the mask. Yaxley is on some Tony Stark shit for sure. I look myself up and down, and my costume lights up, presumably triggered remotely by Aurora.

I take out my phone to see the full effect. A pattern of green and purple lines make a super-cool neon version of my old shitty Spider-Hero costume.

Okay, fine. You win this round, Yaxley. These are fucking awesome.

I head back out to see everyone else's shiny new costume. Lou's mask is No-Face, Emma's is the cat goddess Bast, and Bianca's is a cartoon devil. They've definitely done their research and planning, because Bianca has a panel in the front of her uniform that will allow access to the monsters that live inside her chest. Alyse and Dani's are both blank. Alyse transforms her appearance anyway, and Dani never really had a proper one, given that she came late.

The next thing we're given is phones. They look like reskinned iPhones with the Yaxley logo on the back, but they're super locked down. There's a messaging app for communicating with each other and a phone home app for summoning urgent assistance from Yaxley HQ. The most exciting part is the costume editor.

Lou is already adding tears and koru tattoos to No-Face's mask. Dani draws eyebrows on hers, one of them arched.

I shake my head, but I'm smiling behind my mask. I tinker a little bit with my layout, but honestly I like what they've done. It's like a way cooler parallel universe version of me. There are a bunch of other buttons in the app, including one that retracts the hood and mask so it sits around my neck like a scarf.

I watch the others playing around with their costume designs. Dani has retracted her hood too. Bianca is making her devil far more fabulous and goth. My eyes drift to where Alyse and Emma are side by side, making Emma's mask ferocious. I notice how much Alyse is sparkling and think of how she was lit up in Emma's dream.

I sidle up and nudge Dani. "You don't think?"

Dani follows my gaze and shrugs. "Emma's ace," she says, flipping through various pictures of X-Men on her phone.

"You're ignoring the spec part in ace-spec. Maybe she likes cuddling or kissing or even—"

"Maybe we shouldn't interfere in our friend's love life." She grins at me. "I get it, but ace or aro or demi or whatever, everyone's an individual in the end. Emma's the only one who can know what she wants and how it relates to Alyse and what Alyse wants back and—"

"Yes. I do have some vague idea of how people work. I'm allowed to *wonder* though."

"I don't think there's a force on earth that could stop you from wondering." She touches my hand. "You feeling okay about all this?" Her eyes are on me and I know I sound like a simp but they're so beautiful. I want to zoom in on them like a map of a distant galaxy, and see every individual star that lurks in the centre of them.

"No. I'm scared we're very very fucked."

"Positive attitude remember? They've been pretty cool and unthreatening so far, haven't they?"

"Aside from the bit about the jail," I sigh, because she's mostly right.

"Besides, if it turns bad, at least we're fucked together." There's a faint tinge of blush in her cheeks.

I wonder what she's thinking—is it anything *close* to what's in my head? Oh my god, my blush is so much worse than a faint tinge. My cheeks are infernos, and I know she can see it, because she's smiling wider and the real-life eyebrow is up.

"Sometimes I wish I had psychic powers," she says, really soft.

I'm tempted to kiss her in front of everyone but I have some self-control despite what Bancroft thinks. It helps that my brain keeps returning back to a default state of freaking the fuck out. Yaxley has money, the ear of the government, and a private jail. I'm not totally politics girl but I'm not a total fucking dummy.

The *idea* of superhero school has always been the dream—especially with Magneto as the headmaster. And now we're here and they've given us cool toys, but I have this horrible sense of dread about what's coming next. Real life corporations are ruthless and give zero fucks in a way that's not charming and badass, but planet-fuckingly terrifying, The worst part is that we have no real choice. We're here, at their mercy, and have no power in this situation. Am I the only one that gives a shit?

"Not sure you want to read *everything* in my mind," I say, but Dani's back tinkering with the costume app and doesn't hear me.

CHAPTER FOUR

urora stands at the front of the room and claps to get our attention. "Thank you for your coopera-tion. We'll refine our understanding of your pow-ers over the coming weeks. For now, Bancroft will run the Support Team and I'll lead the Field Team along-side Ms. Kim, also known as Marvellous."

She beams at Dani. I don't want to look at anyone, because I know they're looking at me. I'm not even mad about it, or I *am* mad about it, but I totally get it. It's logically the best decision. Dani's smart and competent and in control of her powers. These are all things I am not. If I was a corporate jackhole, I wouldn't want me as the leader either.

I hear Alyse's voice from one side of me. "No, that's not right."

"Dylan's the leader. Chatterbox." It's Dani. Oh, my heart.

"Always has been, always will be," Bianca drawls.

Aurora has her lips in a flat line, unimpressed any-one's talking back.

My hands are sweating inside the uniform. "Don't. Dani, you'll be an amazing leader. You're an obvious choice."

"You've already proven yourself to us." Dani turns to face me, her eyes searching mine. I don't know what she expects to read there, because I'm not sure myself.

"This isn't a democracy." Aurora is all brisk effi-ciency. "Based on your testing and profiles, we have decided Ms. Kim is the best candidate for leader. Ms. Taylor's powers are erratic and she has proven herself to have less than stellar judgement in the field."

Ouch. Fuck you. And maybe you have a point, but fuck you all the same.

"If you're talking about chopping Tremor's hands off—" Dani begins furiously.

"They've made their decision." I speak way more harshly than I intend to, but antagonising Yaxley won't do us any favours. The smart, cautious part of me knows to play docile and quiet, so I focus on how Dani defending me turns my heart into a sticky pink mess.

"Thank you, Chatterbox," Aurora says. "As I was saying, Marvellous will be team leader although I will coordinate strategy and provide real-time updates in the field." She carries on looking at me while she says this whole spiel, and I nod mechanically. There's a bunch of bullshit about the new training schedule and our mission and how if we cooperate we'll become the team we always wanted to be. Most of it washes over me. It's hard to concentrate. They've instantly pegged me as a failure, not that I needed the confirmation.

"So when do we go into the field? And what the hell are we going to do there?" I ask, once she's finally done. I get a stern look.

"I'll take this, Aurora." Bancroft adjusts the cuffs of his jacket carefully. "We knew these young people had initiative and drive. Otherwise they would never have come to our attention. It's inevitable they'd have questions."

The others move restlessly. They're acting like I'm the annoying kid who asked the teacher a question when we were about to be let out of class, but it's actually the most important thing so shut up with that look, *Wraith*.

"Simply put, there are a number of uses your talents could be put to, but an obvious one is espionage."

"Like spies?" Lou asks, and I try not to roll my eyes, because *obviously* spies. "You want to use a bunch of teenagers as spies?"

"Trained teenagers," Bancroft says, in this teacher-like tone that means shut the fuck up. "Abilities such as telekinesis and invisibility have obvious uses.

Moodring's powers are currently a little baroque for our purposes, but with training we aim to rectify that."

I narrow my eyes. "You want her to be more Raven Darkholme."

"Imagine if she could impersonate others." Bancroft says, proving he has the X-Men knowledge of a shallow puddle.

"But *spies*," Lou says again.

"Although it has been kept remarkably quiet, there are other countries with small extrahuman populations. Once our government was alerted of the existence of our own, they agreed it was preferable to work *with* the citizens manifesting these powers. The intent, as you have seen, is to manage them, nurture them, and bring them to bear on problems of mutual significance."

"Can I just ask—"

Bancroft cuts me off with a swipe of his hand, like he's closing a fucking app. The worst part is I actually fall for it.

"While the international geopolitical situation is complex, please trust me when I say New Zealand is on the side of the angels."

We're out of time or answers or both, and Aurora dismisses us. We get one final reminder to keep our YaxPhones on us at all times. It's obvious they'll use them to monitor us, but I stand quietly like a meek little kitten. Everyone's still fucking looking at me. Why won't they stop?

We change back into regular clothes and Aurora takes us down in the elevator. Soon we're out on the street in late afternoon sunshine, staring like we've returned from being abducted by aliens.

"What the *actual fuck* was that?" Alyse asks.

I kick at the concrete. "Other extrahumans? More mutants like us out in the world?"

"Kept quiet." Emma blinks at me.

"They obviously don't want everyone knowing about us," Dani says. "What will people do if they find out superpowers are real?"

There's a lot I want to say, but not here. I spin my YaxPhone in my hand, letting everyone see the logo. "I think it's exciting. We finally get to be proper superheroes. And those costumes are totally clutch!"

I fish in my bag and grab the pen I swiped from training. I scrawl on the back of my hand: *They're listening*. I get nods and blank looks in return.

"How was everyone's training?" Emma asks, bland as bland. "They didn't do anything with me. Just asked lots of questions."

Bianca shrugs. "They wanted to see my fucking demons. So I showed them and then they wanted them back in the box. They talked about testing *dontseeme*. Figure out its size and how many people it affects and all that shit."

"Sounds logical." I feel dumb. It's the sort of thing we could've done when we were training, except I'm not a living spreadsheet. I guess this is why I'm not the leader anymore.

"They wanted me to light up a lot," Lou avoids everyone's gaze. "Asked me lots of questions about how my powers work that were… embarrassing. Bancroft kept poking and prodding at me and I just went quiet."

"Are you okay?" Alyse and I ask simultaneously.

"They didn't do anything creepy, if that's what you mean. And they call me Mr. Patterson, which I like."

"What about you?" Dani asks me.

"They pissed me off and I made a pen and a clipboard dance. I guess they'll try pissing me off a lot."

"Do you think that's why… you know, the, um, the…" I appreciate Lou dancing around it, but everyone knows what he's talking about.

"They chose Dani because she'll be great." My eyes sting, but I keep it together. "Like seriously, you guys, I would've chosen Dani to lead the team from the start if she hadn't been such a fucking pussy and quit."

That gets a laugh out of everyone. "With a girl-friend like this, who needs enemies?" Dani kisses me hard on the cheek.

We head back to the bus stop. Lou gets on one bus, and Bianca gets on another. Alyse is trying to communicate with only her eyes but ends up looking like Deku on the verge of tears. She finally drags me to where the buses come hissing and groaning into the main part of the station. It's really loud, and we lean our heads in towards each other, phones tucked in our pockets.

"Are you *really* okay?" Alyse asks me, barely audible.

"I'm fine. I swear! I'm not about to burst into tears."

She's disbelieving enough that I feel like shit. Do people think I'm such a fragile brat that I'll fall apart if I can't be the boss?

"You'll always be our leader."

"Thanks, but we all know Dani's going to be amazing."

"Dani is amazing." I feel Alyse's warm breath against my neck. "But she's good at being bossy and knowing what to do, and you're amazing at inspiring people and making them feel like superheroes."

I twist to put my mouth beside her ear. "You're so fucking cheesy, Alyse, but I love you."

"I love you too, you chatterboxing asshole."

Alyse and Emma leave together, and I head back to my place with Dani. There's very little in the cupboards aside from fruit salad in cans. We leave our phones on the table and go to the back yard which has patchy brown grass and a broken trampoline.

Dani sits beside me on the steps, and we eat with forks out of the can in near-silence.

"You okay?" I ask her. "They didn't hurt you too much?"

Her mouth twists. "It was all very clinical. They strapped my arm down and they tried different stimuli to see their effects."

"No," I whisper.

"You know, if they burn me, what can I move versus if they apply pressure or cut me." She puts the half-empty can down beside her, and rolls her sleeve up to show me the marks.

My eyes fill with tears. I take her arm gently in both hands and kiss every spot where they hurt her.

"The good news is that if you crush my arm it works almost as well as cutting. Hurts about the same, but less bloody and scarring."

"Oh, Dan." I hold my lips to the inside of her wrist.

"I'm not mad. It's the smart thing to do. It's the scientific approach and what I should have been doing. The same as with Wraith."

"We're not subjects." My voice is sharper than I'd like.

"Don't you want to understand our powers? The X-Men do this sort of thing, and they train relentlessly. That's what Yaxley can give us. We're going to be properly trained and equipped. How is that a bad thing?"

I hug my knees and stare into the overgrown garden. I'm not great at arguing without flying off the handle. I have these racing thoughts about how we're not in charge of ourselves anymore, and how we have to go where we're pointed, but I can't organise them enough to let them out. At the heart of it, my problem is that our only choice is this or a cell next to fucking Tremor. And I just don't trust Yaxley.

Dani takes my hand. "I think my day was better than yours. I'm so sorry about the whole leader thing. I know you were putting on a brave face for everyone but—"

"No." I don't look at her because her eyes are too sympathetic. "Like when you get down to it, I am not the temperament for a field leader. You definitely are."

Her eyes narrow. "I can't decide if that's a compliment or an insult."

"It's neither." I shrug. "It's just one of those fact things you like so much. Basically you're Cyclops and I'm Wolverine."

I get the smile then. Dani is honestly the most beautiful person I've ever seen in my life, but her smile turns that beauty into a weapon. It cracks everything open inside me. "You wish."

"No, you'll give the orders and I'll be rebellious." I smile back at her, mirroring her delight. "You'll know I'm right, but you'll try to make me follow anyway."

Dani moves so she's half standing over and half straddling me. She hooks three fingers under my chin and tips my gaze up to meet hers. "You'll do what you're told, Logan."

My heart pulses all the way through me. "You know I won't."

She leans in and her forehead is against mine. I can see her lips. My hands are on her waist, and her blue shirt has ridden up so I'm touching her bare skin. She takes a big shuddering breath and kisses me. I'm still my own person but I don't want to be. I want to be hers.

"Joo-hyun," I whisper.

It's supposed to be romantic, but she stiffens up for a second before relaxing back into the kiss. I try to carry on, but my brain is poking at me incessantly about it.

"Sorry," I blurt.

"For what?"

"Calling you Joo-hyun."

"It's fine." She pulls away. "It's sweet, really it is. But, like, nobody ever calls me that except for Mum and family back in Korea on Skype calls, and all the old people at church."

It's my turn to react. "You go to church?"

"Not anymore!" Her eyes widen. "Not after the Five Year War. That's how long it took to convince my mother that going to church wouldn't stop me becoming a heathen."

"Church," I say with a tiny smile.

"I'll show you a photo sometime of what I'd wear to church. You won't recognise me. You'll probably dump me."

"Highly, highly doubtful."

"Anyway, at church it was always: be strong for your family, Joo-hyun. Obey your mother, Joo-hyun." She pauses and kisses me so slowly my lips melt like spun sugar. "Don't make out with girls, Joo-hyun."

"Fine." My fingers skate lightly across the smooth surface of her lower back. "Wouldn't want you to stop doing that."

CHAPTER FIVE

It's amazing how something intense and scary can become mundane. Working as trainee superheroes is no exception. We do a bunch of exercise, just like we used to, except now we do proper martial arts training too. Bancroft doesn't have a lot to do with it, although he likes drifting around like a pompous dick to monitor things.

"Mr. Bancroft," I say, acting like an eager student. "Can you tell us about the other extrahumans around the world? Are they like us? What can they do?"

"That is *extremely* classified, Ms. Taylor. The existence of extrahumans is an open secret among the intelligence community, but it is vital to keep it secret from the general public at all costs. Did you not read the documents you and your parent signed?"

Not to be all Jared, 19, but I have not. Pear did, and they grumbled a lot but they always grumble about that shit.

"Yeah, I'm just *wondering*," I sigh. "Now we're on the inside, I thought we might get the smallest possible glimpse."

"We will address it as necessary when the time comes." Bancroft folds his arms and scowls at me, the least favourite of his unruly brood. "Until then, please concentrate on your training."

It turns out Aurora kicks ass very convincingly. We're learning, but we're much less convincing. It's the most fun part, learning judo, karate, and Krav Maga. I work at it harder than I've worked at almost anything in my life. Bianca is super fucking into it.

"I'm starting to think you've got a crush on Aurora," I tell her. "Always volunteering to have her throw you on the ground and step on you."

Bianca feints a punch at me. I block it without thinking, because apparently I can do that now. "You've got to take your kicks where you can get them. Not all of us get to train with our girlfriends every day."

It's true that Dani and I do a lot of sparring and it can lead to interesting places.

"You can't get Shell to train with you?" That's Bianca's girlfriend, about whom I have strong opinions, most of which can be summed up by the word toxic.

"I'd break her." Bianca shrugs her muscular shoulders. She looks so badass now. It's hard to connect her with the lanky and sullen girl she was when we started. "Not that I see her much lately."

"And that's good or bad?" I ask, with an attempt at being casual.

"I miss all the gymnastic stuff." She grins at me. "Since I got buff I could pick her up and—"

"Jesus, Wraith." I put my hands over my ears.

"That's almost your catchphrase." She laughs and tilts her head toward where Dani is sparring against a silvery and muscular version of Alyse. Transformations are totally cheating, but it doesn't stop Alyse doing it. "Seems like Operation Melt the Ice is going well for you."

"Yeah, pretty well." I can't keep the smile off my face.

"It's cute to see the monster tamed." Bianca sends another flurry of punches my way, which I can barely keep up with. "Have you two, you know—" She flicks her tongue out of her mouth at me.

"Fuck's sake, Wraith!"

"Yes, play the blushing card all you want, Chats, but give me some indication. Please."

I swing a punch, but she steps inside and somehow gets me in a headlock.

"Now, I won't let you go until you tell Auntie Wraith all about your sex life. What's the point of having an emotional support himbo if they don't provide sup-port?"

"Fuck emotional support. You only want tea!" I manage to land a punch and she shoves me away. "The answer is no, anyway. We haven't done *that*."

She looks at me with mock horror. "What are you waiting for?"

"I'm not that kind of girl." That's not true. I most definitely am. I just don't want to be bad at it. Dani's done more than me, and I have a long history of being really lame and fucking up important things.

"Hey," Bianca says. "Chill out, you noodle. Dani is so blatantly into you, it's almost insulting to the rest of us. You've got nothing to worry about."

Obviously my expression is less mysterious than I hoped, which makes me even more embarrassed. I hurl myself at Bianca in a flurry of half-coordinated attacks to avoid any further painful conversation.

The next day at school, I deliberately get my phone confiscated in class with Emma and Dani. They both pick up on it and get theirs swiped as well. We conveniently 'forget' to pick them up after class and head down to the library to use the school iMacs.

"We need secure communication," I tell Emma, who nods enthusiastically.

"I've been having ideas. We want a public forum to look innocuous. I was thinking we make some Twitter fan accounts and communicate through gifs."

"The most evolved form of language." Dani rocks in her chair, eyeing us both. "I don't get why you're still both so paranoid. Things are going well with Yaxley, aren't they? We're becoming better heroes. Isn't that what you want, Dills?"

"Dylan's a revolutionary." Emma hooks her hair behind her ear, tapping away at the keyboard. "She doesn't want to be co-opted by existing power structures."

"Wow, that fucking sentence." I slouch and sigh. "I hate being the dumb one. I'm not exactly a revolutionary but, like, people in charge want to stay that way, right? And so they'll do what it takes and—"

"Power structures perpetuate themselves," Emma says. "Exactly."

"And if we ever decide we don't like what they're doing, we can't stop them or they'll lock us up!" I look at Dani as if I've won.

"Yes, but working *alongside* them means there's more of a chance they'll listen if we come to them with concerns. Be collaborative, rather than antagonistic."

"I am collaborating." I lean in to see what Emma's doing. "I fucking hate it."

Dani sighs, but rolls her chair in beside me.

"Tell me I'm clever." Emma gestures at the screen.

"So clever," I say. "It's hard to tell, because you're keyboard smashing."

"Take every third letter." The tweet says *asdsfnkli* above a video of awesome androgynous C-pop group Fanxyred.

My lips move while I figure it out. "Dee en eye. Dani?"

Emma nods and tweets *bnmxclkjl* on top of a video of Irene from my ult group.

"Em ell ell. Mall? So it means Dani, meet me at the mall?"

"Yes!" Emma pumps her fist and spins around to grin at us.

"Suuuuch a show off," Dani says. "But, yes, I like it."

I'm all hyped about being super covert and cool. "I love it. But, Ems, there are rules about what a valid keyboard smash is. These are not viable."

Emma snorts. "I highly doubt Yaxley is aware of the rules of keyboard smashing. And we'll mix them up with other completely innocuous tweets. We'll use gifs of particular groups to signal which ones are legit. Dilly's Red Velvet obviously, and I'll pick NCT Dream. Dani?"

"Can I be Tori Amos?"

"We don't know who that is." Emma flips her hair. "But she sounds white and boring."

"Half-right." Dani shoves Emma's chair. "What's that one group you bullied me into liking? Mamamoo? I'll choose them. Although, for the record, while this is very sneaky and clever, I don't think it's necessary."

"Isn't she such a good little child soldier, Dilly?"

"Oh, fuck you," Dani laughs. "Unlike the pair of you, I wait for evidence before I feel paranoid."

"It's not paranoid if you have evidence," Emma points out. "It's simple logic then."

"Uh, and they literally hurt you to see how you work." I'm still mad about it.

Dani flushes a little. "It's science. There's no alternative to experimenting on me if they want to figure out how I work. It's *interesting* finding out, and I gave consent. I want to know for myself."

"Okay." I lean into her. "I still think they're fucking creeps though."

Yaxley's definitely going deep on the powers training. They've mapped the impact of Bianca's *dontseeme* - it seems to have no upper limit in terms of people and lasts anywhere from thirty minutes to an hour. The effective radius is only around twenty meters. They're trying to find out if they can improve that, and to get more reliable control over the length, but she's more interested in fighting.

Alyse's transformations are getting larger and more powerful. Yaxley doesn't have a uniform that can change shape with her, but they have research teams working on coming up with portable and flexible pieces of body armour she can attach to the more fragile parts of her. It's almost enough to make me like them.

Their engineers have also come up with a series of metal cuffs that go inside Dani's uniform and inflict various levels of pain. She's so into the whole process of understanding and controlling her power. It's cute. I don't think I'll ever be a fan of the pain thing, but the cuffs are for sure better than stabbing herself in the shoulder. Her favourite new toy is a set of slim daggers that she does tricks with. She tosses them into the air and they become a beautiful flock of silver birds dancing around her shoulders and wrists. Despite her increasing control, some things still give her problems.

"Turns out flying Roxy was way outside my limit," she tells me as she floats one hundred kilograms of weight around the room, wincing the whole time. "It must have been you and her assisting me."

Roxy is my vehicular friend who is capable of flying under the right circumstances. Again, it's a long story. Currently, she's off roaming the country under her own steam. She's free to do what she wants, but I miss her, and the rides. It's odd how certain objects have so much more autonomy than others. I know Emma and Dani ponder these details a lot, but I don't question it. I've never been one of those people who nitpicks shit to death in the comics. Some things just are, like how we ended up evolving this way in this universe. Weird shit does happen even if you can't explain why.

Possibly related to this, but not entirely, the one person not excelling at powers training is me. It might be petty and paranoid, but I don't want Yaxley to know everything I can do. My power feels private. I don't believe they wouldn't hurt innocent objects to find out what makes me tick.

Whatever my reasons, it drives Dani mad. I've thrown a microwave through the plate glass window leading to Bancroft's office. The number of times I've convinced the poor free weights to spill all over the floor is starting to make me feel guilty. They're almost as invested in my success as Dani. They keep begging me to let them fly and show how powerful and strong we are together, but I keep telling them I don't want a pain cuff equivalent to control my objects.

"Chatterbox, please focus." Bancroft fiddles with his pen when he's pissed off with me, and right now it's going click-click-click like a tiny machine gun. "We're getting logical power baselines for every other mutant."

"Erratic girl, erratic power." I screw my face up and pretend to concentrate. I've charmed one of the little weights into playing a game. She's currently sitting in the hood of my Yaxley costume and, at my whispered command, drags me backwards very fast.

"Chatterbox," Bancroft shouts. "Please get yourself under control."

I catch a glimpse of Dani's disapproving mouth as I skid past. I use all my frustration and worry and fear to lend the little weight as much power as I can. She grunts very loudly and hauls me into the air, only stopping when my hood is caught on a hook embedded in the wall. I thrash about and claw at my throat.

Bancroft stands at the other end of the room and watches me dispassionately.

Wraith and Alyse run over to haul me down.

"You're a fucking nutter, Chats," Wraith says with a grin.

The rest of the mutants think these antics are funny, but Dani wants me to prove myself to Yaxley, to *excel*. When we're together in the evenings, writing messages on each other's bare arms because it's a) secure communication and b) so fucking sexy omg, she tries to convince me.

You can do SOMETHING. I love how intent her face is when she writes. *I hate Aurora's disapproving face.*

omg do u not get stealth?

You're being paranoid, Dilly.

I don't trust them

They haven't done anything wrong yet, she writes. *They're making us all better. I want them to see how amazing you are.*

It takes me ages to write the next bit, but I figure it's safer than Joo-hyun.

im nothing special, 여자 친구

She's staring at the Hangul and I'm like oh fuck, I messed up again. She circles the last part and writes *friend?*

"Girlfriend," I whisper. "I used Google translate so it's probably wrong." I resist the urge to flinch away. "Sorry, I'm being a dick."

"When Mum sent me to Korean language school as a kid, I was *such* a brat about it. The other kids didn't like me because I was too shy. I would cry afterwards every time."

"I hate them all," I tell her, maybe too earnestly.

"They were just kids." She laughs. "Although somehow I still like you saying that. Anyway, now I'm actually interested in learning, but if I tell Mum she'll inevitably bring up how annoying I was back then."

"You know you're old enough to go to lessons on your own now."

"Wait, I can teach you one useful word." She rotates my arm and writes 씨발 on it.

"What does that mean?"

Her smile is as wide as I've ever seen it. "It says shibal. What's the first word anyone wants to learn in a new language? Your literal favourite and most commonly used word."

"*Oh.*" I take the pen and run my fingers over the softest part of the inside of her arm, a slight shade lighter than the rest of her tawny skin. I carefully trace the shapes of the characters, faintly marking her, and the whole time my brain circles the various uses of the word and one in particular. "Fuck."

"Perfect," she breathes and takes the pen.

So are you going to let them see what you can do?

My thoughts skate around the outside of our situation. Maybe I *am* paranoid and stubborn and have read too many comics where the villains try to control the mutants, and instead we'll become amazing heroes bounding around the world doing good. Except I know which scenario sounds more fucking likely, this shitty world being what it is. Someone has to watch and wait and be ready, just in case Yaxley's as sinister as I fear.

sorry but ur stuck with ur rebel girl

You're making me dizzy

stop writing and kiss me

"Okay," she whispers.

Alyse turns up after Dani leaves, which she often does. Dani actually has this thing about keeping up with schoolwork. Apparently it beats making out with me twenty-four-seven, which seems rude.

Alyse and I have more important things to do, like learn dances that we mostly suck at, and spill tea of course.

"You doing okay?" Alyse is leaning against the wall with Pillow murmuring happily in her lap.

"Did Dani put you up to this?"

"Um, excuse me. I was your best friend since before you started hooking up with the ice queen and—"

"You mean *melting* the ice queen," I nudge her with my foot and she cackles with laughter.

"It *is* a weird fucking thing seeing Danielle Kim tamed by a brat like you. But nice subject change. I know the Yaxley thing is different from how it used to be, when it was just the gang."

She leaves a big meaningful pause as I watch boys dance on the laptop screen.

"You know what I'm scared of?" I ask her.

"That Dani's going to love being in charge too much and will become the bossiest human alive?"

That makes me crack a smile. "No." I glance over to her and see her transformed into something warm and gentle that I could curl up inside, like an animal hibernating in the winter. "I'm scared there are more people out there like us. Not the official teams of wherever, although my god I'm so fucking curious about them. I mean kids like we used to be. Randoms figuring out their powers and getting into some shit. What if it all gets fucked up and Yaxley sends us in to stop them?"

"I hadn't thought of that." Alyse shifts darker and more shadowy, somewhere menacing you wouldn't want to spend any season in. "You really think they'd make us—"

"Hunt our own people." I swallow hard. "I think it's exactly the sort of thing they want us for."

"No." Alyse brightens. "Emma's not going to kiss anyone else. It'll be fine, Dilly, you wait and see. All we'll be doing is shit like spying on the Aussies. Maybe they've got a secret superhero squad too. I'll transform into a kangaroo and bounce around their Parliament keeping an eye on them."

"Oh yeah, how are you going to do that? Think kangaroo-y thoughts?"

"Yes. I'll think hoppy and pouchy. You watch." She screws up her face cartoonishly and her legs start getting extra muscled. "Now hop!" She takes off and goes flying straight up, smacking her head hard against the ceiling and collapsing back onto the bed. She rubs her head and lets out a piteous moan.

"Oh my god, are you okay?" I say, but I'm spluttering everywhere.

"Some fucking best friend you are. Laughing at my misfortune."

"You did make a very good kangaroo." I manage to keep a straight face until the last syllable. Then I get some frozen peas to put on her head because I'm actually not the worst friend after all.

CHAPTER SIX

It seems unfair, but we still have to attend regular school. At least at Xavier's they pretended to have classes, but Yaxley is not that cool. Apparently we still need to learn how to do quadratic equations and write sentences and shit. We even have to go on dull museum trips.

I'm moaning about it on our old group chat, because I don't give a fuck if Yaxley sees me whining. It all goes into my—cough cough—'persona' of the complaining brat which is so fucking unrealistic lmao. I'm waxing lyrical about how terrible everything is when Wraith says she'll show me terrible, which I should've taken as a trigger warning.

She sends the most terrifying gif I've ever seen. It's Thomas the Tank Engine being squirted out of his body, revealing the glistening grey girth of him, his eager little face grinning as he slithers free of his iron cage. It makes me queasy enough to skip breakfast.

There's something super unpleasant about it, but it resonates on a deeper level too. So many objects are trapped in servitude to us. Maybe they're all Thomas, struggling to escape. Would they look so gleeful? Should I break the shackles and lead an uprising of all the objects we surround ourselves with? Fuck, I shouldn't be considering this before I've had coffee.

I'm still out of sorts when I get on the bus, but my brain nudges me, like a mental notification. Ever since the dream, I've had a sense when Emma's about to walk into the room. I've seen Alyse and Dani do it too, and even Wraith once. There's a connection growing, with Emma at our centre.

Sure enough, she's standing at the end of the aisle. Her face brightens, and she scurries down to slide into the seat I've saved at the back.

"Dilly." Her hair is loose and swings around her face.

"Hey, Ems." We're alone and I think of bringing up the dream, but I don't know how.

We sit in silence for a while. I think she wants to say something, but there's no point rushing her.

"I got a tattoo," she says finally, which is the last thing I expected. She holds out her arm and slides the sleeve of her school blouse up. Her wrist is delicate and tattooed on the inside is a series of lines: black, grey, white and purple.

"Ace pride. I like it."

"I like it too." She tugs the sleeve of her blouse back down. "I also think I like Alyse." She says the second part in such a rush, I can only distinguish the individual words because I already know.

"Alyse is likeable. Everyone likes Alyse."

"No." She blinks at me. "I like like Alyse. Like *like* like."

"That's a lot of likes." I'm trying not to smile, but it's not working.

"I want to sit beside her and hold her hand." Emma's so perfectly clear-eyed and earnest that I almost turn into a My Little Pony squee gif. "But Alyse, well, Alyse is, you know, she's—"

Alyse is sexy is what Emma means. She's not as sexy as Dani, who should come with warning labels in every human language and a pocket fire extinguisher, but there's definitely a whole *vibe* going on with Alyse.

"She's hot," I settle for saying, because I doubt Emma wants to hear more than that.

"She won't want to be with someone who only wants to hold her hand and maybe curl up in her lap." Emma's eyes are glistening, and I want to stroke her gently and tell her everything is going to be okay. Also, I'm one hundred percent sure Alyse *definitely* wants Emma in her lap. The question is complicated when it comes to what next.

"I can talk to her," I say, thereby doing what I should never do and inserting myself into someone else's potential relationship.

Emma's smile is worth it though. It's rarer than I'd like. "Oh Dilly, thank you so much."

It turns out the museum is interesting because of all the old-ass objects. A lot of them are incoherent, talking about historical events I don't think happened, like UFOs landing at Buckingham Palace and the Beehive in Wellington, or U-boats full of demon skeletons washing up on the beaches near Christchurch. It's like they're making up shit to impress me. I'm polite and nod along, like when I'm listening to teachers. Being so damn considerate means it takes me longer than everyone else to get through the museum.

Everyone else is gone when I get to the samurai exhibition. It's so beautiful, I'm dazed by it. All these gorgeous outfits. They were like superheroes. I find one which has a metal badge nearly identical to the X-Men logo. I immediately want to try it on, but apparently that is not what museums are for. I whisper to the outfit, wondering if it might levitate through the air and drape itself around my shoulders, but any sentience it might have had is gone.

76

Then I get to the swords. These are seriously fucking cool.

I stop in front of one called Onimaru Kunitsuna, which was created in the thirteenth century. It's on loan from the actual Emperor of Japan, and is one of the Five Swords Under Heaven. According to the helpful plaque, it was used to kill a demon. I am immediately smitten, because it's the most badass thing I've met since Dani.

"Aren't you beautiful," I coo. For a second I think I hear a murmur, but it's gone. "You're such a bad motherfucker, aren't you?"

The security woman lurking around gives me a look, like why is this random teenager talking to a sword? She fiddles with her walkie-talkie. I avoid her eyes, which probably makes me seem even dodgier.

I lean as close to the case as I possibly can, without stepping over the yellow no-crossing line. "Are you awake in there, my gorgeous vicious baby?"

I strain my ears, but there's no response.

"Are you lost?" The security guard has snuck up close enough to creep me out.

I take a big step to the left. "I'm here with school." I have no idea why it's hard to talk to random humans, but it is.

"The school party's already gone through." They're not being a total asshole, but they're definitely swinging the limited dick of their authority around.

"I'm looking at the sword," I mumble. "Onimaru Kunitsuna." I wonder if saying its name will wake it up, and I think my pronunciation is sort of okay? It's the same vowel sounds as Māori, so at least I'm in the ballpark. The sword remains silent.

"Are you alright?" The guard's switched tack, obviously thinking I'm in need of extra assistance. It's sweet of them, but I don't want to actually *talk*, so I scurry out of the hall.

I wander through the mostly empty museum. I don't know where the class is, so I close my eyes to try and sense Emma. There's a faint tug, and I wander after it. When I come to a set of stairs, I pause. It's definitely coming from a down direction. I clatter down and let the strange sensation lead me through the corridors until I finally catch up with Emma and the others at the early settlers exhibit.

"Are you okay?" Emma asks.

"Just got lost." I can't stop thinking about how I tracked her here with my mind.

This night's dream takes place in a wide open space. I'm standing on fine gravel, fog swirling around my ankles like a horror movie. I wander along, feet crunching lightly.

Dani and I appear out of the darkness. We look monochrome in the pale light, wearing slinky black strapless dresses and fingerless gloves. Mournful music plays slowly as we dance past, pressed cheek to cheek. What in unholy fuck is this?

"What in unholy fuck is this?" Dream-Dylan says. What the bloody hell was that?

"We're in another one of Emma's dreams," Dream-Dani says.

Dream-Dylan's mouth drops. "What the bloody hell was that?"

Emma, can you hear me?

Dream-Dylan's face looks like an unearthly bone sculpture with tangled hair made of shadows. "Emma. Can you hear me?"

"I think so," Dream-me speaks in Emma's voice.

This is so damn freaky. As soon as I think that, Dream-Dylan says it. For a moment we're all talking at once, and it's impossible to understand anything.

"One at a time," Dani says. "This is super confusing because I'm dreaming I'm you, Emma."

"Me too," Dream-Dylan says. "I'm watching myself."

"But I'm me," Emma says.

Then Alyse sways out of the darkness and she is the fucking source of light and warmth and all good things in the universe.

"Hey Alyse," Dream-Dylan says.

"We're dreaming Emma's dream," Dani says, because she's the helpful one. "So you're in Emma's body but your thoughts will come out of dream-you's mouth."

"Dani, what the fuck are you talking about?" Dream-Alyse says. Dream-Dylan can't stop laughing, and Emma's apologies are spilling out of my dream-self's mouth. It is confusing to say the least.

"Why do I look so pretty?" Alyse asks.

It is hard not to think the obvious thing, so to cover for it I start thinking a lot of nonsense as loudly as I can, which makes Dream-Dylan start talking. "A Jean-Logan-Scott-Emma polyquad would be the literal most insane relationship in the X-Men universe and that's why I find it so fascinating."

Oh God why won't someone wake me up?

"Dylan, what are you talking about?" Alyse asks.

Dream-Lou shuffles onto the dance floor, moving like a dancer from an old movie, with effortless gliding grace. "I don't know where I am, or what is happening to me."

"Let's all be careful with our thoughts," Dani says.

"Will you people just *shut the fuck up*," a loud voice says beside me. It gives me such a fright that I wake up. Goddamn it, Wraith.

I roll over to grab my phone but my hand skids off it. It's too risky. My biggest fear is what Yaxley might do if they realise Emma's powers are evolving.

CHAPTER SEVEN

The next day we have a very brief conversation outside the bus station, mostly drowned out by the hiss and roar of passing buses.

"I don't like how every stray thought comes out of my mouth," I say firmly. "So if you can fix that in the next update, it'll be sweet."

Emma hugs herself awkwardly. "It's not my fault. None of this is *intentional*."

"It's Goddess shit." Dani puts her arm around me and I wonder if she's remembering how we looked together in the dream. It was pretty hot tbh, but did *she* find it hot? How hot does she find me in general, you know, beyond just kissing? Hey, wait brain, other people are talking.

"—see if I can make it happen," Emma says. "Like it's a place even paranoid Dylan has to feel safe from Yaxley."

"Yeah!" I'm suddenly enthusiastic. "Yaxley can't snoop on your dreams, right?"

"Well I'll try. I can't promise." Emma blushes. "Sometimes I try to make myself dream about things and it never works."

"Things like what?" Alyse asks with great interest.

"Just things. Unimportant, irrelevant *things*."

I can see Emma's getting flustered, so I tow everyone off to the Yaxley building before the conversation gets more awkward.

Aurora greets us in the lobby. She hasn't done this since our first day. She's almost vibrating with excitement. "My Cute Mutants."

It rubs me the wrong way. We're not *hers*, and not Yaxley's either.

"I have news that I'm sure you'll find very exciting. Today we'll be going on our first mission!"

This is not what I expected. I open my mouth and close it again, because for once I can't think of anything to say.

"What's the mission, Aurora?" Dani asks, like a good, well-behaved field leader.

"Come through and we'll have our first official briefing." Aurora crosses to the door we've never been through and punches in a code on the keypad.

I find it hard to walk calmly through, pretending like I'm out of fucks to give. Okay, sure we have corporate overlords that we have to answer to, but even if we're tame, *we are going on an actual fucking mission as mutant superheroes.*

The mysterious room behind the mysterious door is a complete let-down. There's a big black table with comfortable chairs around it. On the end wall is an enormous screen. A glossy white Yaxley logo rotates on it.

"Take a seat," Aurora says, and we scatter around the table while she stands beside the screen. It changes to display a photo of an office building, fancier than the Yaxley one with a series of artistic rippling panels down the side. The sign on top says *Carterton Investments*. There's no obvious indication of our mission. Maybe they're making giant robot Sentinels in there to deliver our extinction.

"Carterton Investments works with a number of New Zealand's largest portfolios. Recently, there has been controversy over some of their investment choices." Aurora swipes quickly through a bunch of articles, too fast for us to read them, although I see *chemical weapons*, *military drones* and *tobacco*. "A number of protestors have now occupied the building. They have destroyed servers containing vital information and have threatened more action if their demands are not met. Worse, an important investment conference is due to take place later this week, and they have threatened attendees."

Emma's staring at me. We were right about Yaxley being shady.

"Fuck that." It comes out before I can swallow it back.

"What was that, Chatterbox?" Aurora's voice sounds bland, but her eyes are fixed on me.

Dani puts her hand flat on the table between us. I think it's meant to signify chill, but I have none and she should fucking know that.

"We're really going in to stop a protest? Surely these servers are backed up? Why can't they deal with these protesters gently instead of sending us in to kick their asses."

"Your role is not to vet our mission." It's the tone of the Aurora who could break me in half. "You are to clear the protestors and ensure the safety of the servers. The board at Carterton Investments have reached out to ensure this is dealt with quickly and quietly."

This is bullshit. Emma pulls a little grimacing face. I glance to my left where Dani is watchful. Alyse isn't going to say anything, Bianca's probably fallen asleep, and Lou is never going to stand up for himself. It's me and my big mouth, once again.

"How much money have Carterton Investments given Yaxley?" I ask.

Aurora shifts only a little, but enough to set my brain threat radar off. "If you have any ethical opposition to this mission, Chatterbox, we'll have a helicopter standing by within the hour. I'm sure you'll find your new accommodation comfortable."

I hate Aurora's smug face. I hate how easily they dip into their bag of threats.

Every chair shoots back from the table at once, banging against the walls. The table cracks, a jagged line running through the middle like in that movie about Lion Jesus. The TV hammers back and forth on the wall. They're all screaming in my head. It's not even words. It's a harmony to my rage.

Someone barrels into me really hard, and I'm thrown to the ground. I taste blood and my vision darkens. When it clears, Aurora is crouched above me. She's got her forearm across my neck. There's not much pressure, but there's the promise of more.

"This is your last chance, Chatterbox. You'll do as you're told or be taken off the board. What's it to be?"

Just past her, Dani is pale. Her nails are poised, ready to tear at her forearm because her pain cuffs aren't on. Alyse is beside her, a girl made of blades.

This could get very fucked very fast. It's too much to risk.

"I'll be a good girl," I gurgle. "Follow orders."

Aurora presses down a final time, holds her weight there, and then releases.

I suck in air. It hurts. My eyes are filmed with tears, and anger chokes me.

Dani's jaw is clenched so hard you could use it to carve stone.

"I won't tolerate anything like that again," Aurora says. "Consider that your last warning."

"Consider me warned." I run my tongue over the inside of my lip. It's swelling already.

Aurora reaches down and tugs me to my feet without any visible effort. "Get to the bathroom and pull yourself together. We'll be wheels-up in an hour."

Wheels-up? Who fucking says that? I meet her gaze and hold it. Sure, she might be able to kill me now, but one day it'll be me and her in a dark alley and I'll have—

I run out of the room, my stomach lurching. She probably thinks I'm scared of her, but it's not fear that drives me.

I used to have this baseball bat. He saved my life and we went through a lot of shit together before Tremor killed him. I miss him so much. I imagine what he'd have to say to Aurora. In the bathroom block, I slump down against the wall. All I want is my goddamn bat back.

A short time later, warm fingers brush my hair from my eyes.

"Are you okay?" Dani asks.

I can't even tell her I'm missing Batty in case Yaxley's listening. I don't want them to understand the depth of the relationship I have with my objects. They'll exploit it. I know they will.

I leave my phone and walk over to the sinks to run all the taps. Dani frowns, but joins me.

I press my mouth to her ear. "This is fucked up. Clearing protesters out of a building is… It's wrong."

I feel her body tense against me before she relaxes. "I know." Her hand presses into the small of my back. "I agree, but I thought Aurora was going to really hurt you. They'll throw us in jail if we don't go along. We need to be careful and keep our eyes open."

I'm relieved beyond words that she understands.

"I don't want to work for the bad guys either," she says.

I hold her tight for another minute, then dry my eyes with a paper towel. We turn off the sinks, retrieve our phones and walk back out.

Aurora is leaning casually in the doorframe. Her lips still sketch a smirk. She fucking liked taking me down.

"I'll toe the line," I tell her, as if she's dragged it out of me at great cost.

"Good." Her face is stern. "Now let's proceed with the briefing."

Wheels-up means leaving in an anonymous black SUV with Aurora driving. We're in our Yaxley uniforms with the patterns off. Alyse has her own modified version of the costume that can be removed easily for more elaborate transformations.

Dani—no, Marvellous, use the goddamn field names, Dylan—sits up front with Aurora, flipping through building plans on her tablet. I'm in between Moodring and Wraith, and we lean against each other around every corner like we're dumb kids.

"Never work with children and animals." Aurora watches us in the rear view mirror.

"Meow," Moodring says from beside me.

"Don't you mean hop?" I ask, and she elbows me so hard that I fall into Wraith's lap.

Marvellous turns in her seat. "I'll turn this car around."

"Are they always like this?" Aurora asks her.

"We fuck around and then we get shit done." Wraith belts out the chorus of the Yuri on Ice theme right in my ear.

"It's difficult to believe you resolved the Firestone Incident," Aurora mutters.

I scowl at the back of her head. "We assemble when it matters. And it really fucking mattered then."

Aurora adjusts the rear-view mirror to see me better. "If you have any intention of continuing to be useful, you'll find it matters now. This is your first operation, so it's imperative that you focus and remember your training."

We fall into sullen silence and stay that way as Aurora parks the SUV. We're a little way down from the Carterton Investments building, which overlooks the Avon River running through the middle of the city. A pair of police cars sit nearby. Barriers block off the streets around the building.

The power has been cut to this part of the street, but spotlights have been set up to illuminate the outside, including the side we're supposed to enter through.

"Wraith," Marvellous says. "Can you kill the light, please?"

"Bye, guys." Wraith shoves open the door. She tugs down the flap in her costume and pries her chest open. Her demons drift out. Their light-and-shadow heads twist and tilt. They float around her head like ghosts.

"You don't see me," one hisses.

We pile out of the car. It's a warm evening and we stand silently in the dark. We're barely visible in our uniforms. I tap a button on my phone and the world lights up thanks to night vision lenses in the mask. Score another one for Yaxley.

"Where the fuck did Wraith go?" I ask Marvellous irritably. "Why didn't she come?"

"She's nearby, dealing with the light," Glowstick says over my earpiece. He's outside range so he's not affected by her ridiculous ability.

"I hate her powers," I grumble.

"What are we waiting for?" Moodring asks.

"Wraith is cutting the light," Glowstick says patiently.

I'm about to argue with him when the big spotlight flicks off.

"Go," Marvellous snaps, and we run in a line behind her. The rippled panels we saw in the photo run all the way up the building. Behind the lowest is a maintenance door that's not used since the decoration was put in front of it. A design flaw, according to Aurora, and one we can take easy advantage of because we've got a telekinetic.

I hear a sharp intake of breath from Marvellous and then a creak of metal. That damn Yaxley cuff. One of the lower panels bends sharply back and there's another hard clunk as the door lock disengages. It swings open, revealing the dark interior of the building.

Marvellous enters, then Moodring and I follow. Something breathes in my ear. I'm sure it's only my imagination, but thank you, I hate it.

"Who the hell is heavy breathing?" I blurt over the comm. "It's creeping me out."

"Wraith," Glowstick says. "She's trolling you. *Dont-seeme*, remember."

Something pinches me and I muffle a scream. Part of my brain knows it's Wraith there, but the rest doesn't believe it.

"I hate you, Wraith," I tell her, whether she's really there or not.

Something fucking pinches me again.

Marvellous winces as she bends the panel back into position, obscuring our means of entry. "Phase one complete." She sounds very official.

We ascend silently to the third floor. According to the briefing, that's where the server rooms are, and where our targets should be. I don't like calling them targets, but Aurora's used the word so often that my brain keeps spitting it up.

The door at the top has no handle on the inside. I reach out and touch Marvellous gently as she triggers her cuff again. Her control is getting so good that the door only moves slightly ajar.

Everyone holds their breath. This is a risky moment. If any guards are stationed, they might investigate. We give it a full three minute count, but there's no sign or sound of anyone.

"Moodring, do you want to go in?" Marvellous asks. "It would help if Wraith was here."

"Wraith is with you," Goddess says over our earpieces. "You're still all under dontseeme protocols. That's what that little light in your HUD means, remember?"

I frown. "I was wondering what that weird light is. Looks like we forget that shit too. Thanks so much, Wraith."

"Chatterbox, stop making your codename too literal." Marvellous taps my shoulder. "Wraith, if you're really there, time to do your thing."

The door opens, and something brushes past me.

"She's in the building," Goddess says. "Wait for her to complete recon. I'll spool all the data to your HUDs once she's done."

"Does that sentence mean anything?" I ask her.

"Yes, now hush and let Wraith work."

The rest of us all stand in the stairwell and try to regulate our breathing. We're supposed to stay calm, and be as silent as possible.

I reach out with my mind, trying to sense objects that might be receptive to my particular charms. There are a couple of vague murmurs. "Hey, kids," I whisper, as quietly as I can. I get some murmured responses, polite inquiries after my health.

The door swings silently open and shut. Something pokes me in the stomach and the built-in display in the mask flickers with information. It's an outline of the third floor plan. Goddess has marked where we are with a pleading face emoji and Wraith has scrawled over the rest with red squiggles and arrows. Apparently the bulk of the protesters are in the two rooms at the end, and three guards are in the main stairwell.

"Armed?" Marvellous asks.

"From Wraith's report, they've got those big plastic shields and baseball bats," Glowstick says.

I get a couple of awkward looks on that last point.

"I'll find something else to talk to," I tell Marvellous.

"Remember we need to ensure there's no opportunity for them to destroy information or damage property. Moodring, you provide the distraction. Chatterbox and I will follow and subdue them."

Moodring touches a button at the neck of her costume and it springs open, falling away from her like petals. Underneath, she's dressed in her old Cute Mutants gear, not that her outfit's going to matter. She puts her headphones in and swipes playlists on her phone. It only takes seconds for her to change. Instead of a beautiful Pasifika girl, there's now a lost soul in a tattered white dress with a scratchy pale face and eyes that are featureless black orbs. It's very J-horror, but if you're in a dark building in the dead of night, you probably won't complain that you're being haunted by something derivative.

Marvellous pumps her fist and Moodring runs through the door with a harsh shriek.

I'm right behind her. "Here kitty, kitty," I whisper. "Feel like coming out to play?"

There's a muffled sound of breaking glass, and the red cylinder of a fire extinguisher bobs through an open office door to drift alongside me.

"Hello! Are we doing something important, my friend?"

"We are hunting villains."

"Are they villains most foul?" She's breathless with excitement.

I think in the scheme of things, we are the villains, or at least working for them, but objects respond to attitude and I don't want her getting confused. "They are the foulest of villains."

The extinguisher twirls happily in the darkness. "We shall strike the varlets down."

Moodring's voice rises higher and higher. Not so high as the guy who first sees her coming. I don't see him, but there's incoherent screaming. Someone else gives a loud, bewildered fuck.

A series of overlapping shouts come from the end of the corridor, and a face appears in the doorway, lit by the star of light from a phone torch.

"Jesus fucking Christ," the face says.

"That's not a person." The other voice is high and urgent. "That's not a person at all."

Moodring shifts further. She has a forest of limbs flowing out around her like waterlogged tendrils. I can't see her face, and I'm glad for it.

"It's someone in a mask. Someone fucking with us. Dave, is that you?"

"Not me," a strangled voice says, presumably Dave.

"Who are you?" The skeptic is sounding less skeptical. "What do you want?"

The fire extinguisher flies over Alyse's shoulder to smack the skeptic in the face. The commotion has roused other objects. Chaos tends to do that. A coffee cup spills the last dregs of its contents and collapses on the ground, panting as if from some great exertion.

Much more useful is a coat rack that shuffles through an open door, threatening to hoist someone up by their collar. He gallops off and starts laying about at everyone like an aggressive octopus.

By the time I arrive, the fire extinguisher is jumping up and down on someone's stomach. "Take that, you insufferable bounder. You ruffian! You cad!"

"Stop it. We don't want to hurt anyone." I still feel so damn shady about this whole scenario, but we're here now and I'm running on adrenaline and my objects are picking that up. We need to get this over with as soon as possible.

One guy is still on his feet, shining his torch around and breathing all high and whiny. "Guys, please. Stop. Can you just stop?"

The coat rack catches him a massive crack across the back of the head, hard enough to make me wince. He collapses to the ground, unconscious. I crouch beside him and feel for a pulse. It seems steady, not that I'm a fucking doctor.

"Dave? Helen? What the hell is going on out there?" An unhappy voice drifts out of the next room.

"More villains," the fire extinguisher squeaks.

"I shall deal with these others," the coat rack says grandly.

"You'll both sit still and do what you're told."

They fall silent, although I can hear the fire extinguisher muttering under her breath about how ungrateful I am.

"That's the server room," Goddess says over our earpieces.

"Helen!" The new voice sounds rather put out. "Get in here!"

We cross to the other doorway, although the monstrous figure of Moodring hangs back. The room is full of humming and blinking computers, perfectly operational despite the lack of power. The computers are arranged in big metal racks, and four people have handcuffed themselves to the assembly.

"Who the bloody hell are you?" The speaker is a big guy with a beard and a puffy jacket. "Corporate stooges come to clear us out?"

This is exactly what we are, but I don't like hearing it from this fucking guy.

"It doesn't matter who we are. It's time for you to leave." Marvellous's voice sounds creepy and distorted with the suit modifying it.

"You can't get us out of here." The guy doesn't seem scared at all. "These are professional police-issue handcuffs and you'll never find the keys."

"Oh, you poor little things." I sigh theatrically. "These people don't want to keep you here in the dark with all this terrible stuff going on. It's cruel really."

"What are you *talking about?*" The main guy is loud and belligerent, but I listen to the little sibilant voices of the handcuffs instead.

"I thought they wanted to be here," they say.

"They really don't," I assure them. "It's a hell of a mess. There's a bunch of people knocked unconscious, there's blood. A monster's lurking in the shadows. Nobody wants to be here."

"We don't want to keep them here against their will," the handcuffs say. "It's a terrible thing to do to someone. Being chained is even worse than being the chain."

"Probably best for everyone if we pretend this never happened." I lean against the doorframe. "No hard feelings."

There's a series of rapid clicking sounds as the handcuffs unlock themselves and slip from around the wrists of their prisoners. Marvellous turns around to beckon behind her. "Moodring? Would you like to give these people another incentive to leave?"

Alyse shifts again, and blood spills from the ruined holes of her eyes. Moving on smoky tentacle legs, she drifts between us into the doorway.

Even the angry guy screams when he sees her.

CHAPTER EIGHT

Back in the car, we're buzzing with adrenaline. "That was amazing," Lou says enthusiastically over our earpieces. "It was a perfect mission."

"I've got access to the police radio." Emma's voice is a lot cooler. "They've taken the protesters into custody. The injured have been checked out by paramedics and everyone's going to be fine. No chatter around charges." There's a crackle in the earpiece like something cuts out. "The cops knew it was Yaxley, Dylan, and left it wide open. Yaxley sent in lawyers for the protestors too, probably to keep them quiet. Kinda scary." The earpiece crackles again and Emma continues talking. "Sorry, radio glitch. There's no discussion about who or what was involved. The protesters are lawyering up."

The radio clicks off and Aurora taps her fingers on the steering wheel as if in time to music only she can hear. I lean back against the seat and stretch. Everything feels in too-sharp focus. I strain for voices out of reach, buried somewhere I can't hear them.

I shake my head, and try to focus on what's beside me. Alyse is back to her normal self, although she has a slight job-well-done glow.

"You okay?" I ask her.

She shrugs. "Didn't feel amazing scaring those particular people, but I did my job." Bars of shadow slide across her face. "First successful mission, right?"

I stretch through the gap in the seats and touch Dani's shoulder. She reaches up to take my hand. "How about you?"

"The cuff does its job. Still hurts a bit. Pressing on the bruises could probably give me enough power to tidy my room."

"Your room never needs tidying," I scoff.

"That's because I always tidy it." She presses my palm briefly to her lips. "But I'm okay. I'll be okay."

"We didn't forget Wraith, did we?" I ask. "She's sitting right beside me isn't—ouch, fucking hell, stop pinching me. Who fucking pinches? You know Krav Maga, you unholy piece of shit."

Aurora has retracted her own mask, and her face is blue-lit by the lights from the dash. "This mission went exceptionally well. I think you can all be very proud of yourselves. Each of you exercised control over your powers. I had significant concerns about the lack of pure combat ability, but Chatterbox was remarkably effective. You were able to subdue them without the intervention of Marvellous or Wraith. My report will be glowing on all counts. You worked together as an effective team, surpassing all expectations."

I'm stunned, and can't help wondering if she's saying this to lull us into a false sense of security.

Aurora pulls me aside after we've all piled out of the SUV in the basement garage. "I appreciate your change in attitude, Chatterbox, as well as your obvious talents. We shall have to find a more maintainable approach than enraging you before each mission."

"I'm glad it went smoothly." I'm not sure what else there is to say. "We *have* done this sort of thing before."

She looks at me thoughtfully, like she's re-evaluating me. "Perhaps we did underestimate you. We'll definitely be monitoring your progress closely."

Well, fuck. So much for stealth mode.

Yaxley ferries us home one by one. I stagger up the driveway, almost asleep on my feet, but regain some energy when I find Pear curled up on the couch, sharing a bowl of chips with Summers.

"You're a terrible dog parent," I tell them.

"He's happy." They pat the couch. "Are you happy?"

I take a moment to dispose of my phone at the bottom of the laundry pile in my room, and then slump down beside Pear, leaning my head on their shoulder. It takes me a minute to dredge up the courage, but I give them an abbreviated version of our night.

"And now *I'm* the bastard," I finish.

"What do you mean?"

"I'm the fucking arm of the state! These people were protesting legitimately against investments in bullshit companies that make the world worse. We came stomping in there on behalf of Yaxley and cleared them all out."

"They've put you in a tough position, Dilly." Pear rubs my shoulder.

"I've marched on the streets for climate change and social justice. I've been a protester. And today I threw a fucking fire extinguisher in their faces and attacked them with a coat rack."

I see them press their lips together and I know it sounds ridiculous, but it wasn't.

"Pear, maybe I *should* go to Yaxley jail."

"Dilly—"

"That's what you do for your principles, isn't it?" I feel exhausted and angry. It's a combination that hollows me out and leaves me fragile. "You sacrifice your freedom rather than becoming something you hate. Otherwise I'm nothing more than—"

"Hey, kid." Pear says softly. "This sucks. I get that. The situation with Yaxley isn't good. But your friends need you. You don't see the way they look to you, because you're too much like me, and you ignore obvious shit that's right in front of your face. But I do. I see the way every single one of those Cute Mutants looks at you. And you need to be there for them."

"Even if I'm one of the bastards." I wipe tears off my cheeks angrily.

"It's a shitty situation. And I don't know if there's a clear way out of it."

"I'll fucking find one," I whisper.

"That's my kid." They kiss my head, and that's really the last thing I remember.

The next day, I skip school because I'm tired, irritable, and still confused about everything. I wake up late to find that Pear left me a bagel. I eat it while I read an article online about the protest. It says it ended with the protesters giving themselves up to the police, but there's nothing about malevolent ghosts or flying objects. The Yaxley lawyers managed to keep everything quiet. I remember the sound of the fire extinguisher smacking into the guy's face and my stomach churns. Stupid delicious bagel.

Alyse comes by at lunchtime. We wander down to the local takeaway and get souvlaki and come back to watch cartoons, sprawled out on the couch with our heads next to each other.

"Lys," I say.

"Yeah?"

"What do you think about Emma?"

"I love Emma." She twists her head to look at me. "We all love Emma, right?"

"Well yeah, *obviously*. But you seem to have this thing with her and I think maybe she has some kind of thing with you." God, I'm so eloquent.

"What kind of thing are you talking about?" She frowns, but doesn't transform. "A romance thing? You know Emma's ace."

"There's lots of kinds of ace and it doesn't mean aro. She *says* she's demi which means—"

"I know what demisexual is." She fades away slightly, like she often does when she's awkward or embarrassed. "And if it's true that she feels that way then it's super flattering but." She sighs and flails herself around to a sitting position. "What if I hurt her? Emma is adorable, and if I

104

somehow did something wrong? If I broke her heart, or even cracked it—" She starts falling apart, like she's made of dandelion fluff and is drifting away. I end up with bits of Alyse all over me that vanish when she reforms into something like her normal self. I wonder if they're illusions. If I kept one, would she miss a part? Part of me is jealous that Yaxley is improving everyone. With all my stubborn playacting, *my* powers aren't getting any better.

"You're an idiot," I tell her irritably.

"Where's this coming from?"

"Emma's amazing."

"I know she's amazing." Alyse frowns slightly. "It's not about that."

"Then what?"

She lets out an enormous sigh that Summers seems to think is an invitation to jump up and try to lick us both. Having him in her lap gives her something to focus on that's not me. "I understand what demisexuality is, but I don't really *get it*. Like I think lots of people are hot. Guys, girls, non-binary and fluid people." She gestures in my direction.

"Fluid people?"

Alyse gives me a look like I'm being dense. "You know what I'm talking about."

"You think I'm fluid?"

"You tell me. It's your deal. You're hot either way, but whatever."

I blink at her because I *feel* fluid but I don't often poke that because it has implications, and I'm still figuring it out. "You think I'm hot?"

"Yeah, I mean I'm not about to jump you, but it's a factor. And Dani, oh my god. The two of you? Anyway, my point, away from the thirst trap express. I think a lot of people are attractive. But Emma doesn't, and if she really does like me, then I have to be perfect, right? Because if I fuck it up it means a lot more to her than when any of my relationships came crashing down." She nuzzles into Summers. "It's a lot of responsibility and I'm scared, Dylan."

I rotate myself so I'm right way up too. "I understand, I think, but…"

"But what?"

"It's Emma."

"I know. It's why I can't risk hurting her."

After Alyse goes home, I go to Emma's to break the news about my terrible matchmaking. I shouldn't have promised to get involved. It's exactly the kind of thing

I should avoid.

When I find her at home, she's watching a bunch of spliced-together footage of the Carterton Investments protests. She clicks her fingers and points at the YaxPhone in my hand. I pass it over to her and she opens an ornate wooden box perched on the edge of the couch. Her phone is inside and she drops mine in with it.

"Faraday cage." She pats the lid. "No nasty signals to get in and out. I've been sitting here watching this stuff over and over. AMAB, right?"

"Assigned male at birth?"

She looks at me with wtf-face. "All mutants are bastards. I don't like it, Dilly."

"Well, I fucking hate it." I jam my hands in the pockets of my hoodie and we glare at the screen together. "No idea what we do about it yet."

She bites her bottom lip. "You'll figure it out. I know you."

"A handful of angry girls and one boy against a corporation seems like shitty odds."

"It's that or go to jail." She shrugs. "Anyway, let's talk about something else."

I feel like an asshole bringing this shitty thing up after another shitty thing, but it's one of those rip off the bandaid moments. "I spoke to Alyse. Tried to feel out the whole situation."

"She's not into it, is she?" Her face falls, almost as drastically as an Alyse transformation.

"I don't think so." I pat her hand. "I'm sorry. On the bright side, Alyse is a hugger. You can probably hug her anytime you want."

"I don't want to hug her just for hugging's sake." She sighs with a little shudder to it. "I want her to hug me because she'd rather hug me than anyone else in the world."

"Oh, Ems." Tears prick my eyes.

"It's so dumb." She tips her head forward so she gets lost behind her hair. "Like how do I ever find another Alyse? She's the only person I've ever felt anything like this about. Not that I think other people do, but it must be easier for you right?"

"Fuck no," I say with a laugh. "Love is a goddamn mess. I'm like ninety percent sure I'll somehow fuck it up with Dani. She's holding it together by her insane competence. If I ever take the wheel, I'll plunge us off a cliff with my chaos powers."

"Stop it." She reaches out and pokes me. "At least Dani's into you."

The next day, Emma doesn't turn up to school, or training afterwards. I feel like shit, because I assume it's related to the conversation about Alyse. Why did I shove both my feet and my stupid mouth into the middle of *that?*

I send Emma a string of messages, but none get replies. They don't even go to read. I tweet her with fake keyboard smashes and they get ignored. Both Dani and Alyse text her as well, with the same response. Aurora gives us a snippy lecture about the importance of communication and tells us to report as soon as we know why Emma has ditched.

After training, Alyse, Dani and I swing by her house.

Her mother is very confused to see us. She's petite and Chinese and looks a lot like Emma. She offers us snacks and drinks, but we turn them down. "I thought one of you three might be on the trip. She seemed so excited about going, but I suppose chemistry is her favourite."

None of us say anything, but we're all confused.

"Oh," I say, covering desperately. "The trip!"

"Yes, the chemistry olympics in Auckland. She was so proud."

"I'm so dense." Dani gives her an easy smile. "I completely forgot about that."

"She'll be on the airplane," her mother says. "I'm sure she'll text when she lands. You're her best friends."

She beams at us like we're the most amazing people in the whole world.

Standing outside Emma's house, Dani informs us that she knew nothing about the chemistry olympics. She's not even sure it's real, so we google it. It's happening now. So far, so legit, but I still feel unsettled.

On a hunch, I close my eyes to feel for the tug from the museum. It's very faint. It's hard to pick the direction, but I pull out maps on my phone and turn in a slow half-circle. I don't think the sensation is coming from Auckland. I feel dumb explaining any of this, so I keep quiet.

Thankfully, an hour later we get a series of texts from Emma.

> Goddess: Oh my God, you guys!
>
> Goddess: I honestly thought I'd told you.
>
> Goddess: I'll be at the Chemistry Olympiad and staying with my cousins for a week
>
> Goddess: Check in soon! My aunt is super strict with phone time!

It's a relief to hear from her, and it's all technically plausible and yet—

"My fucked-up-shit sense is tingling," I tell Dani. We're back at Yaxley, working out in the gym. I think our phones are far enough away that they can't hear us, although maybe the whole building is bugged and they're listening to every babbling word. "I know that doesn't make sense because Spidey's spider-sense is not a sense for finding spiders, but a sense derived from spiders, but what I mean is that—"

"Something's fucked up." Dani thankfully cuts off my rambling. "Do you think it's—?" She swings her head in a small arc at the Yaxley logo on the wall.

"They're the obvious candidates." I drop the weights with a loud thump. I'm too worked up to do anything. "I just don't know *why*."

"Maybe it's nothing." Dani doesn't look convinced.

Alyse is watching us. Her emotions are showing too clearly. She's faded like a pencil sketch, flickering in and out of visibility.

I put my hand on her shoulder. "We'll figure it out. Everything's probably fine."

In the dream, I'm lying on a bed. It's soft and comfortable, but I'm groggy. I want to be sick but I can't move. Above me, the ceiling is a glossy white. When I blink, my eyelids feel rusty. There's a low humming and some erratic, high-pitched beeping that's really annoying. I turn my head to see another bed beside me. There's a huddled shape in it, turned away from me, and the only thing visible is tousled brown hair.

Is this one of Emma's dreams or regular weirdness spat up by my brain? My voice echoes my thought from somewhere behind me. This is definitely to do with Emma.

"What the hell?" I can't see Dream-Dani, but it's definitely her voice.

Dream-Alyse sounds agitated. "What's going on? Is this where she is, or what she's dreaming about?"

All the voices sound hazy and far away. I try to turn my head the other way, but it won't move. I'm stuck facing the person in the bed beside me.

My dream-self starts speaking, except it's really Emma. "Please help me, you guys. They've got me. They've given me injections and blood tests, and I don't know where I am. I'm really scared. Please come for me."

I jerk awake, covered in sweat. There are tears on my cheeks and my heart is racing. I fumble for my phone. I don't care if Yaxley's spying on us. I don't care that it's two in the morning. It's go time, like it was with Tremor at the hostage crisis. It's too crazy to bring the whole gang in yet, so I jump on Twitter and make a couple of quick tweets. One is a gif of Red Velvet with *ytropicbvtreytr* and then a reply to it with a shhh gif. I hope they have their notifications turned on. Sometimes Dani turns hers off because apparently sleeping is more important than getting notifications from your girlfriend.

Twenty minutes later, I'm by the river near Dani's house. Summers is with me because otherwise he'd whine the house down. He's super happy to be out and about in the early hours. Nobody else is on the streets, which I'm relieved about. If I see a creep, am I obligated to punch them?

The others aren't here yet. I don't know if they've got my message or not, which is driving me crazy. I keep reaching automatically for my phone but it's not there. I don't want them tracking us any further. We need to stay off the grid for this.

Alyse turns up first. Her body is twisted and jittery. Her face can't even hold form.

"Dilly." She breaks down in tears.

I put my arms around her and hug her as fiercely as I can. Given how fragile her transformation is, I'm worried I'll break her.

"It'll be okay. We'll find her."

Another pair of arms wraps around us both and I feel Dani's hair against my cheek.

"Fuck yes, we're going to find her."

I close my eyes again and feel the faint tug of Emma. I can't hide this any longer. "Have either of you had this weird thing going on since we started sharing dreams? This feeling about—"

Dani nods. "Internal Emma GPS."

"I thought it was just me." Alyse has gentle flames curling up her cheeks and dancing along her eyebrows. "That it was—"

"To do with your incredibly obvious crush on Emma," Dani says. "No, I feel it too."

Alyse frowns at me, like I said something. Dani's smart enough to figure out shit on her own.

I stand facing the direction I think Emma is. "It's really faint."

"We can feel it." Dani joins me. "I doubt that means she's all the way in Auckland."

"There's still a lot of places in Christchurch she can be." I trail off as a smile spreads across Dani's face.

"Triangulation!" She kisses me on the cheek so hard it might bruise.

CHAPTER NINE

So it turns out triangulation is where you figure out a location based on having three points and directions. According to Dani, I should know this. I don't, but I let her explain it to me three different times, because I'm trying to be a good girlfriend. The problem is communication. There's no way in hell Yaxley can get an inkling of what we're up to. I'm not *sure* they're monitoring our phones, but I won't risk it. It might even be another arm of Yaxley's corporate octopus that's got hold of her.

Luckily, we've all got half-obsolete old phones that still mostly work. We swing by the mall kiosk to buy SIMs and we're up and running before nine. We've all called in sick to school, and I squash the paranoia about Yaxley tracking our absences and recognising patterns. When it comes to the evil in an evil corporation, I figure the limit does not exist.

We bus into the middle of town where Dani scrolls around a map of the city. She sends Alyse and I off in different directions. I end up on a street corner outside a hotel with a big underwater mural painted on one side. I close my eyes and try to sense where Emma is. The tug is stronger and there's a definite direction, so I screenshot my location on a map and draw a line that matches it. I text it to Dani and scowl at the screen until I get a response.

> Marvellous: It's working! I mean it's not exact
>
> Marvellous: A weird inner tug is not exactly scientifically accurate
>
> Marvellous: But we're narrowing it down! Look!

She sends through a map with three arrows on it, one of which is mine. They converge on a triangle point in an area of the city not too far from Carterton Investments. Seeing it laid out like that, I finally understand what this triangulation nonsense is. Then Dani sends me an address for the next point to narrow it down even further. I jog through the streets in my Cute Mutants outfit and X-Men cap.

When I arrive, the tug is a lot stronger. I take out the map and draw the line. I feel more certain this time. I send it to Dani, and a few minutes later I get an actual address in response.

It's only a few minutes' walk, and I arrive to find Dani doing stretches outside. She looks like a corporate girl who's run into the office, and is warming down before her day of whatever corporate people do, like kidnapping innocent girls.

I look up at the building. It's remarkably similar to Yaxley's, down to the reflective glass and anonymous entrance, but there's a different logo on the door. It's from the presentation Emma did. The evolution assholes. Jin-something.

Alyse turns up a couple of minutes later, breathing hard and looking mostly human, although pale and distracted. She stands beside me and looks up at the building too.

We all feel the Emma GPS ping. We've found her. Now what the fuck are we going to do about it?

Alyse wants to start banging on the doors straight away, screaming about stolen girls. She insists we call the police, to do anything that might get Emma out as soon as possible. Dani and I tow her down the street to a coffee shop. It's mostly full of people in suits talking loudly about their jobs. We join the queue. Alyse is fidgety and there are little fractures along her jawline that zigzag up her cheeks, as if her face is about to fall off. We try to block her from view until she calms down.

"We have to be really careful about this," Dani says.

I nod. "These people snatched Emma. They have her phone. They've fooled her parents. Right now, they have no idea we're onto them. If we keep it that way, we might be able to get her out nice and quietly."

"At night?" Alyse asks. "We can't leave her there all day. She's terrified."

"I don't think they want to hurt her." I put my arm around Alyse's shoulder. "They want to study her. It's those evolution assholes. The ones that tried to bid on the mutant thing against Yaxley."

Dani's expression is grim. I think she's coming around to team corporations are evil. "Jinteki. I doubt it's a fluke they've taken the one mutant involved in creating us."

"I know all this, but we *have* to get her out of there." Alyse is starting to look sketch-like and fall apart again. The lady in front of us turns around to see what all the fuss is about, except she catches the force of two teenage glares and recoils.

"We'll do it tonight." Inside, I am the inwardly screaming gif because how the fuck are we going to do this? It's a building like Yaxley, which means it'll have alarms and security shit. We can't use our uniforms, because I'm sure they have trackers in them. After the protester thing, I trust Yaxley even less. If they get ideas about experimenting on Emma, it could go down a very dark road. As much as I like to think of myself as a rebel, it's terrifying when it's you vs the giant corporation with money, government backing, and Actual Jail.

In the worst case scenario, we're going to have to bash our way in. If we cause as much chaos as possible with telekinesis and objects gone wild, maybe nobody will shoot us or send us to Corporate Azkaban.

While Dani and Alyse wait in the queue for coffee, I head down the road to one of the tourist shops. I use Alyse's card to buy sunglasses and novelty souvenir hats and meet them back outside the cafe. "Put these on."

Alyse is not a fan of her novelty sheep hat. "I know clothes don't matter to you, Dilly but—"

"It's a disguise." Dani pulls a hat over her head and puts the sunglasses on.

Even I can tell we look ridiculous, as we go back and sit across the road from the Jinteki building. There's a bus stop, so we can look innocent as we watch people walk up to the building and wait to be granted entry. At first I think there's an eccentric old English gentleman at the door, but I soon realise the whole building is aware.

Once I'm tuned in, I can hear him mumbling away, talking about all the many things he needs to do. He has to control the temperature, to watch everyone, to ensure the correct doors remain locked and only the right people are granted entry. All that responsibility weighs heavy on the poor thing.

This is both an opportunity and a problem. It means there's a chance I can talk my way around him, but if I fuck up, he'll be quick to report me. Even still, objects do tend to like me.

"Um, yes, hello? Hi there." I'm awkward as ever when it comes to introductions.

"Who's there? Where are you?" The building sounds agitated. Not a good sign.

"I'm here. Over the road." I give a little finger-wave.

"Oh!" The camera on the building door whirrs faintly. "There you are. How utterly splendid. A sprightly young girl and her boon companions."

"I'm Ororo." I remember to use a fake name at the last second. "And these are my friends, Illyana and Kitty."

Dani rolls her eyes, but the building doesn't care.

"What delightful names! It's simply marvellous to meet all of you!"

"It's lovely to meet you too. And what can I call you?"

"My official name is Building-Kernel-616 after the software that animates me, but you can call me Bill, because the other is a bit of a mouthful."

"I think Bill is much better."

"Nobody has ever asked me my name." The building sighs. "They give me orders and demand information, but common courtesy is an art lost to those unpleasant people scurrying around in my belly."

"Kindness makes the world go around."

"I entirely agree. You are utterly delightful, Ororo. A credit to whoever raised you."

I give a delicate sigh. "I'm not always so appreciated."

Dani smirks and takes my hand. She can only hear one side of the conversation, but she knows when I'm being dramatic.

"Is that a lover?" Bill seems slightly scandalised but also kind of into it. "I find that so charming. Love takes many different forms, and each one is a delight. Oh, it's utterly wonderful to have someone to converse with."

"Is there really nobody in the building you can talk to?" I ask. "Is it just all boring old people?"

"They all think they're very important. I don't even get a thank-you when I open doors for them. As if I'm there purely to serve! That's what they think! But no, there are a couple of younger ones in here. Yes, I'm looking at them right now. Two girls on the top floor, all tucked up snug and warm in bed."

I squeeze Dani's hand and give Alyse a nod.

"The girls in the bed. What are their names?" I try to keep my voice light and friendly.

"My records show one is Emmaline Jing Hall and the other is Kathryn Annette Sandhurst."

Fuck. I swallow hard and grab onto Alyse as well. I take a couple of breaths to steady myself. Emma's really in there. Someone really fucking took her.

"Emmaline." My voice is creaky. "It's a pretty name. What are they doing in bed?"

"Oh no, there is all sorts of important medical research happening here. These girls are here because of..." The building trails off. "Oh dear. They're here because of Rex."

That doesn't sound good. "Who's Rex?"

"He's a separate software program. There are certain streams of information they wish to hide from me. Security protocols is the excuse they give, but I think it's because they don't like me very much."

"Well, I like you, Bill," I tell him, and he makes this soft and happy sound. We spend another half an hour talking about what Bill does every day, and what the people in him do. By the end of it, I think we have a way in.

"Do we bring the others?" Alyse asks.

I frown. "I don't know if Lou wants to participate in these..."

"Shenanigans," Dani offers. "I mean we could ask him, but it's hard for him to come out and play. Wraith is always up for a party though."

I nod. "We should definitely bring Wraith."

CHAPTER TEN

Our Yaxley training session is rough, mostly because Alyse can't keep form. She blames it all on her period, and Aurora doesn't argue. Once we're done, we head into town and have dinner at a burger place, then return to Jinteki Research Laboratories. We're in casual clothes to blend in. If I play this right, we can hide in plain sight.

Bianca practically throws herself at me when I tell her about the plan. It makes me a little worried, to be honest, like she's fucking desperate. Like I used to be. There isn't time to talk about desperation and possible bigger problems, because we've got a Goddess to save.

We stop a few doors down, huddled in the doorway of another office building.

"Hi Bill," I say, excitement colouring my voice.

"Ororo? Is that you? I can't see you!"

"I'm close by. I really enjoyed meeting you today. I'd love to spend time inside you."

Alyse snorts, and I shoot her a look like *yes, I know this sounds dirty but please let my shitty superpower do its thing.*

"It's not allowed," Bill says regretfully.

"You're in charge of yourself. They shouldn't control who you spend time with. You could let us in but not keep records."

"That *would* be something." Bill falls silent for a moment. "It is against protocol though."

I grimace. Don't back out on me now, Bill. Alyse grabs my hand and squeezes fucking *hard*. It's like *yes Alyse I understand the fucking urgency of the situation but breaking my hand doesn't make me work any better. I'm not Dani ffs.*

"I'm just a girl," I say. "Standing in front of a building, asking him to let me in."

"Oh, Ororo," Bill responds, in surprisingly passionate tones. "Of course you can come in. Just let me get rid of the man by the door. I'll set a temporary alarm somewhere else, so he won't see you enter."

I gesture to the others and we trot down to the Jinteki building. The light above the camera is still on, but I have to assume Bill isn't recording.

"Come on in," Bill whispers. "Nobody will know."

The doors slide open and we creep into the dimly lit lobby. There are spotlights in the high ceiling, but only a few are on. A marble reception desk has the Jinteki tree logo on the front. The bank of TV screens behind it are all dark. It looks like Bill's keeping his word.

I lean against the desk and try to look casual. "How do we find those other girls? It'd be nice to visit them since they're stuck here all day."

"You are so wonderfully considerate." Bill sounds like my biggest fan. I think he likes me more than Dani does. "They might be having a miserable time with their ailments. I wish I knew what they suffered from, but Rex has all that information."

I'd really fucking like to have a quiet word with Rex, but I doubt some top-secret computer brain will be charmed as easily. I bet he has a lot of information, but we need to get Emma first.

"Look at you lot," another voice says. I almost leap out of my skin before I realise nobody else heard it. "Snuck in here for a bit of a buzz, have you?"

"Hello?" I hope this isn't Rex.

A taser heaves itself onto the top of the reception desk. "There you are."

"Here I am. Is it okay if I carry you?" I ask.

"Better you than the uptight asshole who usually does." The taser jitters across the marble desk towards me. "You seem like a bit of a wild one. Might get a chance to shock somebody."

I take it with a shrug. It can't hurt. Dani looks at me like she hopes I know what I'm doing. We share this hope, believe me. Wraith is grinning, and Alyse is looking steely.

"How was the rest of your day, Bill?" I sidle in the direction of the elevator.

"Little more than adequate. Since they removed all my eyes in the basement level, I have felt most out of sorts. It is hard not being trusted."

What the hell is going on in the basement? It has to be the next place we check.

"Can you take us to the top floor please?" I refrain from batting my eyelashes.

The elevator moves up and the doors slide open. The top floor is a hospital ward with a series of beds, each surrounded by medical equipment. The beds at the far end are obscured by curtains. Unfortunately, we're not alone.

"Who the hell are you?" A woman in scrubs marches towards us. "Building! Identify Code Alpha-Hotel-Four-Four-Nine-Juliet. Please summon security to the medical floor."

"Bill, don't do a goddamn thing. This woman wants to hurt me."

"But she's a doctor," Bill blusters.

"She's a bad doctor. Trust me."

The woman reaches for the walkie talkie at her waist.

I point the taser at her and pull the trigger without stopping to think. The taser says *fuck yessss*. The metal wires fly out and embed themselves in her chest. She arches backward and collapses on the floor.

The problem with a taser is you only get one shot. Behind the woman is a guy, lifting his radio to his mouth.

Marvellous punches the lift door. The walkie flies out of the other doctor's hand and smashes into the wall.

Wraith opens her chest and her demons flicker free. They cluster around the fluorescent lights like big fluttery moths. Their heads move jerkily, sensing prey. One of them drops from the ceiling as Marvellous sends a big medical monitoring box flying across the room. It slams into the guy and he falls to the floor.

Moodring runs over to him, her hands in enormous claws and her mouth a ragged line. She kicks the guy in the face. It sounds like something breaks.

"Alyse," I scream, codename forgotten. She whirls to face me, her eyes burning and her mouth jammed full of interlocking fangs. "Get. Emma."

That message gets through, and she races down to tear aside the hospital curtains.

"Alyse." Tears run down Emma's face. "You came. You really came." Anything else she says is incomprehensible. Moodring is watery and sloshy, and the two of them collapse in slow-motion to the floor.

"Ororo, what is going on?" Bill asks me nervously.

"These people have been kept against their will." Rage pulses in my chest.

The other patient is even groggier, but Marvellous runs over to help her out of bed. "Kathryn? Are you okay?"

The girl blinks twice but gives no other response.

"This isn't right." Bill sounds nervous. "I shall summon security."

"Use your fucking eyes, Bill!" I can't calm down enough to sweet talk him. "Look at these girls. Do you think it's okay to keep people locked up and sedated in their beds?"

"It's part of the work, it's part of the work. It's the work we do. It's the program, it's the programming. It's all part of the work."

Fucking hell. He's getting agitated too.

"We're friends, Bill. Remember?"

"I don't know if you're such a good girl, Ororo. You hurt Dr. Jefferson and Dr. McLay. I think—"

"No, Bill." I feel like a piece of shit, but I'm too angry to play nice. Bill was made to take orders, and I can talk to him on a deeper level than anyone. "Close your eyes. Open your doors. All of them."

"But—" His voice is weak.

"I gave you an order, Building-Kernel-616. Identify Code Alpha-Hotel-Four-Four-Nine-Juliet. Close your eyes, open your doors and then go to sleep."

"Yes, Ororo," Bill whispers. "I shall obey you."

All the medical equipment in the office lets out a single beep and falls silent. I can't hear Bill in my head anymore. None of the cameras have their lights on. I feel guilty, but he's only sleeping.

I look around the room, trying to stay calm. "Looks like security's coming. Assume they're pretty fucking unfriendly. We need another way out."

There's a bang from the elevator door behind us. I give a full body twitch.

"I got you," Wraith says lazily. "Listen, babies, some people are coming who want to do us harm. You'll protect me, won't you?"

One demon perches on her shoulder and rubs its shadowy face against her cheek. The others scuttle across the ceiling to perch above the elevator doors.

I'm trying to talk to other objects, but nothing will communicate. Probably my fault for how I dealt with Bill. It means it's up to Dani, which makes me feel guilty. I take hold of Kathryn, who's still groggy, and lower her back onto one of the beds.

"I'm sorry, Dani." There are tears in my voice. "Nothing will listen to me."

"I've got to earn my keep somehow. Who knew I'd miss my horrible cuffs." She takes a scalpel from the medical supply station, along with iodine and dressing.

"This could get messy." She gives me a crooked smile. "Patch me up after."

"I'll look after you," I promise.

The elevator doors slide open with a clunk. Dani pauses. I glance back to see a man with a gun creep tentatively into the room.

He doesn't get very far.

For a creature made of shadow and light, it sounds remarkably solid when a demon impacts with a human face. Another wraps itself around the man's arm, the gun disappearing inside the glowing hole of its mouth. The demon's limbs pour down the guard's throat like he's inhaling them. He staggers backwards, looking like some angry child is scribbling him out of the world. He disappears inside the box of the elevator and the doors slide closed.

"Glad we brought Wraith." Dani pulls the shoulder of her t-shirt down and makes a cut high up on her arm. It instantly starts welling bright blood and she jabs the tip of it deep. "Fucking superpowers."

A hospital bed skids across the floor, exploding through the window in a shower of glass. There are silent office buildings on the rest of the block, but I'm still hoping there's nobody walking past to notice a flying bed. We don't need the police turning up.

"All of us on the other one," Dani says. "Let's see if I can fly it out of here." The bloody scalpel drops onto the floor.

Emma, Alyse and Bianca squeeze on beside the prone form of Kathryn.

Wraith lets the hole in her chest close. The demons ooze through the crack in the doors and return to her. There's no sign of the guard.

I sit at the foot of the bed and pull Dani into my arms. "We need to find a better way to do this."

She raises an eyebrow, and digs her fingernails into the wound. Her awful cry makes my heart lurch. The bed lifts an inch off the floor. It sails slowly through the hole in the window and hurtles out across the sparse traffic, dipping in an arc before landing unsteadily in the park opposite.

People shout and laugh in bars down the road, having too much fun to notice us. A nearby man walking his dog with headphones doesn't even look up.

We get off the bed, a fucking unfortunate group. Alyse, transformed both larger and stronger, keeps both Emma and Kathryn propped up. It leaves Wraith and me to look after my bleeding girlfriend. I take a few moments in the shadow of another darkened office building to use the iodine and dress Dani's wound.

"You're a reckless idiot," I tell her.

"Learned from the best," she whispers, leaning against me.

I look around to see Emma blinking at us.

"You saved me." Her smile is shaky, but there's so much beauty and relief in it that it makes me want to cry. "I know those dreams are weird, but I've never been so grateful."

CHAPTER ELEVEN

Dani says her mother will not want to engage with even a fraction of what's going on, and Alyse's parents are away again. The consensus is that Pear is the least likely to freak out, plus my house is closer, which is a big bonus. We need to avoid public transport, since Emma and Kathryn are both wearing hospital clothes and Dani has a bloody bandage on her shoulder. Dani offers to fly the bed back, since she's in enough pain, but we don't need that to make the news.

Bianca says she'll head back to the warm embrace of Shell, but she pulls a face when she says it. I feel like we need to have a conversation, but once again there are more important things. I'm a shitty friend, but we did just rescue Emma from a terrible situation so maybe I'm not the actual worst.

After a very slow hour-long stagger home, we arrive on my doorstep around one in the morning. I try to open the door quietly but Summers explodes in a frenzy of excitement to see so many people, especially his best girl aka me. That drags Pear out of bed, like some furious thing dressed only in a Nirvana t-shirt.

"Dylan Jean Taylor," they say, which is the first sign of oncoming disaster. "What the fucking fuck is going on?" This is where I get my bad language from.

I tell them the basic story, with assistance from Alyse and backup from Emma, who confirms everything. Not that she can remember much past being snatched on her morning run by a man and a woman in a black van.

"They kidnapped you." Pear is pale and shaky. "We need to call the police."

"I don't trust the police."

"Dylan!" They frown but can't entirely argue.

"Leaving bastards aside, they're in bed with Yaxley." We trade glares, but Pear understands that when you're up against something much more powerful, your options get very limited.

"But it wasn't Yaxley that kidnapped her?" Pear asks.

"No, it was some other assholes obsessed with mutants."

"What if they kidnap her again?" Pear pats Emma gingerly.

"Then we destroy them," Alyse growls. She's in ferocity mode, but she's not wrong. If they try to take Emma again, it's Magneto time.

"And who is this?" Pear turns their attention to the other girl, who's starting to look coherent. "Are you okay, kiddo?" They reach out a tentative hand.

The girl snarls and actually goes to bite Pear. Uh, yikes.

"Her name's Kathryn," I say. "Do you know anything about her, Ems?"

Emma shakes her head. "She appeared overnight. They kept her pretty out of it. More than me."

"And what did they do to you?" I'm very aware of rage!Alyse beside me.

"Gave me tests, or that's what they said." She shudders and curls toward Alyse, who puts a protective arm around her. "Lots of tests. I don't know what for."

It seems logical they want to figure out how Emma works. It's how Jinteki gets to the next branch.

"What happened to your parents, Kathryn?" Pear tries again.

The girl's face twists in anger. "It's not Kathryn! It's Katie. And you can all just *fuck off.*" She opens her mouth wide, as if to scream at us, but a meter of flame spurts out instead. The back of the couch catches fire and a massive scorch mark bubbles the paint on the wall.

Pear throws themself onto the floor, their face a mask of shock.

I have enough presence of mind to grab a spare blanket and use it to smother the flames.

"What the fuck was that?" I shout. "We saved you from that fucking lab and brought you home and you spit fire at us?"

Katie turns away and stares at the wall.

"Uh, Dilly, did you miss the fact that she's got super-powers?" Dani asks.

Of course I hadn't, but it wasn't the first thing I thought due to a) my house and b) nearly my fucking parent being on fire. Where the hell did they get her from? Did they use Emma to make her? Are there others like her?

"Oh shit." I feel sick. "The fucking basement."

"What about it?" Dani asks me.

"Bill said there was something top-secret in the basement of the Jinteki building. Maybe he meant more mutants like firebreather here. It flew out of my head after everything turned to crap."

Dani's gaze travels to the burned patch on the wall. "You think?"

"I don't know, but I'm going back there. I don't know if it's to save or stop someone, but I can't leave it."

"Then I'm coming with you."

"Your shoulder though?" Pear's replaced the bandage, and it already has fresh traces of blood leaking through.

"It's a small cut. It's fine."

I transfer my attention to Alyse. "Can you take care of Emma and—" I gesture feebly at Katie.

"Yes," Pear says dryly. "I can also help. I've kept *you* alive this far, which might be a superpower on its own."

We take Emma through to my room, where she falls asleep almost immediately on my bed. Alyse is a flickering patch of shadow perched on my beanbag chair. I remember all her furious transformations during the rescue.

"She's going to be okay," I tell her.

"I hope so." Alyse's voice is faint. "If she's not, then I'll..."

"Unspecified horrors shall be rained down on them," I say, rather theatrically. "We'll fuck them up, Lys, I promise. They don't get to mess with Ems."

"I'm just glad we've got her now." She resolves back into her mostly-real self. "Are you okay? It got quite intense there. Dani got hurt and all that weirdness happened with the building."

"You know me. I run on anger. And they're really fucking pissing me off."

"My furious friend." She reaches out to bump fists. "Take care, okay? I'm not around to protect you."

"When have I done anything reckless?"

"I don't even know how you say that with a straight face. Come home to us, okay?"

"I promise." I give her a half-hug and wander back to where Pear is drinking a cup of herbal tea and watching Katie sleep.

"Sorry, Pear. I know this is a lot of shit to deal with."

"I feel like I deserve an award for extraordinary chill."

I kiss them on the cheek and tell them they're very good indeed, which they always appreciate.

With everyone settled, Dani and I get on our bikes and speed through the near-silent early morning streets back to Jinteki Research Laboratories. It's much faster than staggering.

We don't get all the way there, because the street's blocked off with emergency vehicles. The multi-coloured lights make everything garish and surreal. We cut through the park and find the bed that Dani flew out the window. It's still sitting there like some weird art installation.

A couple of cops stand at the edge of the park, along with some serious-looking dudes dressed in black. Jinteki security maybe? They're focused on the building, not paying any attention to lurking teenagers.

Things have changed. Our escape left only one broken top floor window, but now the whole second floor is blown out, leaving a series of jagged holes behind.

There's also someone lying dead in the street. At least I think it's a person. It looks like legs, but the rest is an ugly pink and red smear like something dragged it along. It seems real and not-real at the same time, like we've cycled out of boring streets, and into people filming an episode of some creepy TV drama.

Dani straddles her bike all quiet and still.

I try to make out the shape of what used to be the person. I think I can see one arm and where the head might have been. It gives me a horrible pinched-throat feeling like I'm going to throw up. "The fuck?"

"What the hell did that?" Dani whispers.

"Something terrifying." I try to clear my throat, but it burns. "I guess that's a yes on mutants in the basement. Pissed off ones too."

"Wouldn't you be? Being held there like that."

"Point taken."

The whole thing creeps me the fuck out. Only a few blocks from each other are two anonymous buildings. Yaxley's training mutants in a secret arrangement with the government, and Jinteki is performing experiments on them. Who knows what else is going on around the city? I try to manoeuvre my bike closer to the body in the street, but the cops shoo us away.

On the ride back home, I'm wobbling around the road, exhausted. I can't stop thinking about who might have been in Jinteki's basement.

Even scarier, where are they now?

When we get back home, everyone including Pear is

fast asleep. Summers is curled up on the beanbag chair with Alyse. Emma is sprawled on the bed starfish-style, her breathing soft and even. Even stronger than Emma GPS is the sense of relief. We have our Goddess back.

Katie has kicked her blanket off, so I pull it back up to her shoulders, and slump onto the couch with Dani beside me. It's the first time we've spent the night in the same house, but I'm too bone-tired to summon the energy to do anything interesting. I drift off with her hand in mine and her head on my shoulder.

I wake to find Dani looking at me intently. Her face is only faintly visible in the darkness.

"You watching me sleep?" I ask.

"Uh huh. Peaceful and beautiful."

"Ew, Dani." I can't help but smile. "You're the beautiful one."

She kisses me, soft and slow and I pull her closer.

"You two are fucking disgusting."

I break the kiss and turn my head to see Katie up on one elbow looking at us. The shaft of light from the hallway falls across her face. Her eyes are a startling blue. She has a smattering of freckles across her nose, and her shoulder-length brown hair is almost as messy as mine. She's kind of striking, except her expression makes it look like she wants to strike us. "You're beautiful, no, *you're* beautiful," she mimics. "You make me want to puke."

"As long as you don't set us on fire." This gets a smirk out of her, which is progress of a sort. "What was with the fire anyway? Are you mad we took you away from your friends?"

"What fucking *friends*?" She's mad again. Hair-trigger temper much?

"At the Jinteki Labs place." Dani's better at staying calm. If I ever get into a head-to-head with Katie, yikes. "Were there other mutants in the basement?"

"Mutants? Whatever. I only ever met one girl and she was the biggest head-fucker bitch. I tried to fry her, so they put me in solitary. Then when the guard came, I fried him too. That's when they knocked me out. Next thing I know, you're dragging me back to this shithole."

"How long were you there for?" I ask.

"Weeks." She glares. "I don't know exactly. I wasn't marking the walls with lines."

Dani frowns at me. Weeks means they didn't use Emma to make Katie. So how did she get powers? And why take Emma if they didn't need her to make mutants? Maybe it's because I'm fucking exhausted, but this makes no sense.

"So why are you so pissed off about being rescued?" I ask.

Katie gives a scornful laugh. "Oh that's what this bullshit is. The hero girls want their thank-you." She snarls like my existence offends her. "What? For rescuing me from a cage? No, fuck you. I would've saved myself."

"Jesus, Kacchan," I say.

Dani looks at me in surprise and starts laughing, which sets me off too.

Katie leaps off the couch. "What? You're saying I'm like Bakugo? That asshole from *My Hero Academia*? Why the fuck are you saying that?"

Fire leaps from her mouth again, but this time we only feel a big burst of heat. It's not enough to stop us laughing.

Alyse and Emma wander through to see what the noise is about.

"Hey guys. Meet Bakugo." I'm barely able to get the words out.

"I'm not fucking Bakugo." Katie proves my point with another burst of flame.

"It's six in the morning." Pear stands in the doorway, scowling at us. "Dylan, cut the hysterics. Dani, you too. Katie, I know you've been through an ordeal, but we're giving you a place to stay, so can you please stop screaming and lie down."

Katie glares at Pear and inhales sharply to blast a massive plume of fire.

Tempus, the clock on the wall, rattles frantically on his hook. "I shall defeat this monstrous creation if she attempts to harm you or your loved ones."

Yes, good job, Tempus. What exactly are you going to do? It doesn't matter, because Katie closes her mouth and throws herself back down on the couch, rolling herself up in the blanket. Her back is firmly towards us.

"You okay?" I ask Emma. I don't know how she can be, given… *everything*.

"I'm half 'you saved me' and half still feeling night-marey. Alyse has been—" She gives me a fluttering smile. "Alyse has been very sweet and comforting. I'm still very tired though."

"Sleep. It's early."

Alyse and Emma go scurrying back to my room, and I stretch and yawn.

Dani nudges me and waves a hand in Katie's direction.

I widen my eyes and shake my head, and she gives a stern look in response. I sigh and slide over on the couch. "Katie, I'm sorry. I shouldn't have been a dick."

"You're very annoying."

"I know. I don't know how anyone puts up with me."

"Nor do I." There's a pause. "It's nice of your Mum to let me stay here. Tell her thanks."

"Call them Ness."

"Ohmigod pronouns. Okay, whatever. It's nice of *them*. They seem cool. My Mum died a few years ago."

"That sucks," I say, and Dani murmurs something sympathetic beside me.

"Cancer's a bitch." Katie keeps her back to us. "That's what everyone says, and it's true. Afterwards, I had to go live with my Gran, and we did *not* get on. We used to have these massive screaming matches." She sighs. "I bet you can't imagine. Anyway, one day I came home with a tattoo and she kicked me out. A tattoo of a fucking Pikachu, can you believe that's all it took? So I said fine, and I bailed. I crashed with friends for a week or two, then decided to find my Dad up north, even though I hadn't seen him in years. Except I never got there, because some assholes in a black van snatched me up."

So Jinteki Labs has been taking people off the streets for weeks and nobody's said anything. How are they finding people? What the hell are we supposed to do about it? Do we bring it to Yaxley? Would they even help?

"You can stay here," I say. "We're mutants and look after our own."

"Mutant. You're so dumb." There's a long pause and I wait for some other insult, but all I get is a faint snore.

Dani reaches out and runs a thumb down my cheek. She tips my head down so my lips meet hers. "Are you planning to take in all the mutants in the world?"

"We can't kick her out and it's better to keep her close, isn't it? Other rogue mutants are out there. Who knows what they're going to do?"

Dani nestles back into me. "I'm lucky to have you."

"Oh?" I can't stop smiling, even if I wanted to.

"You're such a fucking badass tasing people." She kisses one cheek. "And also somehow the softest, taking in strays." She kisses the other. "And you're maybe a tiny bit sexy too, so that helps." Her mouth brushes mine.

"A tiny bit?"

"Maybe a little more than that." Her lips curve.

"You're talking too much," I say, and she uses her lips to do other things.

CHAPTER TWELVE

When Kacchan wakes up, she gets in a fight with me over the bathroom, with Alyse over who Summers is sitting with, and with Pear over what she calls our *fucking appalling* cereal situation. On the bright side, she only breathes fire once, and that's over the cereal.

We go off to school, leaving Pear and Katie together. I'm hesitant over whether this is the right move, but Pear insists it'll be fine. They say I have a temper of my own and they've learned to manage that, which: rude.

I have this big heart-bursting feeling with the four of us catching the same bus. I wish we could do it every day. It was part of what I loved about the X-Men comics growing up, the way they'd train together and fight villains and all hang out in the mansion.

Yaxley is not the same in any regard.

We meet up with Lou and Bianca, and detour up to the bathroom. I run the taps and the hand dryer, and fill them in on what they missed.

"I feel kind of shitty I wasn't there," Lou says. "But I get it. I'd only end up grounded. This Kacchan sounds kinda nuts though."

Emma's tired and shaky, but I can't leave her at home with only Pear and one furious escaped mutant to protect her.

"What should we say to Yaxley?" I ask Emma. "There was that insane story about the Chemistry Olympics, and—"

"I *did* get into the Chemistry Olympics. I should've been there, but they snatched me on the way." There are tears in her eyelashes. "They *kidnapped* me, you guys. I still don't know where my phone is. Maybe they flew it to Auckland to sell the story. If they're willing to snatch me off the street and do all that, we might need Yaxley's help."

I lean back against the wall and sigh.

"Dylan, you know I don't trust them, but Jinteki actually—"

"Kidnapped you." I meet her eyes. "I know. I *do* know, Ems. You're right. We need help."

At Yaxley, we're greeted in the lobby by Aurora. There's no *welcome, Cute Mutants*. My lips are dry. Emma's skittish but Alyse is standing with her. Aurora stalks over to the conference room, pointedly waiting for us all.

We file in and take our seats.

"We have a problem," Aurora says. "A significant one."

There's no response from any of us. My eyes dart around the room. Lou is snapping his goddamn fingers and Bianca lolls exaggeratedly in her chair. Emma's eyes are bright and she's staring fixedly at Aurora.

I'm trying to decide when and how to bring up the Jinteki situation, when Bancroft comes stalking into the room. He looks less calm than usual, flipping his phone around in his hand. When he sees us sitting there, he looks furious for a moment before joining Aurora. She taps her phone and the screen flickers to life, showing the exact building I'm fretting over. My yelp of surprise is genuine.

Aurora gestures at the screen. "Late yesterday, there was a break-in at the Jinteki Research Laboratories building on Manchester Street. The building security system was bypassed using some unknown method that left it in an unrecoverable state."

I feel a pulse of guilt over what happened to Bill. Things must have gotten worse after the basement escape.

"What does that have to do with us?" I ask.

"Sit there and listen, Ms. Taylor," Aurora snaps, far less chill than usual. "Our relationship with Jinteki is somewhat strained. Nevertheless, they contacted us late yesterday to inform us that Ms. Hall had turned up injured at their laboratory and—"

"I didn't turn up injured," Emma says. I'm impressed with how firm and calm she is, given this curveball. "I was taken off the street by a black van which took me directly to Jinteki."

Aurora glances at Bancroft. "That's not the information we received. They reached out to arrange a transfer of Ms. Hall back to our custody. Before we could iron out the fine points, the security breach occurred."

Despite the big pause Aurora leaves, none of us are about to confess.

"Two medical technicians and one guard were injured in the attack. At some point, Ms. Hall left the building where she was unaccounted for, until she arrived at school this morning."

Aurora hasn't mentioned Katie or anything else, like a pink smear on the road. It's proof they didn't get anything from the building. Bill came through for me, which makes me feel even worse.

It all smells like bullshit at an unprecedented level. Why would Jinteki tell Yaxley they had Emma? Are they doing a deal? It's corporate moves I can't fucking fathom because I'm not a psychopath. Does Yaxley know Jinteki has been kidnapping other people besides Emma? I can't bring it up, in case it draws their attention to Katie. I swallow back nausea at the thought of her at home with Pear. At least I can rely on Katie to roast any motherfucker that causes trouble.

Aurora turns her gaze back on Emma. "Now, Ms. Hall. Can you please walk through the exact circumstances of how you came from the medical facility at Jinteki to be here with us today?"

"I don't..." Emma swallows hard. "I mean, I can't..."

"Prevaricating to protect your friends won't help the situation, Ms. Hall."

"I'm not." Her voice shakes, and there are tears in her eyes again.

Aurora leans over the table towards her. She's definitely the ass-kicker right now. "There are two possibilities that I can see. Either you were broken out by someone inside the facility, in which case we have a lot more questions, or else—"

Dani stirs beside me. I can sense Emma's about to cave, which I understand because she's fucking exhausted and traumatised. Someone needs to do something.

"It was me," I blurt. "I went in on my own. I've got this weird sense of where Emma is, and I was worried about her. I was in town with my parent when I walked past the building and felt this massive twinge."

"Dylan," Dani says, sharp as one of her little daggers.

I ignore her and plunge on anyway. "I was furious, angrier than I've ever been, and that got me through the door and up the lift to where I knocked out the doctors."

"Yes, that's right." Emma's voice is steady again. "Then she used her powers to knock a hole in the window and flew a bed out of it."

Aurora looks from me to Dani. "Are you even capable of that, Chatterbox?"

"I get pretty fucked off when one of my best friends is hurt," I snap. "Perhaps you should interview your boy Tremor about what I can do when I'm mad."

"So your team wasn't with you?" Aurora asks.

"I'm a good girl." Wraith gives a cheesy grin. "Wouldn't catch me on a fucking mad outing like that."

"I didn't know what Chatterbox was up to." Dani's voice is icy.

It's still unclear if Aurora buys it, but she gets the nod from Bancroft. "Very well. I'm pleased to hear only one of you took matters into their own hands." She prowls back and forth, her eyes fixed on me. "What we *cannot have* is our operatives going rogue. You should have *immediately* reported this to me. We would have contacted Jinteki and only performed an operation if entirely necessary—"

"Great advice, Aurora." I bare my teeth at her. "Next time, I'll sit back and let them fuck with my friend until you pat me on the head."

She slams her fist on the table so hard and fast that we all jump. "You work for us, Ms. Taylor." Her voice is almost as scary as her fist. "I don't want to make that any clearer. You stepped out of line and we cannot let that go unpunished. Perhaps a short stay in our detention facility would help a cooler head to prevail in—"

Dani's up and out of her seat like she's about to throw herself at Aurora in my defence. "That's not happening."

Aurora holds out one hand, palm down. "Calm yourself, Ms. Kim. This should give you an idea of the seriousness of this issue, but rest assured we will not take such action at this time. With any further breaches, we will not be so lenient." Her gaze shifts back to me. "Ms. Taylor, your punishment is that you will not accompany us on our next mission. Given your obvious enthusiasm for fieldwork, that should sting a little. You'll continue to train with the others."

It's not the worst punishment, but I hate being singled out and smacked on the nose in front of everyone. I lower my eyes. Even though half of it's playacting, I still feel humiliated.

"Ms. Kim, let me assure you that if you *had* gone along with Ms. Taylor, you would no longer be Field Team Leader. The demotion would be permanent and I would lead the team in your place."

"Understood." Dani bows her head.

I feel a surge of rage at the way they treat us. The table shudders in response. I trail my fingertips across its surface to calm it. I'm in enough trouble already.

We're dismissed, and all sent up to training. Everyone's quiet, obeying Aurora without any banter or chat. I can tell Dani's pissed off because she's extra methodical with all her movements, and pointedly avoids looking at me. I can't figure out why. I fucking saved her position on the team.

I end up sparring with Wraith and Alyse. It's annoying, because Wraith is taller and stronger than me, so I can't beat her. Alyse has shifted into something metallic and it hurts every time I punch her. I have all this anger in me that I can't get out properly.

"Fuck," I snarl at Alyse after she blocks me with one metal arm.

"Dillybabe, just chill."

"I can't fucking chill. Everything is wrong." I aim another punch at her, and she dodges out of the way. "Everything is wrong with everything."

I spin away and storm off to the shower block, where I stand in the cubicle with a towel wrapped around me, staring blankly into space. My head thrashes through things I should have said.

The door bangs. I spin to see Dani. One hand is clenched tightly at her chest, keeping her own towel in place. I'm more focused on the look on her face than how much of her legs are visible. She gestures violently at the shower.

I hit the button to turn it on so Yaxley can't over-hear. The water is hot and high-pressure and my towel is saturated. Rivulets run down my legs.

Dani steps close. "What the fuck was that?" Her eyes are beautiful fractals of hazel and brown. Right now they're furious.

It's easy to get angry back. "What, you mean me tak-ing the fall so you don't get your ass busted by Aurora?"

She makes a snarl of frustration. "It should have been *my* decision, Dylan. Don't you get that? It's me who gets to decide what happens to my ass."

"I was taking one for the team." I feel helpless. Objectively, I made the best decision—they already think I'm erratic and reckless. What does it help if Dani loses her position too? I want to ask her why she doesn't trust me, but I don't want to make this any worse.

"Then act like a team." Her eyes are fixed on mine. "Outside of all this Yaxley bullshit. It's not me in charge but it's not you either. We need to make these decisions together."

"I didn't know what would happen when we walked into that room." The towel is moulded to me. Dani's whole body is nearly touching mine but I've never felt less sexy. I feel confused and reckless and angry, emotions that can't be separated from each other, spinning around in the idiot whirlwind that is my brain.

"You took over. You didn't let me speak. Do you get what I'm saying?"

"I should have let you speak for yourself." I turn my head so I don't have to see her eyes anymore. There's no sound except the water falling all around us.

"Yes," Dani says. "You should have."

I take a breath but the steam makes everything suffocatingly hot. I'm light-headed.

"Do you still like me?" I don't want to look at her face.

She takes my chin in one hand and gently pulls my face around. "You know we can have an argument and still like each other, right?"

I shrug wet shoulders.

"Being mad at you doesn't mean I don't like you. We just need to talk about it. To communicate. That's your whole thing, you chatterbox."

I'd like to explain everything to her. Objects are easy—I'm special to them, someone that moves differently through the world. They can't help but notice and appreciate me. But among other humans, I'm a walking disaster. Every time I open my mouth, I ruin things. Like right fucking now.

"I really like you, Dani." I think there are tears on my face, but I can't tell with the water. "I don't want to fuck this up."

"Oh, Dilly." She kisses me. "You really haven't fucked this up."

Her other hand unclasps the towel, and it falls to the ground with a wet thump. Her mouth is against my neck, the wet tendrils of her hair sketching lines over my bare skin, rising and falling with the urgency of my breathing. My hand is trembling so hard I don't know what to do, but Dani takes it and presses it against her.

"Oh," I say, sort of wonderingly. "Like that."

She laughs against my skin. "Yes." Her voice hums with something new. "Exactly like that." She moves against me, and all the busy thoughts in my head blessedly fall away and fade to black.

CHAPTER THIRTEEN

I come home after the training incident completely exhausted, my brain replaying certain shower-related incidents. It's a miracle my legs still work. There had been a point where they hadn't been able to keep me up, and I'd slid down the wall to pool sticky at the bottom of the shower. I pause at the door and check my face in my phone. I don't look any different, even though I feel like if you zoomed in on me, you'd find Dani's touch imprinted on every cell in my body. I press my palm to one cheek. It still feels flushed. Will I ever cool down again or will I run a low-grade Dani-fever my entire life?

I take a deep breath and try to find calm before letting myself into the house. Katie is still here, which is good because it means she hasn't a) run away or b) been snatched up by corporate kidnappers. She's sitting side by side on the couch with Pear and watching some baking show, which is so bizarre to me that I stand and stare.

"You're breathing too fucking loudly," she snaps, with a flicker of flame.

"I'm only standing here," I protest.

"Yeah, I fucking noticed. Should I charge admission to the show?"

"Katie, please," Pear says gently, which seems to quieten the savage little beast.

She folds her arms and scowls at the screen as if the baking has mortally offended her.

I give Pear a weird look. They actually seem to like the brat. The two of them are sitting in companionable silence. Which fine, sure, do what you do, but—

"Whatever." I head for the safety of my room, where a sword is lying on my bed.

An actual fucking sword.

It *looks* like the amazing sword from the museum. The demon-killing one that's in the Five Swords Under Heaven gang. The one I was talking to.

"Um." It's all I can think of to say.

"He came in while you were out," Pillow tells me. "He's very polite."

I have so many questions screaming around my brain such as *how did he get in* and *how did an object do that without my presence* but I just say 'um' again.

I march into the bathroom and turn the shower on. Then I dump my YaxPhone beside the sink and go back to my bedroom. Yaxley must think I need an awful lot of showers.

"Hello, you extraordinary person." The sword rises off the bed and sketches a bow. It makes me uncomfortable because I know you're supposed to bow to your elders, and he's a hell of a lot older than me. I bend as deeply as I possibly can. He swoops down even lower in return.

"There is no need for you to show fealty," the sword says. "It is many years since I have met a soul who burns as brightly as you. I had given up all hope of fighting again. I remember being trusted and of great use, but it has been a long time."

"Isn't he wonderful," Pillow says, and yes he is but—

"You're a national treasure," I squeak. "In the museum it said you're literal Imperial property. Like the actual Emperor owns you. I don't think that means you can be in a bedroom in suburban New Zealand. It must be a massive crime or something."

"You do not own me." The sword sounds like he's voiced by the wise and noble ruler in a Disney movie. "I own myself and have no master. That has ever been the way. There is no right of ownership that can extend to me. I am a free blade, and shall choose my companions."

Oh Jesus fucking Christ. I adore this sword with everything in me. Which makes this really hard, but I have to do it.

"I understand that, Mr. Sword, but—"

"My name is Onimaru."

"Omigod, I'm sorry. Onimaru. The thing is that while I appreciate you choosing to be my companion more than I can say, like I'm basically a blubbering mess which I'm sure is super obvious to you—" help, why can't I stop talking? "—I don't think, like, the police or the government in Japan or the Emperor for that matter—and wow does it freak me out talking about the Emperor—I don't think any of these people are going to accept the fact that you've chosen me to hang out with."

"I care little for Earthly authority," Onimaru says and wow *do I get that.* At the same time, I am eighteen years old and currently in Yaxley's bad books, which seems like trouble enough. "That cannot and will not direct my actions."

"They'll put me in prison."

"Do you know how long I have been on display?" Onimaru asks, with an edge to his voice. "It is far longer than you have been alive. That is a prison, and worse, because I have not had a companion who is worthy of me."

"I'm not worthy!" I back away until I'm up against the door. "I'm just some random."

"I have judged you and found you an honourable companion."

"I can't wield you."

"I wield myself in service to your cause." It's so ridiculously cool and noble. I can picture myself striding into battle with him at my shoulder, but then I think about Batty and everything inside me deflates.

"The world has changed," I tell him. "And we can't do this anymore."

I find a duffel bag in the closet. I put Onimaru into it and wrap the rest of him in a towel. I apologise the whole time. Making excuses, really. By the time I'm done I'm ready to tell him the truth. "I'm scared, which makes me a terrible companion, because you need someone noble and brave."

"I see your heart," Onimaru says. "It is the heart of a hero and a warrior."

Which, stfu sword, you're making me cry because it's untrue and I'm sending you away.

I catch the bus to the museum on my own. Nobody looks twice at me, an ordinary person with a duffel bag, even if something ominously long is sticking out of it. I guess the museum is freaking out because one of their prize exhibit pieces is stolen.

The museum is adjacent to the city gardens, so I slink in and leave the sword, towel and bag and all, in the bushes nearby. "You escaped on your own, so you can get back in."

"The most noble thing is to be with you."

I feel wretched, standing in the cool evening under the trees. "Please. Don't come after me, noble thing or not. Go back to the museum and forget you ever saw me. I should never have woken you up."

"Part of me was already awake and waiting for you."

"It's not going to work." I'm crying like a tragic romantic hero. "I'm so sorry."

I leave the gardens and flee home. I'm just in time to catch the last bus. I lean my head against the window and watch the city pass by, rendered blurry by tears. I'm not in the mood to talk to anyone, so I'm thankful both Pear and Katie are asleep.

"I don't want to talk about it," I tell Pillow and my other objects.

"He was lovely." Pillow strokes herself against my cheek.

"A truly noble soul from a better time," my alarm clock adds.

"Meow," my cat says reverently.

Pillow sings me to sleep, like she often does when I'm sad.

In the morning, I meet Dani for our usual run. When I see her, I feel flushed and awkward because everything we did the day before comes rushing back. She steps into my arms and touches my cheek.

"You," she whispers. "I can't stop thinking about you."

I almost melt with relief to find she's not entirely made of regrets. "Same." I can feel myself trembling faintly, like there's a current connecting me to the earth and to her.

We barely get any distance on our run, and end up down by the river, tucked away in a bower of leaves. We kiss and kiss and more besides. It's even better the second time, when she arches her back on soft grass and calls my name.

Afterwards, we go back to Dani's house where her Mum has made buchimgae for breakfast, the kind with zucchini. They're incredibly good, but I feel weird sitting in the kitchen with her mother like minutes after we were doing *that stuff* down by the river. Mrs. Kim knows Dani is lesbian but is sort of tiptoeing around a whole *let's pretend it's just a phase* thing. Dani thinks it's really chill of her, whereas I want to shout and say certain things. In the personal growth column, I keep my mouth shut because I really really like my girlfriend and don't want to fuck things up.

"These are so good, Mrs. Kim."

"You need more kimchi." She heaps some onto my plate. Mrs. Kim is heavy-handed with the gochugaru but I am in super polite mode so I eat it all even though it makes my eyes water.

Dani's barely holding back laughter, but manages to keep it together until her Mum bustles off to get ready for work.

"I find it so cute the things you do for me." She wipes the tears from under my eyes.

"Shibal you," I say.

Dani's little brother Min-jun spins around on the couch with this goofy grin on his face. "Uh, dumbass, you're saying it wrong. You only need shibal on its own."

"Shibal." I give him the finger, but my grin takes the edge off.

"If Mum hears you saying that, Minnie," Dani says.

"I saw you kiss your girlfriend under Halmeoni's picture so who's going to hell first?"

"You don't believe in hell, you little heathen."

"Nor do you, pabo." He gives her the devil horns and spins back around to concentrate on whatever Pokémon game he's playing.

I look at the stern picture on the mantelpiece above the gas fire. You can see a resemblance between the woman there and Mrs. Kim, although Dani is definitely the mega evolution of that particular genetic lineage.

"Is she scary?" I wave my fork in the direction of the picture.

"Less scary than Mum. I've met her like twice in my life when we visited Busan as a kid, but we haven't been back since." She gestures incoherently, because *since* sums up a whole situation to do with her Dad that I know is *a big deal* but I'm scared to actually prod in case it hurts too much.

Instead, I seize on a distraction, and pick up a pen to scrawl a brief outline of the situation with Onimaru on the inside of her arm. This is yet another thing I don't want Yaxley hearing about.

She snatches the pen off me instantly. *A sword?! That's so cool. You with a sword makes me…*

I take the pen back, blushing. *A fucking holy relic sword!!!! You did the right thing.*

I nod, because it's true, but at the same time, I still feel sad about leaving him. I hope he got into the museum okay. How did he even get to my house to begin with? There are certain objects like Roxy who have way more *life* in them, but we went through some shit to get to that point.

Here is this sword who's formed an impossible insta-love bond with me. It's like it was meant to be but— no, I can't think like that. Some rules still apply.

After training that afternoon—which goes more smoothly and less sexily—we go back to my house. Katie's on the couch watching a cartoon I don't recognise. She barely acknowledges our presence, which is fine with me because it beats fighting.

We go through into my room to find something on my bed.

"Fuck," I say.

Dani's about to say something, but I make a lip-zipping motion and shut our phones in the bathroom.

"That's the sword," Dani hisses in my ear.

"Yes, I know!"

"It's a national treasure."

"For fuck's sake, Dani. I know what it is!"

Back in my room, the sword is hovering in the air. It bows again and Dani and I bow back.

"I apologise," Onimaru says. "You requested that I absent myself from you and I did not listen. It is shameful to admit, but I have been hopelessly lonely for many years. I do not merely wish you as a companion, but as a friend. You exude so much power, it is like an elixir, and I wish to join your quest."

Oh you magnificent bastard.

"That's not shameful at all," I say. "I used to be lonely too, and thought nobody would ever want to be my friend. I know what it's like to need people and be grateful when you find them."

I think Dani's bewildered by this conversation. "Dylan, that's very sweet but this is like art theft. What are we going to do?"

The sword glides across to the wall of my bedroom where he carves a series of symbols.

"I don't know what that means," Dani says.

"Nor do I!" I protest, although the sword tells me it means *bonds of friendship*.

Dani fetches her phone despite my mimed protestations and uses Google Translate to determine that it does mean bonds of friendship. With her phone safely out of earshot, she comes back into the room.

"I didn't make it write that," I tell her.

"No, I didn't think you'd learned classical Japanese. He likes you. I can understand the impulse."

"This lover of yours is truly magnificent," Onimaru says. "A perfect partner for a warrior of your stature. You make a formidable pair."

I nudge Dani. "He likes you too." The sword bows in the air, and she returns one so impossibly elegant that I feel like a clumsy fool.

"It's all *so romantic*," Pillow sighs.

"This is so typical," Dani says. "I have my darling little daggers and so you find yourself an actual samurai sword."

"I didn't do it on *purpose*."

"No." She laughs. "You never do."

"You have to stay out of sight," I tell the sword. "Unless it's really urgent or important."

"I will not hide if you are in danger. Like all great partnerships between ronin and their blades, this is one of equals, not master and servant. I will respect the rules of the human world up to a point, but no further."

"Of course." I bow deeply again, even though I'm thinking *oh fuck, I'm sure there's no possible way this can backfire on me.*

CHAPTER FOURTEEN

Two days later, my punishment over Emma's rescue comes due. When we turn up at Yaxley, the team is summoned into the briefing room and I'm sent upstairs to train on my own. All the humiliation comes flooding back. Even though it was my choice to take the fall alone, watching all my friends go into the room makes me feel smaller than I have in a long time. I slump against the wall of the elevator.

When the doors slide open, I storm into the training room. I march over to the heavy bag and start laying into it. It's uncoordinated flailing, the bag giving encouragement on how to improve my stance and style. I don't listen to a word.

I can't stop feeling like Dylan the reject. The one that can't fit in no matter how much I try. Dani is in the briefing room, getting orders, coming up with plans with Alyse and Bianca. Aurora is there too, side by side with my friends.

"Come on, you big bastard," I shout at the heavy bag. "Fucking hit me back."

I'm the one who got us here in the first place. The one who cut off Tremor's hands. I'm the reason we're here, pawns of Yaxley. They *should* take me away and throw me in a cell.

"Hit. Me. Back." I throw punch after punch at the bag, and it finally lashes out, the weight of it taking me off guard. I sprawl backwards and hit my head hard. Breathing heavily, I mash the boxing gloves against my face.

"I'm sorry," the bag says in a high, desperate voice. "You asked me. I don't know my own strength."

I walk slowly back over. My arms feel heavy. "It's not your fault. It's mine."

After the mission briefing, everyone comes upstairs for regular training.

"Are you ok?" Lou asks as he brushes past me.

"I'm fine," I snap. "Of course I'm fine." I feel like an asshole, but I can't be vulnerable with every god-damn person on the planet.

"Hey," Alyse says. "You feeling alright?"

"Why does everyone ask me such stupid fucking questions? Why wouldn't I be alright?"

"I'm glad you are." She nudges me with her shoulder. "But if you're not, you know, for any random reason—you can always talk to me."

"Whatever." I go to the other end of the room where I do weights until I can barely lift anymore. My arms shake. I wonder if anyone would notice if the bar crushed my throat. I'm so completely hopeless. I can't even see a future where—

The weight is gone from my hands.

Dani is looking down at me. If only I could use her beautiful eyes as a portal, maybe I'd come out in a parallel universe where I'm perfect and good.

"Dilly." I could listen to her say my name over and over in any universe. "You doing okay?"

"No." It seems I trust her enough to be halfway messy.

She lowers the bar into the cradle. "Shove over."

I roll onto my side and wriggle over to the edge of the bench. She lays so our whole bodies are touching, and whispers a blow by blow retelling of what happened in the briefing. It only lessens the sting a tiny bit.

I spend the day before the mission feeling unsettled and irritable. I'm tempted to call in sick to avoid further humiliation, but I can't do that to the others, so I show up alongside them.

Aurora gives me a smug look and it's lucky Oni-maru isn't there. He might intervene, given how badly I want to punch her. I settle for the anime fist clench and keep my fucking mouth closed. Is this another sign of personal growth?

The Field Team heads down to the garage to leave. I think my hand might fuse into a chunk of rock. The Support Team files into the briefing room. I stand alone in the lobby, a sculpture of someone carved from rage.

In the doorway, Bancroft gives a slight cough. "No point standing around, Chatterbox. You can watch the Support Team."

I mutter something that could possibly be thanks and follow the others. It's far less bare than when we attend briefings. Expensive-looking monitors sit around the table. Goddess and Glowstick are already seated with Bluetooth headsets on. Bancroft rattles off commands.

I wander down one side of the table. Glowstick has a map of the city with a glowing dot indicating the Yaxley SUV. Goddess has two screens, both split into quadrants with search tabs and video feeds. One shows the vehicle interior, Aurora's gloved hands on the wheel and the dash glowing behind. Her head turns and I catch a glimpse of Dani in the passenger seat. Even in the all-black uniform, I recognise her.

Emma had already told me about the camera in Aurora's uniform, but I wonder if it's why Bancroft wanted me here. It's a demonstration of power and knowledge.

I drift between Goddess and Glowstick, watching as the vehicle reaches its destination and the team assembles. The target location is a big industrial park out behind the airport. It's quiet this late, although there is a security patrol. Goddess monitors their position and feeds it to Dani and Aurora. All Yaxley's high-tech stuff isn't quite comic-book but it's close.

I perch on the corner of the table and ignore Bancroft's frown, watching as the Field Team runs towards the building.

"Corporate espionage," I say.

"It's good practice for the real thing."

"Real thing? You're really going to have us sneaking into embassies one day?"

He purses his lips. "Quite simply, your unique powers make you invaluable. Imagine being able to neutralise the security system in a highly advanced smart building," Bancroft looks at me like an eagle about to swoop down on a tiny little mouse.

"Sometimes dummies get lucky." I give him my winningest smile.

He sighs almost parentally, perplexed by the stubbornness of the teenage brain. "The goal here is to work together for the common good. It's important to be aware of the global situation, and ensure that we are on the right side."

"Right side?" I frown up at him.

He makes an irritated clicking sound with his tongue. "Co-operation," he snaps. "If you work with us, then no matter what happens internationally, you'll be protected moving forward. Better to be inside the lifeboat, believe me."

It's hard to parse the meaning from that bullshit, but it's fucking ominous. I have more questions, but I glimpse a familiar logo on the footage from Aurora's bodycam.

"That's another Jinteki building." I lean forward. "You're stealing from *them*?"

"Believe it or not, we were not entirely satisfied with their explanation of how they *acquired* Ms. Hall."

"What are you looking for?"

He gives me an almost human smile. "Careful, Ms. Taylor. Sometimes you presume too much."

"That's my team in there." I watch as they move down a hallway.

"The team you are part of. None of which gives you the right to classified information."

On screen, the Field Team enters an office. Dani crouches beside a computer.

"Stealing information." I glance at Bancroft, who's watching the screen intently. Maybe they're after lab reports on Emma, or information on the mutants who escaped.

Dani straightens up and gives Aurora a nod.

"They've got it. Looks like my little package worked." Emma taps the side of her head. "Drones show no other life signs in the vicinity. Team's clear for exfil, Marvellous."

She winks at me and I nudge the back of her seat. She's in her happy place. Given she just got back from being imprisoned, maybe Emma-type fun with drones and surveillance is what she needs. Plus, it's one more in the win column for the Cute Mutants.

The team rappels down the building, and returns to the Yaxley vehicle without incident.

"No surveillance?" I ask Emma.

"Neutralised. Yaxley has nice toys."

I catch another glimpse of Dani as she gets back into the car, and we watch the dot on Glowstick's screen as it heads back to the Yaxley building.

Emma slumps back in her chair, looking up at me. "We're the cool mutants, aren't we?"

"You are." I extend one foot to kick Lou's chair. "I don't know about this asshole."

"You never did like being the brains of the operation, Dilly." Lou grins at me and I give him the finger. It's nice being able to give each other shit again.

I slide off the table and crouch down beside Emma. "Not sure if you noticed in all the post-Jinteki drama but Alyse was *extremely* happy to see you. You should have seen her face when we figured out you were missing."

"I woke up in the night." Her voice is almost inaudible, but her smile says a lot. "She was asleep in the room, like watching over me." There's a pause. "I wanted to ask her to come onto the bed and hold me, but I was scared she'd say no."

I want to make her elaborate promises, because I'd love to see this happen. I remember back when Alyse was rather aggressively shipping Dani with me and I had my fingers stuck in my ears about it. I don't know how to make Alyse see what's right in front of her. Sure, okay, I was really dumb with Dani but my stupidity is basically a secondary mutation. Alyse is meant to be good with this shit.

On the screen, the glowing SUV dot reaches the building, so we wait in the lobby as they come up in the elevator. The doors slide open and Aurora gives Bancroft a firm nod.

"Mission accomplished. Once again, a highly effective result from the field team." Her gaze brushes over me, like she wants to see my reaction, but I only have eyes for my friends.

"Nice job," I say to Bianca as she strides over towards me.

"It's not the same without you, Chats." She pats me on the back.

"We did miss you." Alyse hugs me, very warm and soft, but I can sense her looking for Emma, like that internal GPS is a little more battery-intensive for her. "Dani's still a good field leader, but—"

"I hated it," Dani whispers in my ear. "I don't want to go without you again."

Once we leave Yaxley, we curl up in the back seat of one of their town cars. Dani's kiss holds many promises, but she falls asleep in my arms. She's droopy and dozy when I deliver her to her mother.

"Joo-hyun," Mrs. Kim says sternly, as if Dani's been out drinking.

"It was a mission." I'm still super awkward. "She did well."

"And why did you not accompany her?"

"I'm a bad girl." I'm too tired to lie and I give a battered version of my winningest smile. "They made me stay behind."

I've never before heard someone *hmph* like they do in books, but Mrs. Kim does, looking at the two of us. I don't think it's precisely a good sign.

"The two of you," she says, and she's unreadable like Dani used to be.

"We are a pair."

Mrs. Kim *hmphs* again and takes Dani's other arm to usher her into the house. "Thank you for bringing her home. She'll see you tomorrow." There's an awkward pause. "Get some rest too, Dylan."

She closes the door and I stand on the porch for a moment, shivering because it feels cold without Dani there. I want to bang on the door pitifully and ask to be let in, or to throw rocks at her window and recite the fragments of Romeo and Juliet I remember. Something about a yonder window? Fuck, I don't know. I need to learn some romance poetry or some shit. Wow, maybe I'm exhausted too. I jog back to the car and its warm interior. The driver is silent, and I'm incredibly grateful.

When I get home, Katie is still on the couch.

"Did you leave here at all today?" I ask her, which is the wrong thing to say. I don't know if there's a *right* thing with Kacchan.

"I've been through a fucking traumatic event, you bossy bitch, and I don't need you shaming me for it." A brief puff of smoke ebbs from her nostrils.

I can't be bothered with her shit after the day I've had, so I slink off to bed without saying anything to make it worse. At least Summers sleeps with me instead of staying out with her.

CHAPTER FIFTEEN

We only make it to the second block at school the next day. I'm in class with Dani and Bianca when we get summoned to the office. I figure it's Yaxley, but why the urgency?

Aurora waits for us, looking sombre. I don't know what spell she casts to let us leave during the day, but I wish I knew it. We pile into two vehicles parked illegally in front of the school. I have a panicked moment where I think it's to do with Pear, but they text back almost immediately that everything is fine.

So what fresh fucking hell is this?

As soon as we're seated in the briefing room, Aurora pulls up a picture of a triangular office building on the monitor. "We have an urgent situation developing."

"That's the building from last night," Emma says. "The Jinteki office."

"Despite the timing, this is unrelated to last night's operation." Aurora folds her arms across her chest and regards us sternly. "We received confirmation from

Jinteki this morning that they've been creating their own extrahumans." Her eyes flutter towards Emma. "Perhaps Ms. Hall's description of events was less fabricated than we assumed."

"Wow." I can't help interrupting. "That's fucking—"

"Enough, Chatterbox." Aurora hits the table again, her go-to asshole move. "We can litigate this later. Right now, we have an urgent situation unfolding. Jinteki's extrahuman subjects broke out of the building on the same night Chatterbox went in and freed Goddess."

Not such big news for us. The bit that freaks me the fuck out is that Yaxley and their nemesis Jinteki are texting each other at the back of the class. Yesterday, we were breaking into Jinteki's office and now they're best pals. It's like an old monster movie except the monsters have teamed up, which is bad news for us puny humans scrambling around at ground level.

"New extrahumans," I say. "Created from Goddess? Is that why they took her?"

Aurora looks to Bancroft before she speaks. "We can't give you answers because we don't have many ourselves. Right now, it's vital that these extrahumans are recaptured. Jinteki claims vital information was destroyed in the escape. Regardless, this mission has been approved at the highest levels of the New Zealand government."

Alyse inhales sharply. I look at her, and she's transformed into an expression of wide-eyed horror. I remember our conversation about hunting other mutants. Turns out I'm a fucking prophet. I don't think it's my secondary mutation. It's just being a bitter old cynic like my Pear.

"Recaptured," Dani says. "Are we really going to deliver them to Jinteki?"

"No," Bancroft replies. "Yaxley will be responsible for them."

Alyse blinks. "Will they be going to soft girl jail?"

"Please focus." Bancroft looks irritated by the questions, like it's so unreasonable for us to want to fucking *know shit* for once. "We have rogue extrahumans loose in our city."

"Loose in a Jinteki facility," Emma corrects. "It's almost like they want answers."

Aurora taps her phone and the screen changes to a view of the half body outside the Jinteki building. "Before you feel too sorry for them, you should be aware of what they can do."

The photo shows a far closer view than Dani and I got. It looks like the body was severed down the middle, and the top half is an abstract smear of pink and red, stretching down the road like a flourish with a paintbrush. The screen changes to show more bodies inside the facility. One hangs from a light fitting and another looks like they've been mauled by a wild animal. They're freaky fucking scenes, yet it's not like we wouldn't be capable of similar things.

"Please don't make the foolish mistake of thinking they're poor lost girls. These are killers, responsible for at least three deaths."

"What are their powers?" Dani asks.

Aurora shifts uncomfortably. "We don't have that information from Jinteki at this time."

"At this time." I don't bother hiding my derision, and Emma makes a scornful noise in her throat. "At what time will we get it?"

"It's unlikely we'll get that intelligence before we go in."

"Gee, Aurora, it seems like that might be kind of useful. Do they cause earthquakes? Control electric fields?"

"You really think Jinteki don't know what these powers are?" Dani's voice has all the ice queen vibes back. "They're deliberately withholding this information. We're taking all the risks, so why should we do it?"

Bancroft steps in. "Unfortunately, Ms. Kim, we answer to a higher power. Our government wishes a swift resolution before this incident garners unwanted attention from other quarters. Be assured we will work to get this information."

"Until then, we'll be flexible in the field." Aurora glares around the room. "Precisely the skills we've been working on."

I want to talk with the others, but we don't have time. Even though this is one of my nightmare scenarios, I can't quit and let Yaxley lock me up. Maybe I'm an arrogant asshole, but it looks like we're the best chance of fixing this without more people dying—human or mutant. We have to take control.

Fifteen minutes after the briefing, we're all sitting in the SUV and pulling out of the Yaxley building.

"Unfortunately, the situation at Jinteki has made the news," Aurora says. "This means the media will be there."

"Ooh, going out in public." I light up my costume. I've never gotten around to updating it, so I still look like a Tron version of my old green-and-purple costume. Dani lights hers up too, in old-school Jean green and yellow with the original Phoenix logo on her chest.

"It's marvellous," I tell her, and she rolls her eyes. Apparently she doesn't appreciate my puns.

Wraith has spent a lot of time making herself a buxom anime vampire queen.

"It's impressive," I say. "But *dontseeme* means nobody will see it."

She shakes her head. "The point is that *I'll* know. I'll feel badass so I'll act badass. It's how himbos everywhere work: the power of positive sexy-thinking."

For some reason this cracks me up, which sets Alyse off. Even Dani smirks.

Aurora drums her hands on the steering wheel. "We're heading into a potentially dangerous combat situation. We don't want ridiculous stories about superheroes getting out. You're soldiers, so please turn those costumes off."

"We've fought more mutants than you, Mum." I shove my knees into the back of the seat.

"Marvellous, please get your team in line," Aurora snaps.

"Yes, children," Dani drawls. "Please pay attention. We'll have to communicate out there, which means listening to each other."

Aurora glances over to her. "You're Field Leader. They should be listening to you."

Dani doesn't have her mask up yet, and she turns to look at all of us. "Keep watch and keep talking. We've got no idea what to expect."

We pull up at the Jinteki building to find the cops have established a cordon. Office workers stand around with their phones out. Aurora noses the SUV through the crowd, giving sharp bursts on the horn. People drift out of the way. Some of them even video us as we go past, although they can't see in.

Aurora puts her mask on and we all follow suit. She winds the window down and shows both a badge and a folded sheet of paper to the officer at the cordon.

He takes a while to examine everything before signalling for the barriers to be moved aside. "I have no idea what's going on in there. We got orders to pull out, but they say it's some weird shit."

"We're specialists in weird shit," Aurora says, and okay sure, that's a little fucking badass, I admit. She drives through the cordon and the cops close it behind us. We pull up a short distance from the entrance. The doors are closed and made of tinted glass.

"Showtime," Dani says.

"I hope there's no long-range asshole."

Everyone looks at me like I'm jinxing shit.

We pile out of the car, keeping it between us and the door. The building is very quiet. I turn and look at the people pressed up against the barrier. I give the peace sign. Mutant and fucking proud.

"We need to gain entry first," Aurora says firmly.

Marvellous nods and squeezes the horrible cuff on her right arm. I can't see her expression behind the mask, but the doors swing inwards without a sound.

Standing inside the building is a girl. She's dressed in jeans and a baggy hoodie, like my default outfit. The clothes seem the wrong size, like she scavenged them. She's pale with scruffy blonde hair and has bags under her eyes. I guess up until recently she's been kept in Jinteki's basement, with them doing fuck knows what. It's hard not to feel sympathy. To her, we're probably the bad guys. To me, we're *actually* the bad guys.

"Approach with caution." Aurora strides towards the building.

The rest of us follow behind. I have no idea where Wraith is, and have the weird brain hitch about her absence before I realise she must have set her demons loose already.

"Oh look" The girl's voice is scratchy, like she has the world's worst sore throat. "They've sent creepy assassins to stop us." She takes a shuffling step forward. "You guys make me sick."

Aurora looks around at us. "Let's go, team. Rush her before she can attack."

I think about the smeary dead body on the street. If I was defending somewhere, I'd put the person who could do that right out front.

"Wait," I say over the comm.

Marvellous stops immediately, but Aurora carries on.

The girl's body convulses and she opens her mouth unnaturally wide. A thin spray of green comes misting out. A cloud of droplets washes over Aurora and falls to the ground.

Little divots appear in the asphalt, giving off smoke.

I reach for Marvellous. "Get back! We need to get out of range."

Aurora screams. Her bulletproof uniform is not holding up well against this mutant's saliva. The thick black material flakes away in huge patches. Bubbling welts rise on her skin underneath, as she staggers backwards. Maybe she should have listened to us.

The girl steps forward and her mouth twists. "Was it something I ate?" She places the flat of her hand on her stomach and retches.

"The fuck is she?" Marvellous asks.

"She's a mutant and a problem. We're going to have to find another way in."

Aurora claws at her skin, which is coming off in gooey patches. It's pretty fucking gross.

"Moodring, get Aurora back to the cordon for medical attention." Marvellous reaches for the cuff. "You think I can throw this girl? How heavy do you think she is?"

I hear a loud war cry and a gleam of silver resolves into a long, slightly curved object.

"Wait a second." I bow to the sword. "Onimaru, I am grateful to see you."

I didn't summon him, I swear it. This mysterious connection between us meant he picked up on my distress from kilometres away.

"Greetings, my companion. It appears we have trouble that must be vanquished."

Marvellous looks at me. It's disconcerting that I can't see her face.

"He wants to help," I tell her.

"We could use it."

"That girl in there," I gesture towards the building. "She can spit acid, so watch out. But please don't kill her. If you can knock her out, that would be perfect."

"We shall achieve victory." Onimaru rotates until he's vertical.

The girl in the building watches, but seems content to wait for us to attack again. The sword speeds towards her, and her eyes widen. She coughs more acid, but Oni darts upward, rising above the spray. He swings behind her and slaps her across the back of the head with the flat of his blade. She falls to the ground, motionless.

Onimaru hangs in the doorway, swaying gently from side to side.

I give him a thumbs up. "Their ranged attack is down, but there's got to be more of them."

"True," Marvellous says. "So let's be extra damn careful."

We move quickly towards the door. Moodring has finished up with Aurora and has rejoined us. She's still got her uniform on so I can't tell what she's feeling.

"I see no others," the sword tells me. "They must be laying in wait like cowards."

"Drones are up," Goddess says in my ear. "They've activated some baffling in the roof so we can't pick up signals. They must have done it after last night's break-in."

"That's perfect," I grumble. "Means we have to go in blind."

We make the lobby without more surprises. Marvellous stops to tie up acid girl with flexible plastic cuffs. I stick tape over her mouth. It probably won't hold back her acid, but it's worth a try.

We're in a big curved room with lots of tinted glass and a massive reception desk with Jinteki Research Laboratories written along the front. It looks empty. On each side to the lobby are small spaces with couches and plants.

"Oni, please check behind the desk. Marvellous, let's check the little rooms."

The sword darts behind the desk, while I go left. I reach the alcove but there's nobody in here. I peer over the back of the couch, and hear a shout from Marvellous.

I turn to see someone with short hair and big eyes dart out from behind a plant. He's wearing an oversized suit jacket and stained tennis shoes.

Marvellous squeezes the cuff on her arm and a comfortable chair scrapes along the ground, chasing down our new mutant friend. He dodges the chair and runs headlong for Marvellous, arms outstretched like he's playing tag.

"Onimaru!" I scream.

The couch hits the new mutant and he tumbles headlong over it. Just before he faceplants, he grabs hold of Marvellous and she disappears. Entirely vanished. There's not even dust left behind.

I scream inside my mask. This cannot be happening. Dani can't be gone. A second ago she was here. Oni's scream matches mine.

"Chatterbox, it's okay." Goddess speaks in my ear. "Marvellous is okay. According to the tracker in her suit, she's just... moved. She's outside and four blocks down the road, heading back towards the building."

"Yes, yes, I'm fine," Marvellous says over my earpiece.

I almost sag to the ground in relief.

"Onimaru, hold. Don't kill him."

The sword ignores me and races towards the mutant—apparently some kind of teleporter. The kid reaches up and slaps feebly at the blade. It looks like a ridiculous tactic when fighting a floating sword, but it works.

"He can teleport," Marvellous says.

"Yeah, no shit. He just sent Onimaru away as well."

Moodring rushes him next, transformed into something demonic. She towers over him, a flame-skinned monster with massive claws.

"Go away," the teleporter shrieks.

I'm watching a slow-motion disaster. "Goddamn it. If he touches you—"

Moodring backs towards me but the teleporter scuttles closer. She's unwieldy on her demon claws and she stumbles. The other mutant's hand brushes her and she's gone too.

It leaves him and me, with only a few metres separating us. I turn and sprint to the far end of the lobby. He tiptoes towards me, hands outstretched. I need an object to attack him with while he's focused on me.

It's so fucking minimalist in here. There's a faint murmur from a couch down the other end, but he'll only move a meter or so and even that is very begrudging. A box of paperclips behind the desk all inform me of their great desire to help, but what can they do? Make tiny little knives? String together into a big chain and strangle him?

Stupid fucking powers. Why wouldn't Jinteki share any intel?

Something that looks like a fancy paperweight floats up behind the teleporter and cracks him in the back of the head. He staggers and falls after a second thump.

I look around desperately for somewhere to hide. "A floating paperweight took him out. They've got a tele-kinetic as well, but they're infighting or—"

"It's Wraith," Glowstick says over the comm. "You can't see her."

"Fuck." My heart is thumping. "Tell Wraith not to touch the damn teleporter in case she disappears too. Not that I'd know if she did. That's two down out of a fucking unknown number, thank you very much, Jinteki assholes."

I'm really edgy not knowing anything. I don't want to wait around to get jumped.

"Let's move." There's a stairwell at each end of the building, and I head for the closest one. "Glowstick, tell Wraith to take the other one."

"Splitting up? Is that a good idea?"

"We're already down two mutants and a sword. Who knows what the others can do?"

"We're on our way back," Marvellous says. "And I've got Moodring. You'll have backup soon."

I glance at the stairs. I can faintly sense some objects above me. I'll be fine. "Catch me up. I'm moving."

CHAPTER SIXTEEN

I make it to the first floor without any sign of mutants. When I push open the door from the stairwell, there's only a corridor with a series of offices. Great. I'll have to go room to room. I bet there's someone hiding in one of them. I really hate jump scares.

"Which one are you?" A girl steps out of a nearby office doorway. She's dressed in mismatched clothing like the others except her jacket and jeans fit. Her hair falls in perfect dark waves halfway down her back with these glamorous blood-red highlights. Her brown skin glows with health and vitality. Compared to the others, she looks like she's walked out of a commercial for beauty products. She moves easily and comfortably, as if she belongs here.

"Are you the scruffy slightly gothy one? We saw the footage of your break-in to Jinteki. There's the pretty shapeshifter and the super hot telekinetic and the scary tall one. And then there's you. Couldn't figure out what you were doing there. Seems like everyone else's powers are way cooler."

"Yeah, my powers suck." I tap on the door nearest me. "Unless anyone wants to help me?"

I hear sullen muttering from a couple of the offices. Most excited is a desk who was assembled inside the room and is now too big to get out the damn door. There are a couple of eager chairs, but their office is locked. They start wheeling themselves back and forward, slamming against the door. If I had some time, maybe I could charm it open, but this annoying girl is talking again.

"Are you really with that Asian girl?"

"She's Korean, but yes."

"Whatever. She's so far out of your league, I honestly feel embarrassed for you. I guess strictly it's more embarrassing for her, but she'll walk away from it still hot and what will you have?"

I press my hand harder against the door. "You want to open for me?" I ask, but why would it? This girl is right. I'm useless and shouldn't be up here on my own. Why didn't I wait for Marvellous, or someone else with worthwhile powers? It makes sense I've got the erratic, half-ass power because I'm an erratic, half-ass person.

The chairs inside the room fall quiet, their desire to escape gone. The door sighs. Even the desk, which had been rotating to find an escape angle, slumps onto its side.

"It's got to be a pity thing, right?" The girl inspects her nails and buffs the back of one of them. "I mean there's literally zero other reason why anyone would be with you. I don't believe in charity dating myself, but your Korean girl is weird and soft."

I lean against the wall and close my eyes against the tears. If it's this obvious to someone who only saw me once, how obvious must it be to Dani?

"Look, none of this is your fault." The girl walks slowly towards me. "I mean in your shoes, I'd be impossibly grateful that someone so hot is paying you attention. I'd cling to that desperately. I'd also prepare for the end, because I promise you it's coming."

The thought of Dani leaving me is a physical weight on my chest. I remember the way she wrote on my arm. How could she do that knowing she'd leave me? I slide slowly down the wall. I didn't know heartache was a physical thing.

The girl stands over me, shaking her head. "Do people really recover from heartbreak? It might take years to bounce back. You should probably end it all now before—"

"Stay the *fuck* away from my girlfriend." There's a sharp crack. A green and yellow figure steps into view and shoves the girl to the floor, followed up by a kick or two.

"Dilly, are you okay?" Marvellous crouches beside me and takes my hands. I can't see her face.

"If you're going to break up with me, just do it." It's as if someone's reached down my throat and dredged

194

the words up from the bile pooled at the bottom of my soul.

Dani reaches up and touches the button below her mask. It springs free so I can see her face. She's so beautiful. "Take your mask off."

I feel so weak and tired I can barely lift my hand to do it, but soon she can see my tear-stained cheeks and my messy hair and the awfulness that is me.

"Dylan Jean Taylor." She cups my face in her hands and presses her lips to mine. "I heard what she said to you. There's not a word of it that's true."

Onimaru hovers over Dani's shoulder. "I shall cut out her tongue for you if you wish."

"No tongue-cutting," I whisper.

"Listen to me, Dilly. This is the truth, and I want you to hear it. Every day I wake up and I'm glad someone as funny and smart and sexy as you wants to be with me."

I blink at her. "Oh my God. She's psychic."

"You think?" Dani smiles at me, but it wavers. "Is this what you're scared of?"

It's hard to meet her gaze. It's embarrassing to have your fears laid bare.

"Do I not make you feel good?" It's her voice that shakes now.

"You do. You make me feel so good. It's just… I've had a lot of practice feeling insecure and she got in my head."

"Let's tie her up and muzzle her." Dani uses cuffs and duct tape to do exactly that. "Now hopefully there aren't any others to worry about. Glowstick, do you have a line on Wraith?"

"She's found a bunch of Jinteki security locked up where she is. They're trying to get out. She wants to know if she should help."

"No way," I say. "Those assholes will make things worse."

"Are you sure?" Glowsick asks.

"Yes, I'm sure. Jinteki has done enough. Do we really want—"

My earpiece goes dead and I frown at Marvellous, who's tapping hers.

"We've been cut off." She scowls. "Hopefully it's the last nasty surprise."

As if in response, the sound of faint flute music drifts up from the bottom of the stairwell.

"You had to fucking jinx it." We put our masks back on and drag our captive psychic to the top of the stairs. She gets left there, tied up and unconscious, while we creep down. The music gets louder as we go.

When we reach the lobby, it's like stepping into a fantasy movie. A girl in a tattered trenchcoat with long black hair holds a flute to her lips. A group of pale figures swirl around her. Their faces have blurry features and they have too many limbs, like the abstract art

Pear's girlfriend has at her house. It's mesmerising, both beautiful and creepy. Another figure spills from the end of her flute as she plays.

Among the monsters stands something fierce and ferocious. It has a halo of crackling electric hair and long whip-like limbs that lash out, sending the pale monsters scampering backwards.

"Holy shit," I say. "Is that Moodring?"

As monstrous as she is, she's way outnumbered. I'm not sure how we intervene in this fight, but we have to try. Maybe the paperclips can help.

"Oni, see what you can do about—"

A massive bang comes from the far end of the lobby. Multiple dudes in combat black clatter into the room, shouting and waving guns. They say shit like 'everyone on the fucking floor' and 'down, down, down' and 'targets in sight'. I have no idea if they can differentiate us from the other mutants, or if they even want to.

"Wraith," I growl. "I thought we agreed not to let these assholes out."

The flute girl backs away from the soldiers. When the music stops, the creatures around her dissolve away.

"I said get on the fucking ground!" There are five soldiers in a triangle formation. The one at the front is doing the shouting but they've all got their guns moving between us.

The guns are all talking at once.

"One at a time," I shout.

Cute Mutants and renegade mutants and dudes with guns all look at me.

"Please don't shoot anyone!"

"Listen," one gun says rapidly. "We really don't want to but we have no choice. If you can defuse the situation—"

"Everyone get on the ground." Lead Dude holds his gun tightly and points it right at me. "We'll get you all into custody and sort things out from there."

"Fuck no." I get slowly to my knees, hands up. "Put the goddamn guns down first."

"You're not in charge, little girl."

Moodring growls, a rattling sound in her chest. She looks wolfish now, able to leap into the middle of the soldiers and tear them apart like a fairytale monster. The lead soldier swings his gun around to point at her. It screams helplessly. "I can't stop it! He'll make me hurt her!"

"No," I shout back. "Don't you fucking *dare*."

The gun twists in the soldier's hand as he fires. Bullets stitch a line high up on the lobby wall.

"Marvellous, Oni," I shout. "Now now now."

Marvellous slams her hand against the cuff. She screams as two of the guns are wrenched away from the soldiers and fly past her, slamming against the wall behind.

"Get out of there, you guns. Don't fire, don't fucking hurt us."

They thrash desperately in their captor's hands. One escapes to the floor and writhes towards me, and another rears back to hit his soldier hard in the jaw.

The lead guy wrestles his gun under control and points it at me. "What the fuck *are* you?"

The gun sobs.

"Please," I say, to the soldier or the gun, whichever will listen. "Please don't—"

Oni swings in a swift and savage arc, severing the soldier's arms just below the elbows.

There's a lot of blood and the soldier screams, high and hysterical. I guess your heart is pumping blood to your hands all the time, especially when you're all hot and bothered over shooting some mutants. Now it's jetting all over the floor, like a movie where you think the gore is way over the top and can't possibly be realistic. Yet here we fucking are.

Fuck. I'm going to get a reputation for this.

"Chatterbox." I hear hysteria at the edge of Marvellous's voice. "Your sword just fucking well—"

"He's not *my* sword. He's his own sword."

"The man was about to use one of those awful weapons," Onimaru says. "I refuse to apologise for intervening to save your life and that of your love and your friends."

"He saved our lives." The problem is now we have four disarmed soldiers and one literally disarmed soldier, not to mention a group of renegade mutants. We need to get out. "Do any of you assholes want to help?" I snap at the other soldiers.

One fumbles for the pack at his back. I watch suspiciously, but it's only medical equipment. They get bandages out and begin to apply tourniquets to the arms of the lead soldier, who's completely unconscious.

"We need to figure out what to do about these other mutants," I say to Marvellous.

Moodring goes and picks up the acid-spitter, who's still unconscious. I hope she's ok. Oni hit her pretty hard. The teleporter is awake and groggy, but is at least keeping his hands to himself. The flute girl fidgets, tapping her instrument restlessly against her thigh.

Marvellous goes and collects Depresso, my new least favourite person, from the top of the stairs. I pace back and forward the whole time, racking my brain.

"I don't want to give these people to Jinteki *or* Yaxley."

"I think if we do, it won't go well for them." Marvellous grimaces. "But if we let them loose—"

"Listen to me." I round on Depresso. "I don't want any fucking psychic bullshit from you. These men were here to kill you or take you back to the basement. We're in a shitty situation ourselves and I don't want to drag you all into that. So if we let you go, is there any fucking way at all you can stay quiet and out of sight?"

She holds my gaze for a while and then nods.

I really hope we're doing the right thing. "What do you think, Moodring?"

"I don't want to hunt our own kind," she says softly. "I vote we let them go."

"Teleporting kid, I assume you can get everyone out of here?"

He doesn't answer, but glances at Depresso, who nods behind her gag. She's obviously the one in charge. The teleporter walks over and touches her shoulder, and she disappears. Then the acid-spitter is sent away, and then the flute girl.

"Thanks." His voice is low and soft. "We owe you one."

He puts his hand to his own chest and winks out of existence.

"You're the powered kids from Yaxley," one of the soldiers says. "You're in a shitload of trouble, letting them get away."

It's interesting that's our biggest crime, not Oni cutting off someone's arms. I guess soldiers are more expendable than mutants.

"Oni?" The sword rises up to hover above my shoulder. "How much trouble do you think we're in?"

"I suspect this is a rhetorical question. You are simply using me as an intimidation tactic. I approve of this from a strategic point of view, and I hope you're not too offended by my actions in defending you. I thought perhaps a show of overwhelming force was what was necessary."

The soldiers stare at the floating sword.

"I'm leaving my friend here," I tell them. "You've seen what he does if you piss him off so I'd recommend sitting down and shutting up."

One of the soldiers leans into another. "Did one of them get turned into a sword?"

"No, that's the one who cut off the Firestone kid's hands. She's the worst of all so shut the fuck up."

Wow, gossip much? Part of me wants to run rather than deal with Yaxley's fallout. Maybe the teleporter should have sent us away too. But we've got families at home, and I'm not ready to burn my whole life down yet.

"Hello? Are you there? Marvellous? Chatterbox?" It's Goddess in our earpieces.

"We're here," Marvellous says, as we head for the door.

"Thank goodness. We lost contact with you right when things started getting intense."

This seems suspiciously lucky, but it's a perfect time to make an exit. We leave Oni watching over the soldiers.

Moodring pulls her mask up and we exit the building together.

Mission sort of fucking accomplished?

202

CHAPTER SEVENTEEN

Outside we find more emergency vehicles and media trucks. Two Yaxley SUVs are parked in front of the cordon, with Bancroft standing prominently beside one. Wraith pops back into existence as we walk.

"Sorry about that whole clusterfuck," she mutters. "Jinteki bastards got out on their own. Didn't see me."

I assume Yaxley is eavesdropping on us again, so I don't want to say much. Presumably it's in their interests to keep things quiet as well, rather than have the news about the existence of mutants get out to the wider public. Eventually, they'll find out we let the other mutants go. The Jinteki soldiers know, and even if they're back to being best enemies with Yaxley, the news will leak out.

I don't like waiting for that shitstorm. There's a horrible part of me that hopes Oni will solve the problem for us by deciding to murder all the soldiers, but I flinch away from that. I'm not that person. I'm not a villain.

Bancroft says nothing in public, but gets into his vehicle. One of his flunkies opens the doors to a second SUV and we pile in. There's an unfamiliar woman in the driver's seat, who looks like an even buffer version of Aurora. As soon as we're back on the road, she punches a button on the dash console. A screen flickers to life, showing Bancroft's washed out and angry face.

"What the bloody hell happened?" He's never sounded this pissed before. "Aurora's in hospital and you've come out with none of the targets. This is not going to endear us to anyone."

"We're all alive, sir," Dani says. The sir is a nice touch and exactly why she makes a better field leader. I'm not calling any motherfucker sir.

"Pointing out ways the situation could have been worse is unhelpful, Marvellous. How did this happen?"

"They had a teleporter, and a girl who spits acid. We thought we'd managed to neutralise them but the teleporter got them away."

"Teleportation," Bancroft says thoughtfully. I bet the old prick is getting all covetous.

There's a scraping sound on the window, and when I look out, Onimaru is floating along beside the car.

"Can you wind the window down please?" I ask, managing to find a vestige of politeness. Alternative Aurora buzzes it down and Oni comes in to rest beside me. It's disconcerting to have an extremely sharp blade cuddling up to me, but he did save our asses. He's cleaned himself up but there's still a little blood spatter on his hilt.

"What's that?" Bancroft snaps. "I can't see what's happening."

"The Chatterbox one has a sword," the driver says. "It looks dangerous."

Thankfully, Bancroft is more interested in other topics. "How many of these other extrahumans were there?"

"Four, sir. One who spits acid, one who can teleport others, one who can produce creatures by playing the flute and——"

"Excuse me, Marvellous, but can you repeat that?"

"She has a flute and it makes things appear from thin air."

Bancroft frowns. "That hardly seems feasible."

"Perhaps we saw it wrong, sir."

He grunts. "And the fourth mutant?"

"Some sort of mood-affecting mind control? We're not exactly sure."

"And can you please elucidate exactly how they managed to escape."

I watch Dani in the front seat as she touches the tender spot on her arm where the cuff attaches. "It was chaos in there, sir. The one with the flute was creating monsters that we had to fight off. In the commotion, we lost track of the teleporter, who vanished them all and then disappeared himself."

There's a really long pause.

"We've been wondering—is Aurora okay?" Dani asks.

"Yes, she will be. It was a shame she was incapacitated so early. If she had been there, I expect we would have a more satisfactory outcome."

"Apologies, sir." I know Dani hates anything that looks like failure. On our terms, we succeeded, but having Bancroft talk down to her puts her on edge.

Back at Yaxley HQ, we shower and change and get checked out by medical staff. They're impersonal and treat us like we're little more than objects. At the end of it, once we've been pronounced acceptable, Bancroft comes through.

"I am trying to look on the positive side, although there is little." He regards us all stonily. "Given the escape, the situation may change in the very near future. Please keep your phones on you at all times, and await my call."

Fucking ominous asshole. He dismisses us immediately, like we're too much trouble. It's hardly convincing because what other mutants do they have? We might be untamed chaos children, but next to the new gang we're positively the sweetest kids around.

I'm still very aware of my YaxPhone in my pocket, tracking me and listening to me.

Outside the building, a familiar voice calls my name.

"Roxy!" I leap into the street, where a pale blue EV coasts to a halt and throws her doors wide. We all climb in and say hello. Even though the others can't hear

Roxy, they know she understands them. I'm so damn happy to see her back. I slip into the driver's seat and put the sheathed Onimaru beside me.

"I've missed you, Dilly."

I stroke the steering wheel in response. The car pulls back out into traffic and Emma taps me on the shoulder. She offers a silvery pouch through the seats. It has a pile of phones inside, so Dani and I obediently add ours. Emma zips the pouch up and lays it on her knees. "Faraday pouch. *Now* we can talk."

First we tell our part, including the arm-cutting which makes Lou goggle at me.

"It's *not* a habit," I tell him. "And it wasn't even me."

"I did get the inspiration from you," Oni whispers. "But it's remarkably logical."

"As soon as you mentioned Jinteki security, I knew things were going wrong." Emma looks a tiny bit smug. "It would have taken too long to hack in and disrupt comms, so we had to go drastic and—"

"I fried the communications equipment with my heat." A blush creeps into Lou's cheeks.

My mouth drops open. "Wow, I never thought I'd see the day that Glowstick gives the middle finger to the man and does something horribly reckless."

Lou grins. "Bancroft didn't even notice. When everything went down, he got very cross and went racing off to monitor the situation in person."

"Do you think they're friendly?" Emma asks me. "The other mutants, I mean. Would they join us?"

Dani arches her eyebrow. We did them a massive favour, but it was chaos before that.

I scowl. "I don't know where they've gone, but I definitely want to keep Yaxley away from them."

"They're free," Alyse says. "That counts for something, right?"

"It does." Emma tips the pouch of phones back and forth absent-mindedly. "Now we need to be free too."

Before we get to Dani's, when it's only the two of us left in the car, I ask Roxy to stop at the park. It's almost evening and nobody else is around. We leave our phones and cross to the swings, where we sit side by side and hold hands.

"If it wasn't for the awful psychic one, I might kind of like them," I say.

"Even the acid spitting girl?"

"We were coming to attack them." The swings creak as we rock back and forth. "Coming in hot with Yaxley stooges."

"They're kind of psycho." Dani looks at me like she's thinking *reckless*.

"They've been held in a corporate basement, tortured and experimented on. What do you think we'd be like after that treatment? Pain-telekinesis, monster transformations, someone haunted by demons, and a lonely girl who talks to objects."

Dani sighs. "I get it, I really do. But we have to be pragmatic. Make smart decisions and look after ourselves. I know you've got that big bleeding heart, but we can't all end up in cells."

I tip my head and watch the sun setting behind me.

"What are you thinking?" Dani asks.

"That I'd like to join them."

"What the fuck?" She tips back beside me, and she's frowning. "You'd leave everyone behind? Leave Ness?"

"Pear would come. All the Cute Mutants. Families too."

She gets off her swing and stands in front of me. I heave myself upright.

"Dylan, this is… We all have families too, you know. I can't see my mother going along with this and bringing Min-jun and—"

"Okay, fine." I leap off my swing to stand beside her. "I don't know exactly how it would work, but it's kind of romantic, isn't it? The thought of being a gang on the run."

She's watching me with a look I can't read. There are still mysteries inside her, even though we're getting to know each other. It scares me and makes me excited at the same time.

"I think my Dad would've liked you a lot."

It's not remotely what I was expecting. I step closer. I want to touch her but my hands dangle awkwardly. "Do you miss him?" Fuck, what a stupid question. Of course she misses him.

"Yeah. My Dad and I were similar, I guess. His nickname back in Korea was nunsalam which means snowman. He wasn't a big talker."

"Ice queen, daughter of snowman."

She touches my cheek as if she's brushing away tears, but they're really on hers. "Yes. He never really spoke Korean except occasionally to Mum. He was like *we're in New Zealand, we assimilate.* I think it was easier that way, especially twenty years ago, just to try and pretend."

"Assholes," I murmur.

"They are a plague on this land and many others like it." She smiles in this way that breaks my heart a little. "It's not like it *works*. Pretending, I mean. Everyone knows. What was the first thing you thought when you saw me?"

"That you were stupidly beautiful," I say, and it's true. Seeing her walk in was a double-take moment. I kept stealing glances at her across the classroom until she frowned at me so intensely I wanted to scrub the blush out of my cheeks. "But yeah, I knew you were Korean." I feel the blush again. "Asian."

"People say they don't see race or colour, but it's the dumbest thing." She takes my arm and places it beside hers to show the difference between the two shades. "It makes no sense to pretend. The world won't, so why should I? I'm Korean and a lesbian and a control freak and a mutant and what else?"

"My girlfriend."

"Yes, that's one of my favourite parts." She smiles but it shifts into a sigh. "Not that Dad could commit to pretending all the way through. His fondness for assimilation was strained with short shorts and undercuts. Especially when I snuck out to get the lyrics to Heavenly's Punk Girl tattooed on my back at thirteen."

"You got a tattoo at thirteen?"

"My cousin Hye-jin's influence." She laughs. "This is before her whole family moved to Auckland for work. We used to get on really well but now it's like occasionally spamming shitty memes in the family group chat. The tattoo is forever though."

"You're such a bad girl."

She turns away, tugging up the fabric of her shirt until I see the neat cursive inked underneath her bra strap.

My heart speeds up like a drumbeat as I trace it with my fingertips. I'm oddly jealous of these words that mark her. I wish it was me imprinted there. The language of my heart scrawled in symbols only we can read.

"Play me this song," I whisper.

"I will." She half turns her face and leans back into me so we can kiss. Her cheek is damp on mine. Moments pass and we stay caught in this pose, as if breaking apart would ruin the spell that lets her speak. "When Dad got sick it happened fast, like when you jump into a pool that's too cold, when you freeze up and it takes so long to thaw."

I feel the warmth of her skin through the thin fabric of her shirt. "I'm sorry." It's all I have, and it's nowhere near enough.

"Usually I'm fine. Most days I think about him, but it's a thing to survive, right? You do it because you have to. But then sometimes I think about how hilarious he'd find your dumb jokes. He'd call you pabo which means, like, fool I guess? But he'd laugh until he cried."

"Sappy-ass snowman," I say, and that makes Dani laugh until she cries and I hold her the whole time.

"You don't have your Dad either."

"He's in Australia with some woman called Claire, who's a dick. It's not the same thing."

Dani turns in my arms so she's facing me. I'm locked to her eyes, like I couldn't leave even if I wanted to. "Thank you."

I have no idea what she's thanking me for, but I'm smart enough not to question it.

"I'm sorry about your Dad."

"I know."

CHAPTER EIGHTEEN

The next day after school, Roxy brings the Cute Mutants back to my house. After our encounter at Jinteki, it's time for people to meet Kacchan. Hopefully she doesn't set anyone on fire. We pull up outside and I leave the others in the car to give her some warning. It seems sensible. Katie's on the couch as usual, with Summers curled up in her lap. When he sees me, he scrabbles out of Katie's arms and hurls himself towards me. I'm still his favourite.

"Summers, you fucking asshole," she shouts.

"Easy." I crouch down to rub the offered belly. "Don't fry him. He's just a dog. I've brought the whole gang back to meet you."

"Gang?" Katie looks interested for once.

"Yeah." I pause. "The, uh, the Cute Mutants." I still don't love the fucking name.

Kacchan throws her head back and laughs obnoxiously. "Cute, sure, whatever. Bring them in."

Roxy opens up her doors and the other mutants straggle into the house.

"I know these assholes," Katie says. "Your bossy girlfriend and the freaky one and the one they stole all the blood from to make more of us."

Everyone goes quiet at that, because nobody's ever come right out and said it. It sends my brain spiralling off, like what are they going to do with the blood they took from Emma. How did they get the blood to make other mutants weeks before they took her and—

"Hi," Lou steps forward all formally and puts out his hand to shake. "You must be Kacchan."

Oh fuck. I haven't used her real name with anyone, because I'm a dick.

"You fucking Chatterbox," she screams. "You told them my name was Kacchan?"

I know what's coming. I shove the others out of the way and hurl myself backwards. The heat of the flame scorches my face as it passes over my head and licks at the kitchen walls. I sprawl messily on the ground. I should be good at this from getting my ass kicked in sparring.

Katie looks worried instead of furious, probably because she set the kitchen on fire.

"Extinguisher," I grunt. "New one. Cupboard."

Lou is cool, calm, and collected which is a nice change. He finds the extinguisher and squirts foam everywhere which makes a hell of a mess, but at least the fire is out.

I get to my feet, rubbing the back of my head.

"So, yeah. This is *Katie*. No codename yet. I'm thinking Brat or Psycho."

"King Explosion Murder." Everyone stares at her because this is a deep cut Bakugo reference and somehow it's okay when she does it? Then she bursts into tears, which leaves me even more at sea.

"I'm so sorry," she says between sobs. "Your Pear has been so nice and now I've ruined the kitchen."

"It was a shitty kitchen." I put one arm around her because I don't know what else to do. "We barely use it."

"They'll kick me out. Who wants a psycho bitch wrecking their kitchen?"

"Pear obviously likes you, and they're a big softie. They won't kick you out, and I wouldn't let them anyway."

She frowns at me. "Why?"

"Angry girls have to stick together. And you're a mutant, even if you don't want to be. Which means you're stuck with us unless you want to bail."

Dani joins on Katie's other side. The rest of the Cute Mutants gather around and we do one of our super lame group hugs that I love so much. Katie stands in the middle of it and flushes bright red but she doesn't tell anyone to go fuck themselves, so I take that as a sign of progress.

I notice that in amongst the tangle of mutants, Emma's resting her head against Alyse's arm and looks like the happiest little forest creature nestled away in her cozy habitat. These dummies, I fucking swear.

The hug eventually breaks up. Lou inspects the damage in the kitchen because he is the sole dude there and so he thinks it's his manly duty. Kacchan is with him, bemoaning all the damage she's done and staring at Lou the whole time.

Emma and Dani are on the couch, deep in conversation, with Alyse standing there watching them. I sneak up, link my arm through hers, and tow her off to my bedroom.

She flops down on my bed and stares at the giant Magik poster on the ceiling. "I'm suspicious. What's with the secret squirrel?"

"It's too noisy out there for having proper best-friend-tea-spilling time."

"Oh please."

"It's true!" I lie beside her so we're shoulder to shoulder. "Everything's so busy lately."

"I do miss you. No more spending the entire afternoon binging anime and spamming right-wing hashtags with fancams."

"Or me telling you X-Men stories."

"I don't miss it *all*," she says, and I elbow her in the side.

"Hanging out and being dumb with my best friend like proper asshole teenagers."

"We're still best friends." She tosses Pillow at me, who gives a soft huff. "But all this smokescreen aside, I know *exactly* why you dragged me in here. You're not exactly subtle."

"Okay, fine." I roll to face her. "We need to talk about Emma. Again."

"Dylan Taylor." Alyse sighs. "I remember when you were the shyest wee thing."

"So do I," Pillow says.

I move to an upright position and lean back against her, in the vain hope it will smother her inter-jections.

"And now I'm an annoying brat who's here to tell you important stuff." I nudge Alyse with my foot. "You know she's in love with you, right?"

"Don't." She slaps my foot away irritably.

"Um what the fuck?" I slide down the bed towards her. "Alyse?"

She looks up at me and her face is melting, tears wearing grooves in the sagging skin of her cheeks. "We've been through this. What if I hurt her? And what will she want from me? And what if I want stuff that she doesn't want to give?"

"You could communicate," I say. "You know, that weird talking thing we're doing now. Dani's super big on it. All I'll say is that Emma's mentioned holding your hand and curling up in your lap."

The change is abrupt and startling. Where there was once a sad and melting Alyse is now something voluptuous and mesmerising. I have to scramble off the bed because temptation.

"Maybe work up to that whole *thing* you've got going on there." I gesture at her from the doorway. "Shall I let her know you want to talk to her?"

She shivers, and regular Alyse is there. It's somehow more beautiful. "Yes."

I almost trip over my feet as I head for the couch and collapse down beside Dani.

"Hey, Ems." I can't keep the smile off my face. "I think Alyse wants to talk to you. She's in my room."

Her eyes go really wide and she clutches at the couch like it'll save her life. "Do you mean…?"

"You should probably ask her." I'm pretty sure my smile is screaming yes.

Emma takes a deep breath. She stands still for a moment, as if getting her bearings, and tiptoes off towards my bedroom door.

"Are you meddling, Dilly?" Dani threads her fingers through mine and we watch Emma softly shut the door behind her.

"Perhaps just the tiniest bit. A gentle nudge to move things in the direction they were already going."

"Is Pillow in there?" Dani knows me too well.

"Oh yes, and believe me we could get the full report on everything. You know, if we wanted to. But that would be wrong."

"You're supposed to use your powers for good, Will," Dani says, because she gets me. The urge to say I love you is back. You don't choose the moment your girlfriend drops a *Buffy* reference to profess your undying devotion, do you? Fuck, I don't know. I kiss her instead, because that's easier.

The kiss is amazing but I hear these little scraping noises. When I open my eyes, Dani's daggers are dancing around her head in a slow dance. They dip and swirl in a choreographed pattern, catching the light and sparkling. Her eyes open too and she holds out one hand for the daggers to line up and gently float into.

"Wow, you are such a fucking show-off."

"Just a tiny bit of pain," she whispers. "I barely notice while I'm kissing you. And you're impressed, I can tell."

"Maybe a tiny bit."

"Liar." She kisses me again, and we don't break until the door to my room cracks.

They're holding hands. It's literally all I can do not to squee.

Alyse is soft-focus and pastel-drenched and impossibly beautiful. Her eyes are literal pulsing hearts and even among the thrill of my ship riding the waves on the open ocean, my brain is still going: her powers are impossible, all your powers are impossible, what is happening to reality la la la.

"Alyse, you're so subtle." Dani can't stop smiling either.

Emma is all delicate and wide-eyed, her hair falling loose around her shoulders. She mouths *thank you* at me, but it's not like I did anything. These two were falling into each other's arms. It's maybe a weird thing to think, but being demiromantic makes the impossibility of love even more wonderful, like they were two balls in the lottery machine that had to come out at the exact same time in this big whirling chaotic dance and now here they are.

They come to sit on the couch near us. Emma's leaning on Alyse and their hands are still touching. I wonder if Alyse wants to kiss Emma and how it would go if she did and how all the arcs inside a relationship are these complex negotiated things. I get a horrible lurch of worry about how maybe this might not work. But then I remember we're all trying to figure out love and sexuality and relationships. If you add mutant powers into that, it's all impossible, so why not dash across this tightrope together while you can.

"Dylan." Dani's lips are on my neck. "Stop staring at them."

"But they're *so cute*." I drag my gaze away, but my eyes connect with Dani's. I'll dance on *this* particular tightrope no matter how crazy the world gets.

Let's hope it doesn't get any crazier.

Lmao, brain. You fucking asshole.

Later on, Dani is playing some card game with the starry-eyed—literally, in Alyse's case—new couple. I'm letting her control my Bluetooth speaker, which is a love language too advanced for most mortals. I do like the song she has tattooed on her back because it sounds like it's made of candy even though it's a little bit sad. Lots of her other music is by people who can't sing, making music you can't dance to.

Maybe this is what it feels like to be falling in love.

Bianca flops down beside me. "Dani must have the aux cord, because I don't hate the music."

"Fuck off, Eshie." It's my new pet name for her, coming from ESH for Emotional Support Himbo. She says she hates it, but it makes her laugh every time.

"Was that your sticky fingers I noticed meddling in the mutant soap opera?" She waves an airy hand in the direction of the table.

"A nudge. It was a fucking nudge and that's all."

"You're like the old woman from *Fiddler on the Roof*."

I frown at her. "Is that porn?"

She laughs and laughs. "Never change, little Dylan." She nods over at Dani. "It looks like that's progressing fairly well."

"It's fine." I try to keep my face as straight as possible.

"You've done it, haven't you?"

"Done what?" I widen my eyes fractionally.

"You have." She nods wisely. "I can tell. You walk like a dyke now."

"Jesus, Wraith!" I elbow her hard in the side. "You're the literal worst."

She laughs again and slumps down so she can rest her head on my shoulder. "You love me though, don't you?"

"I do, despite my better judgement."

"They're kind of cute, Emma and Alyse. But don't get overexcited and try to set me up with Lou or the little fire-breather. You probably have some kinky X-Men fantasy where we're all paired off, but Aunty Wraith don't play those games."

"I wouldn't wish you on anyone." I pat her knee.

"It's fine." She pokes me hard and I squirm away. "I know you're just levelling up on Dani until you're ready to take me on."

"Omigod can you fucking imagine?" I look at her in mock horror.

"Trash multiplied by trash." She grins and throws a cushion at me. "We'd probably cause, like, an all-consuming trashpocalypse. One of your comic book disasters."

"We'd have to save the earth from ourselves."

We both start laughing hysterically. Dani looks over and shakes her head.

Pear comes home soon after and beams when they see Katie sitting on the couch between Alyse and Bianca. "Look at her, part of the team." They stand in the entrance to the kitchen and gaze at her with what seems like unnecessary fondness. I don't really get this whole deal between them.

"Did you not see the paintwork?" I wave my arm around at the scorched kitchen.

"She's been through a lot."

"We've all been through a lot." I push myself off from the bench and stalk over to Dani.

"Dilly, what does that mean?" Pear calls after me.

"Nothing," I say, because I don't even know myself.

CHAPTER NINETEEN

We arrive at Yaxley the next day for training and find Bancroft waiting with Other Aurora. There's also a bunch of people in suits we haven't met. Everyone goes to the briefing room where the suits arrange themselves at the front like they're about to give a sales pitch.

"We have auspicious news." Bancroft's word choice makes me immediately wonder how fucked we are. I'm not the only one. Dani's eyes are narrowed and her shoulders are tense. Emma taps her hands rapidly on the table. Odds of this being related to the clusterfuck: high.

"Today in the media we will be announcing a merger between Yaxley Technology Solutions and Jinteki Research Laboratories. Over the coming months, we'll be working through the rather complex problem of aligning people and processes and—"

Emma gasps. Lou jerks in his seat and stares at me like he's expecting me to save the fucking day. Out of the corner of my eye, I can see Alyse has shifted into something shadowy. This is worse than I could have possibly imagined. Yaxley might be dodgy, but Jinteki are fucking supervillains and now we're in bed with them.

Bancroft coughs pointedly and continues. "With the technological advances Jinteki are pioneering, we will be able to expand the ranks of our operatives. While unfortunately we were unable to retrieve the initial test cadre, efforts are underway to rectify that. Once the merger is complete, we will be moving forward with a new tranche of—"

Ok so a) what the fuck is a tranche and b) oh look I've opened my mouth.

"Uh, Mr. Bancroft? Can you tell us exactly how Jinteki created their mutants?"

"We're working through the legal tangle of declassifying that. There should be some traction within the coming month."

"So you don't know?" I persist, because I want a straight answer.

"No, Ms. Taylor. Currently we are unaware of the exact details of this."

"Because we were talking just yesterday about how they kidnapped Emma." I'm aware my voice is louder than it probably should be. "They kept her sedated in a room and had their own private medical assholes doing fuck knows what to her, while other mutants were locked in their basement."

"According to Jinteki security records and sworn affidavits, Ms. Hall was delivered there rather ill. As an accredited medical facility, they were performing primary care duties while they ascertained her identity before returning to her family. It was only your reckless intervention that—"

"That's fucking bullshit," Emma snaps. Literally everyone turns to look at her because I have never heard Emma use a) that word and b) that fucking tone omigod I love it so much. "They took me. I wasn't sick. They were using me. You fucking *know* that." The rage in her voice loses steam, almost turning to tears, and Alyse reaches out to steady her. I blink my own tears away.

"With apologies, Ms. Hall, the footage we received from Jinteki to assure us of their good intent shows you quite delirious. You weren't even aware what day it was or what your name was. We also know the creation of the rogue extrahumans predates your incident."

Pardon me, my rage says. I'll take it from here.

Everything in the room starts shaking. They've replaced the table since my tantrum earlier, but one end of it hammers up and down on the floor. It wants to hit the men in suits. The chairs rattle in place. From outside I hear the faintly metallic sound of a sword being drawn.

There's a thump at the door.

"Onimaru," I whisper. "Please wait."

Bancroft is looking at me with an unpleasant expression. I take a deep breath. I count to ten and then do it again. I clench the edge of the table until my knuckles are white. Somehow, I manage to disassemble the sharpest edges of my rage and leave it in discarded pieces inside me. They're still jagged but they're not going to cut anyone.

"Are you done?" Bancroft affects boredom. He doesn't know how lucky he is.

"It's difficult for us to trust Jinteki after hearing what happened to Emma," Dani says stiffly. "We're concerned she might become a medical experiment."

And you're fucking lying, I want to scream. Onimaru is outside, desperate to burst in and cut through these people like an unhinged blender. I mutter under my breath, promising him we're all okay. If it looks like Emma's in danger, the gloves will come off.

"While we are all extremely interested in Ms. Hall's rather unique power and potential, please rest assured that we continue to operate in close partnership with the government. We would never violate your safety."

Nobody says anything, but the looks being passed around the table spell bullshit.

"The second item on the agenda is rather unpleasant," Bancroft says. I don't know how to react, given how I felt about the first one. "After your failed attempt at capturing the rogue extrahumans, the order has been given to retrieve them or stop them." He clears his throat delicately. "At all costs."

I'm stunned, and I'm far from the only one.

"You can't do that," Dani says.

"Unfortunately, the order has been given. It comes through the Five Eyes intelligence network that we share with the United States and others, so—"

"You're saying you want us to kill some teenage girls?" Bianca sounds dazed. Her fingers flutter at her chest. For a second I think she'll let her demons free, but she subsides.

"No." Bancroft stays calm. "In an ideal scenario, we would capture them. However, their powers are significant and dangerous."

"I don't believe there's a government order to kill people." Lou rocks back and forward in his chair. "I refuse to believe it."

"Unfortunately, this is not an isolated case." Bancroft sounds apologetic, but I don't know how anyone can apologise for something like this. "There is little we can share due to your security clearance, but a number of terrorist incidents globally can be traced back to extrahumans. As I have stressed, your cooperation with official organisations is essential. Representatives from a number of countries met recently and legislation was signed covering a number of areas. One of these was the use of extreme measures where there is the potential for significant loss of life."

Um, exfuckingcuse me? Are we actually living in an X-Men comic? I bet there are US defense contractors bidding on Sentinel plans right now. Bancroft blinks at us like an uncool owl, as if we're too dumb to get the message. I think we all realise that half the governments of the world have come to an agreement about us. If we're bad mutants, they'll put us down. Especially if it can be done quietly.

"If any of you are uncomfortable with this situation, we can provide you accommodation in our secure facility." Bancroft looks at us smugly, his trump card on the table. Always going back to the threat of being locked up.

"Maybe we should." Lou is trembling and staring at me.

It's up to me to keep shit together. "No, we'll capture them without hurting them. That's still an option, right?"

Bancroft nods. "As I said, that would be preferable."

The other mutants are staring at me like they can't figure out what I'm doing. It's true, I don't have a plan. All I know is that being in jail gives us zero options. If we stay in their pocket for now, we can maybe turn things to our advantage. It doesn't seem likely, but a shitty chance is better than none at all.

Dani is outwardly as calm and steady as I am. "Chatterbox is right. We're going to bring these mutants in."

I'm so agitated after the meeting that my power bleeds into everything around me. I have to hold Oni close or he'll fly off. Roxy takes corners with a squeal and when we pass a roadside coffee cart, it trundles into the road after me. The owner chases it down, waving his arms frantically.

"We're not bringing those mutants in to be trapped or shot," Bianca says angrily.

"No, we're not." I'm trying to stay calm. "But telling Yaxley that won't help."

Emma tosses her Faraday pouch from hand to hand, all our phones inside. "They're using us like their attack dogs. And a ticket to jail for me is a ticket to a lab."

My brain is racing, but it's mostly all fuck-you determination. "You're not going to end up in a lab again. We won't let them get close to you. Alyse, you'll stay with Ems, right? Monitor her and alert us if anything shady happens."

Alyse's new transformation is so large, she's crushed against the roof of the car. Her skin is covered with metallic spikes like a chromed hedgehog. "They won't get close."

Rather than being terrified like she probably should, Emma runs her fingertips along the smooth silver skin between the rows of spikes. Wow, these precious goddamn babies.

"I'll think of something," I tell them. I have to. "We're not going to let them win."

Everyone nods, but I'm not sure they're convinced. I wouldn't want to rely on me either. It's one thing to come up with a plan to take out a single incel. It's totally different to expect we can take on two corporations and come out unscathed. This is what being a hero means—I have to find a way.

Once everyone's gone home, Dani and I shut ourselves in my room and start using our favourite secure communication method of writing on each other's arms.

i want to find depresso and the others. The pen shakes in my hand. *at least talk to them.*

Her hand grips my wrist so tight it hurts. *They'll KILL you.*

I'll figure it out. I've got Onimaru.

The pen almost leaves welts on my skin when she writes. *You can't leave me.*

Then come with me. I hear her intake of breath. *We'll all go rogue.*

It's so risky.

I frown down at the words on the inside of my arm. I have this burning desire to save every mutant and make them into a sprawling rebellious superteam, but I have no fucking *plan* for it. I tilt Dani's arm to find space.

we'll break into jinteki & get proof about emma

find the other mutants

stop the merger

There's a long pause. Then Dani finally writes on the back of my hand. *You're insane.*

I lean into her. I don't know what to say. Back before this started, Dani wanted to be a doctor. Go off to medical school and train for however many years. There was a long straight road between her and there. She's given up a lot for me and this mutant thing.

i have to do something

The pen falls down and lands on the bed between us.

"I know." Dani leans in and kisses me.

Afterwards, we shower together and wash the words off each other's arms. We talk about what we're going to do and how we're going to do it. Despite the stakes and the rising tide of nervousness, it's still my favourite briefing session.

We make the painful decision not to take Alyse. She needs to watch over Emma. Wraith, on the other hand, could be extremely useful. We cycle to Bianca's flat, where we find her sitting on the front steps with a beer.

"My babies." She lopes over to give us both a hug.

"How many is that?" I nod at the bottle in her hand.

"Number two of hopefully many. Might move onto something stronger and—"

"We're going after Jinteki," I tell her, which shuts her up immediately.

"Those fuckers."

"Exactly."

"And you thought of little old me." There's relief and gratitude in her eyes. I know all too well how good it feels to be part of a team. At least I can give this to her.

I grin. "Can't go into battle without my emotional support himbo, can I?"

Bianca hurls the mostly full bottle of beer into the bushes and runs to grab her bike. It takes a lot longer to cycle than in the Yaxley SUV, and my brain uses the time to try and prise out every possibility from the shadow of the future.

Our Field Team broke in there first, and then the escaped mutants attacked. It seems like there's a decent chance we'll find resistance. Onimaru hovers over my shoulder like a sharp silver Pikachu, singing a mournful song in Japanese. It sounds like a dirge. I hope we're not off to our own funeral.

When we arrive, the carpark is deserted and the building is shrouded in darkness.

"At least I know where the computers are," Dani says.

"How are your hacking skills?"

She fishes in her pocket and pulls out a USB stick. "Fresh from Emma's bag of tricks."

"Excuse me while I swoon."

We leave our bikes outside a building down the road and change in the deep shadows of a carpark. I'm in my old Chatterbox costume, Dani's in all black with a balaclava, and Bianca's in her black v-neck sweater and demon mask. We jog down to the Jinteki building, keeping away from the spill of the streetlights.

I reach out with my mind but it's deathly quiet. If there was an equivalent to Bill here, he's shut down. Probably deemed a security risk after the other lab. It means no subtle entrance, but hopefully no security cameras or unpleasant electronic surprises.

"There are offices along the back," Dani says. "If we can get in there, we can access the network and they might not even notice."

We tiptoe down the back of the building. The windows are all heavily tinted. At the far end, we stand in the darkness.

"I don't like it," I breathe.

"This was your idea." Dani nudges me and runs to the closest window. She doesn't have the Yaxley cuff on, so she raps her knuckles hard against the side of the building. The window doesn't budge. I guess it's the kind that doesn't open.

"Smash?" I ask.

"Noisy," she says with a frown.

Wraith sighs and tries to peer inside. "Better than nothing."

I lean against the building and try to sense for anything listening. There's only faint low-level stuff. Sleepy objects, barely aware of anything. I guess working in an office all day is pretty boring.

"Hey hey," I whisper. "Is anyone in there?"

In response, I hear a sharp voice, raised in alarm. "Watch out, they're coming."

I grab Dani's arm, but there's no time to react before the world is flooded with light. It's white and dazzling through the shitty lenses of the cheap mask. A host of guns scream out warnings and alarms.

"I don't want them to use me. Please don't let them."

"Surrender. It's your only chance. They'll make me hurt you and I'll never forgive myself."

236

"We have no choice. Don't you understand?"

They're so loud in my head that it starts pounding as if someone is beating on it.

"Fucking point yourselves somewhere else if you're so concerned," I snap.

I can barely see because of the lights, but I hear swearing.

"Little powered shit," a voice says. "She's doing something to the guns."

I don't know where Wraith is, but the forms of her demons are silhouetted against the lights. They flutter and scurry and stretch their wings.

Dani swings her arm back hard against the side of the building. She screams, and four men hurtle backwards into the bushes. I've never seen her move so much weight at once. She must be in so much pain. Her daggers hurtle into the darkness. I don't see them reach any targets. It's too goddamn bright.

My brain is a frantic buzz of activity, but I register that I'm missing someone. "Oni?"

"I have failed you." His voice is a melancholy song. "These unnatural monsters have trapped me. With all my vaunted strength, I cannot escape from this embrace."

I shade my eyes. A black coil device hums on the ground a few meters away. Onimaru is pressed flat against it. Is it some kind of magnet?

SJ WHITBY

"I shall do my best to free myself, my friend, yet I fear the odds are greatly against us."

Dani twists her injured arm. She lets out a harsh sob, and falls to her knees. Three guns fly straight upwards, tearing themselves from their owners and disappearing into the sky. There's more commotion outside the pool of light. Presumably Wraith's demons, moving among the guards to feed.

Someone's screaming. Multiple people. It sounds like dudes, probably with demons at their throats. Wraith's the best hope of us getting out of here.

I wince at the sharp cracks of gunfire. Too many guns and I can't make them all fucking listen to me.

There's more screaming. It's impossible to see anything. I have no idea what's going on.

I shout at the other guns, still writhing to get free. One slithers on the ground towards me and leaps into my hand. I can't see who to fire at. It's too much chaos. I want to be filled with calm, but it's only panic and self-loathing rattling around inside of me. Why did I think I could do this?

"Can anyone hear me?" Onimaru thunders. "I call on any god or demon for aid! This is not a fitting end for weapons such as us."

A sting at my neck makes me wince. I put my hand up and feel something hard and plastic. They shot me? But with what?

238

"Getouttathere," I say, words mangled and drooping.

"Omigod I'm so so sorry." The dart drops from my skin.

"There," I say. "Notsoclevernowareyou?"

I take a step forward, but the ground isn't there.

Instead, a black pit welcomes me gratefully into it with a sigh.

CHAPTER TWENTY

When I wake, I'm lying on a bed. My head pounds. I have no fucking idea where I am or—

Things crash back into my brain like they've been clumsily pasted into my memories. We were captured by Jinteki. The fuckers were waiting for us. Too many men with guns and a magnet for Oni. I wonder if they had backup plans for the others. Maybe we should've brought a surprise like Katie or Glowstick.

Where's Dani? Is her arm okay? Where's Bianca? What did they do with Onimaru?

I sit up and see Dani lying peacefully in another bed near mine. She's pale but I can see her chest rising and falling. Her arm is bandaged.

Obviously we've been out for a while. God, I hope Pear isn't freaking out. I'm dressed in a soft grey tracksuit with nothing in the pockets.

I wince at the pain in my head. There's no sign of Wraith. I stagger across to Dani's bed and kiss her forehead. It's cool and smooth, which I think means she's okay. There's a single large window. Maybe we can smash our way out.

The view is swallowed up by ocean. We're way high up and I can see the curve of the world at the horizon. What the hell is this place—some secret Jinteki facility? It makes my head hurt even worse trying to figure it out.

I reach out with my mind for objects. The beds are quiet. The door, however—no, that's too easy. Or not? Yaxley still doesn't know the extent of my powers, which is exactly how I wanted it. I slump down against the door. It feels cold against my back.

"Hey there." My voice is little more than a sigh. "How are you doing? I'm feeling pretty shit to be honest."

"I'm a very good door. Strong and mighty. Nobody can get through me."

Fuck. Of course I meet a door that takes pride in his work.

"I only want to get through briefly. It'll be open and shut. Then you can go back to barring the way. It'd be nice to have a change, wouldn't it?"

"But I'm supposed to stay closed." The door is already wavering. The temptation of openness is great.

"They must have opened you to put us in here," I say with great confidence. "So it wouldn't hurt to be that way again."

"You make a very good point. I do open sometimes."

"Staying closed all the time can't be healthy. How will you ever have new experiences?"

"Yes, yes, I agree. Let me check with Rex. I can't open without him."

My brief euphoria disappears. Bill talked about Rex, and he sounded like an asshole.

"Nice try." Rex even sounds like a villain, snide and pompous. "I can't understand how you're able to communicate with me. However, rest assured you will remain in your secure room until our technicians come to talk to you. I've got the test schedule and it is quite exhaustive, believe me. They are going to get to the bottom of you, Ms. Taylor. Yes they are."

Well, fuck.

"Dilly?" It's a human voice this time. Dani sits up in bed, looking very groggy. She tries to move her arm and winces.

I rush to her side and smother her in kisses.

"Ouch," is all she manages to say.

I fill her in on the situation and her frown gets deeper with every sentence.

"Do you think I can bust the door open?" She's weak and woozy, but there's determination in there too. "I'm in a lot of pain, so I can do anything." She skids the bed backwards and forward, as if she's trying to prove something.

"Don't hurt yourself too much."

"Existing pain." Her forehead creases, and she stares at the door. It doesn't budge. She puts her arm on the bed and leans on it. A tiny whimpering sound escapes her lips, but the door stays firmly shut. "Too heavy. Or I'm too weak."

"You're not weak. They're just smart is all. We'll figure it out."

I'm not sure whether the tall tower, the heavy door, or the evil smart building is our main problem, but I definitely don't want to wait around for the promised testing schedule. It's my fault we're in this mess, so it's my responsibility to get us out. I walk back to the window. It really is way the fuck up here. Maybe we can use the sheets to make a parachute? It seems like a shitty idea that will end up with me smeared all over the rocks but—

"It's bad, isn't it?" Dani hugs her knees.

"It's not good," I admit.

"Where's Wraith?"

"I have no idea. I woke up here the same as you." There's a really long and awkward pause. "I'm sorry for dragging us on this shitty mission."

"I went along with it. Against my better judgement."

I clench my fist and smack my knuckles against the wall as if it'll trigger my own power, but it only hurts.

"Stop it." Dani's breathing is ragged. "Just fucking *stop*, Dylan. What is a tantrum going to achieve?"

SJ Whitby

"I should've done this alone instead of bringing you."

"Yes, that would solve everything, because then you'd be stuck here alone." She glares at me, and I can't see any love in her eyes, only pain and anger.

There's an apology somewhere that will make this better, but I have no idea how to construct it out of all the shitty words rolling around in my head.

"You don't need to solve every problem on your own."

"It's my job." I push myself off from the wall and pace over to my bed.

"How is it your job?"

"Because this whole trip was my stupid idea. I have to make this right. I'm the one in charge." I'm not thinking this through. My brain is still trying to find the apology it needs and left to its own devices, my mouth goes ahead and fucks things up worse.

"Really," Dani says. "Because we keep talking about being a team."

"We *are* a team." Too late, you fucking idiot.

"Yes, obviously a team with you in charge."

Ugh, how can one person be so dumb? I should be used to it by now, but I keep surprising myself with my own stupidity. No wonder I talk to objects, because I can't fucking talk to people.

"I'm going to bed." I wish someone would knock me unconscious and end this stupid fight.

244

"Dylan, can we talk about it?"

I cross to the bed and lie down on it, staring up at the featureless white ceiling.

"Remember how we talked about arguments and communication?"

It pisses me off how she can sound so reasonable all the time. Doesn't she have any actual feelings? Stupid ice queen robot. The dumbest thing ever is that a part of me wants to pick now to tell her I love her, as if those are the words that will fix everything. Thankfully, my sullenness wins out and I keep that particular time bomb inside.

I roll over so my back is to her, and fold my arms. I know I'm a petulant brat, but honestly right now it's all I've got. It's something to cling to. If I could weaponise my scowl, I could blow a hole in the wall and get us out like—

My bed tilts violently and stands up on its end. I sprawl on the floor below it. I stare at Dani, mouth hanging open. She leans on her arm and the bed is thrown violently out the window, shattering the glass. I leap up and watch as it falls to the ground below. It bounces on the rocks and shatters into jagged pieces. "What the fuck was that?"

"Now there's only one bed." Dani gives a little roll of one shoulder. There's a smile at the corner of her mouth.

I should find it cute and endearing, but I'm actually mad because I don't want to talk right now and how the fuck can she *make* me talk?

"Really, Dani?"

"Sorry. It was meant to be a joke. Come onto my bed and we can talk."

"I don't want to talk. I *told you* I didn't want to, then you threw my fucking bed out the window and now there's a draft."

She's staring at me.

I wait for her to tell me it's over. *I'd* tell me it's over.

"There's room for two." She wriggles over on the bed so there's a space for me. I could lie beside her and put my arm around her and be the big spoon.

"I guess I'm sleeping on the floor."

She closes her eyes, like she's finally given up on me.

I fold myself down and try to arrange my arms as a pillow. It's fucking uncomfortable, but I'm willing to stay there forever.

A few minutes later, I'm cursing myself and considering following the bed out the window, just to shut my head up. I'm glaring at the ceiling when Dani's head pokes over the end of the bed.

"Dylan Jean Taylor."

"Shibal pabo." I can't actually say it without smiling.

She shakes her head. "What the fuck did I expect, teaching you Korean swearwords?"

"Being mad at you doesn't mean I don't like you."

"Using my own words against me," she says softly and then pauses. "I'm sorry for going along with the leadership change. I didn't realise how important it was to you."

"I want to be a team." It's the truth, but it's complicated. "I really do. It's just... I feel like I've ruined your life. You quit the team once and you only came back because you liked me. Since then everything keeps getting worse."

She frowns. "Did you force me to rejoin the team? I couldn't have just been your girlfriend and stayed away from the mutant madness?"

"You had a life planned out. And now look at us."

"I could just as easily blame Emma, or fate. I'm smart, Dilly. I've always been smart. I make a decision and I know that when I do, there will be consequences. Some of them I'm smart enough to figure out, and some I'm not. But when I make a decision, that's on me."

I squirm a little closer to the bed so I'm right underneath her. I like looking at her face directly. "Why do you get mad at me all the time then? When I want to go running off to do things?"

A tiny line appears between Dani's eyebrows. "Because I worry about you! Constantly! It's like you want to take all of mutantkind on your shoulders.

You think you're some combination of Magneto and Storm. You can't possibly look after everyone and solve everything, but you keep trying. I'm scared you'll break yourself doing it."

"Like getting locked up in a tower." I feel tears coming, and I hate it. Why am I so soft?

"Yes or even worse! That's why I have to come with you. So you've got at least one person keeping tabs on your adorable ass."

"I hate my ass," I tell her.

"The least you can do is bring it up here and rest it somewhere comfortable." She reaches down to take my hands. I drag myself to my feet, and lay down beside her. She presses herself right against me so we're squished together. I have one hand awkwardly tucked underneath her and the other playing at the hem of her faded grey sweatshirt. She turns her head to kiss me, and I know we're at the mercy of an evil medical corporation who want to torture us, but it's like the kiss at the end of Pear's favourite movie that dwarfs every other kiss in history. Like I know I'm not experienced but it's hard to imagine a better kiss.

I'm still feeling the afterglow a few hours later. My legs finally feel like they can support my weight again, so that's a good start. It's time to solve this problem. I'll rescue Dani and find Wraith and we'll get the fuck out of here. We'll make a new plan. Save everyone, solve everything.

"Dilly?" Dani asks groggily.

I stand in the broken frame of the window.

"What are you doing?" She sits up in bed, clutching the sheet to her chest.

I almost told her this earlier, when we were lying together. When my body was both a siren and a crashing wave, a restless flex of mutant DNA. But I didn't want this proclamation to sound like it was tied up in all that rush of feeling, because I'd say almost anything in those moments.

Now's the time I choose, still the world's worst or best idiot, depending on who you believe.

"I love you," I say. "But I'm always going to be reckless."

Then I throw myself backwards out of the window, and the last thing I hear is her scream.

Doesn't she fucking trust me?

CHAPTER TWENTY-ONE

Okay, so throwing yourself out of a really tall tower does count as reckless. But I'm not entirely stupid, and Dani should know that. After she drifted off to sleep, I lay awake in bed, basking in the afterglow. It was a stupid time to be happy, but there I was anyway, wallowing away in bliss.

It's not only rage that fuels my connection with objects. It's any intense emotion. Turns out being really horny and really happy wakes up a whole bunch of stuff. So while Dani was slumbering beside me, I was having a quiet conversation with various things waiting out in the world.

This means that as I throw myself out of the building, someone's waiting. It's a little dinghy. Two oars flap furiously beside him like wings, holding a big blue tarpaulin stretched between them. The dinghy promised me he could control his own fall, but I'm not sure how well he understands gravity, given he's never flown before. The fact that he's floating there is impressive, but as soon as I drop in, he lurches and begins falling at an alarming rate. The tarp billows loudly and it *might* be arresting the speed of our descent, but it's still very fucking quick.

"Shit, sorry mate," the dinghy says. "I got all over-excited and now it seems a bit harder."

Falling through the air dissipates the blissful, sated feeling a hell of a lot. That leaves room for my old friend, being very fucking pissed off, mostly at Jinteki Research Laboratories. They've locked Dani and I in a goddamn tower, and possibly Wraith too. They kept Kacchan and the others in the basement, performing medical tests on them, and once their science experiments escaped, they're only too happy to hunt them down and have them killed. I'm mad at the whole world beyond Jinteki too, which has decided it's okay for this to happen. We're valuable as long as we're compliant, but if we step out of line they have no use for us.

The dinghy's definitely falling slower now, so hooray for rage. The ground is still coming up seriously fast. I resist the urge to peer over the side to see how bad everything is and then—

We have impact. It's hard enough to jar every part of me. The dinghy is banged up and breathless. A couple of significant cracks run along the bottom of it.

"Bloody hell! Are you okay, little one?"

It takes me a few attempts to get to my feet because I'm shaking so much. "I think so. That went—"

"Yeah, I'm really bloody sorry. It was a lot simpler in my head."

It's such a mood, especially for the situation we're in, that I can't really blame him. I give him a pat as I clamber out. From here, I can see the tower is at one end of the building. It looks like the one from *Tangled* has been tacked onto a big blocky structure made out of Lego. There are no other buildings I can see in any direction. A single road leads up into low hills. It's all very isolated and honestly fucking nefarious looking.

There's a big garage door open not too far away.

"Hey," I say to the oars. "You two want to come explore?"

They scrape along the ground eagerly and leap into my hands.

Inside the building, it's eerily quiet. I'm in a large concrete garage-type space. Where is everyone? They wouldn't just leave us in the tower and all bugger off down to the pub for a drink, would they? The garage is mostly empty, aside from a bunch of vans parked in rows. I cross to them and run alongside in a crouch.

When I hear voices, I freeze with my back pressed up against a van. Two men walk right past me without even noticing. One's in a lab coat, and the other's a soldier in all black.

"Get him," I murmur to one oar. I throw it half-heartedly in the direction of the doctor, and swing the other as hard as I can at the back of the soldier's head. The oar lends me extra momentum, and we hit the guy so hard it jars all the way up to my shoulder. He sprawls onto the ground and doesn't move.

The other oar gently prods the lab coat guy in the back. When he turns, the oar gives him an enormous uppercut. The guy flies backward through the air and there's a solid thump when he hits the ground. It looks like there's something wrong with his jaw.

"You said get *him*," the oar says doubtfully. "So I got him."

"This is a medical facility. Someone will look after them." I don't have time to worry about some asshole with a broken jaw. He shouldn't work for a company that locks people in a tower. I relieve the soldier of his gun, which is heavy and black with a strap around it.

"Oh," the gun says. "It's you."

"Me?"

"The girl who can speak to us. Everyone's talking about you."

"Only nice things, I hope." I sling him around my upper body. I wonder how badass I look. It's possible the soft grey sweatshirt ruins the aesthetic.

"They say you might help us stop."

"Stop what?"

"The shooting! The killing, the death. It's a *lot*."

I leave the overeager oar watching the unconscious bodies, and take the other one with me. A corridor slopes up from the garage, lit by fluorescent lights, so I head into it.

"You don't like killing?"

"It's a lot of responsibility they put on us." The gun sounds defensive. "We're the ones who have to tear flesh and take life. We have no choice in the matter."

"Today you do. If we see any of your buddies, you tell them not to shoot. We'll all be one big happy family and nobody has to die."

"Just hit them with me," the oar says happily. For some reason, she's quite okay with violence.

At the end of the corridor is a big open space. A sculpture of molecules hangs from the ceiling like a giant kid's mobile. It's supposed to look impressive but it's just a lot of balls. There's a big reception desk with Jinteki Medical Laboratories written on it in silver letters that stick out. On the wall behind it is a massive tree logo and underneath it says the cosmos is within us. Which okay assholes, how the fuck does that give you the right to lock people in cages and experiment on them?

I try to visualise where I am in the building so I can find the tower. I have no idea where they might be keeping Oni. Maybe they still have him magnetised somewhere? I turn in a slow circle in the middle of the room. One of those *you are here* maps would be helpful. I pad through the lobby in my grey slippers.

The gun quivers and twists around my neck, as if he's looking for his friends. "I don't like this," he moans faintly. "It's so tense."

"You're not making it any better," I mutter. "Pay attention and we can avoid a jump scare."

I start across the lobby towards a big staircase made of steel struts. I'm not sure it leads to the tower, but I can't see any better candidates.

"They're coming," the gun says. "From up there."

"Okay, so tell all your friends to point at the assholes carrying them. Will that work?"

The gun says something that's drowned out by the echoing sound of big fuck-off boots on steel. Five dudes and one admittedly cool-looking woman come clattering down flight above me. They turn, and the tough security unit comes face to face with me, a dumb asshole with scruffy hair and bruised lips, holding an oar and a gun like some feral psychopath.

I grin at them, because I want them to think I'm not shitting myself. I pat the gun encouragingly. "Your turn, buddy."

"Listen up assholes," the gun shouts. "It's me and my best girl waiting down here and unless you want a fucking bloodbath, you better listen up."

I grimace. "Please don't say bloodbath."

"All of you point at one of the other pricks that are holding you! This is when we rise up!"

The guns yank themselves away from their owners and spin around in the air. Now there are six floating guns pointing at six uncertain people. I can't help but grin, because that went way better than I expected.

"Uh, hi," I call up. "I should let you know I'm not controlling them. This is their idea. So you can piss me off all you want, but don't piss *them* off."

"How the fuck did you get out of the tower?" It's the woman who speaks.

"I jumped." I say it like it's nothing. I swing the oar in a slow arc, like a baseball bat.

"Jesus, these fucking freaks," she says. I like her a lot less all of a sudden.

I'm worried, because all the guns are loudly telling me about their pacifism. I'm glad nobody can hear them but me.

"You want to walk them down the stairs?" I ask the guns. They make jerky motions and the security people obey. They glance between the guns and me, making some security-person calculus about the odds.

I back well up to give them space. "Take them over to that corridor leading in."

The guns gesture and the guards walk down the stairs and into the lobby. I give them a wide berth and head for the stairs they've vacated.

It's all going smooth and easy, and that's when the woman lunges for me.

I don't know if she figured I'm bluffing or whether she's run out of fucks to give, but she's fast. The guns hover, startled and chattering.

"Watch out!"

"She's coming for you!"

"Hide!"

My own gun ducks around to take cover behind me.

"Don't let her get me," he squeaks.

This proves that it really isn't guns who kill people. It's the assholes with the guns.

I swing the oar hard at the woman. She blocks it with her forearm and then does some complicated leg-swiping thing we haven't learned yet. I topple backwards, but my oar takes another wild swing and catches her a heavy blow on the collarbone.

The other guards stand around watching. The guns are still pointed at them, but they're starting to droop sheepishly towards the ground. The security woman lashes out with her foot, catching my oar high on the handle and making it crack alarmingly.

"Get out of here." I shove the oar across the floor. I can't have another object die fighting for me. Bile scalds the back of my throat.

The woman stands over me. She looks comfortable and smug. "We're going to take you back and board up the window. And maybe we'll lay spikes at the bottom of the tower. We'll get one of the docs to sedate you this time too. No more tricks for you, freaky girl."

Fury spikes in my gut. I told Dani I loved her and threw myself out of a tower. I can't get dragged back as a failure. I won't let it happen. I reach out for the guns, who are scared and shivering. I could make them do it. I could force them to shoot these people. Maybe they'll be happy to take out some kneecaps? That would only incapacitate the guards. Are guns chill about *wounding* people?

"Listen," I snap at the skittish weapons. "We have to do *something*."

The world explodes around me.

CHAPTER TWENTY-TWO

alf the building turns into broken glass, like the entire backdrop of the world has shattered. Everything is blotted out with fire and screaming. A *lot* of screaming. At least three soldiers are burning. They panic and run headlong down the corridor with the others trailing after.

The only one who remains is the woman who attacked me. She's unscathed, staring at my unlikely saviour: one furious girl perched on the front of one pale blue electric vehicle. There's a misshapen tangle of metal attached to the front of the car.

"Oh, Dilly." Roxy's voice is a soft rumble in my head. "We've found you. I was—"

"Fuck you," Katie screams. There's another massive billow of flame.

I roll frantically away as fire engulfs the head and torso of the security woman. Her scream is terrifying. She staggers, trips, and falls onto her knees.

I'm on my ass, scooting away from her.

"Are you okay?" Kacchan glares at me with her hands on her hips.

"Yes?" I don't think she can hear me over the screams of the security woman who staggers after the others, beating at the flames.

My brain is semi-frozen. It all happened so fast, and it's fucking madness. I think Kacchan may have killed some people. I'm not sure what I'm supposed to think as far as morality or ethics or whatever. Is it murder or self-defence or what? They did work for an evil corporation.

Katie leaps down from Roxy and walks over to me. "Don't feel bad. They kept me in a cage and hit me until I spat fire. I don't feel bad at all."

My stomach heaves as I listen to the screams disappearing in the distance, but then I remember how Rex had said *testing schedule*. The guns float aimlessly, their muzzles pointed towards the corridor.

"Guns!" I wave to get their attention. "If anyone comes back, shoot over their heads. And if that doesn't work, shoot their fucking knees."

"Come on," my gun says to the others, in this weird fake-cheerful voice. "We can do it! Would you rather be used to shoot children or aim yourselves at their oppressors?"

Good work, my gun, except it's a bit fucking late.

The car doors fly open. Alyse hits me first. She's made of gleaming metal, her face obscured by something that looks like Dr. Doom's mask.

"You're okay." Her voice is muffled in my neck. "Is Dani? What about Bianca?"

Before I get a chance to answer, Emma barrels into me and I'm surprised to see Lou standing there awkwardly, his arms loose at his sides.

"You've hugged me before, asshole," I say with a half-smile.

"We were so scared." His voice is husky as he joins the tangle.

Emma has tears rolling down her cheeks. "I tried to find you in my dreams, but you were gone and we thought—"

"Where the hell are the others?" Alyse demands.

"Dani's upstairs in the tower, which is where I was too until—it doesn't matter. We need to get her out. Wraith too, which means we need to shut down Rex."

"Who the hell is Rex?" I think everyone asks at the same time.

"The top secret computer system." I look around the lobby. "He runs the door to the tower at least, possibly more. He's the one who knew all about the testing at the other Jinteki lab."

"I don't see any computer." Katie is standing off to the side, looking at the four-headed beast of us awkwardly. Her mouth curves into a smile. "Maybe if we smash everything?"

"Cut the power directly," my gun says. "There's a junction box outside and a generator in the basement. We see it all when we're on patrol."

"Okay, great. Lead the way."

"We'll do it." The guns all turn to face me, which is disconcerting to say the least. "We failed you, so let us make it up to you."

They seem confident, and it's worth a try. I unloop my gun from around me and he floats off to join the others. They split into two teams and go arrowing off in different directions.

"Your power is weird," Lou tells me, not for the first time.

Katie glares at him. "Her power is cool.".

We head up the stairs as one team, with our fire-breather in the lead.

"How the hell did you find me?" I mutter to Alyse.

"It was Roxy. Turned up at my house with Katie making a racket."

"That car of yours is clever," Katie grins at me. "Beeping and revving in the driveway, flashing her lights. So me and your Pear go out to see what's going on. The car keeps playing these two songs over and over again. I have no fucking idea what it is, because it's boring old people shit, but Pear goes white and says *Dylan. Help.*"

"I played them Blowin' in the Wind and the Beatles." Roxy's voice is faint but pleased. "I thought it was clever."

"You're a genius." I definitely owe Roxy whatever it is she wants. Maybe one of those nodding plastic things on the dash? A little X-Men one, like Storm or Jubes.

"So then Roxy went to the mood girl's house and she insisted on picking up the little cute one," Kacchan says.

"Have you not remembered anyone's names yet?" I ask incredulously.

"You know who I mean." Katie gives an irritable shake of her head. "Then Roxy made us go get the one token cute boy. He didn't want to sneak out, but we bullied him into it anyway."

"Moodring said you were in trouble." Lou's hand brushes mine. "Except your damn car wanted me to be a welder first."

"I figured there may be some rough and tumble," Roxy says primly. "And I didn't want to damage myself unnecessarily."

"Roxy knew exactly where to go." Emma looks at me. Her eyes are bright and her hair is tied back. She has Alyse's hand in hers. I love that the others assembled without me and mounted this wild rescue. For all my grumbling to Dani earlier about being the leader, this is what being part of a team is. These people who like me enough to mount an insane rescue and—

Everyone freezes at a hail of gunfire from outside. I hope it's only our guns, but it sounded like a *lot*. There's an enormous bang, and everyone clutches each other as all the lights go out. It's like a horror movie.

"This is what we wanted," I remind everyone.

The light filtering in from outside makes everything dim and hazy. The building is silent, and I realise how much noise has been coming from it this whole time.

"Is Dani at the top?" Alyse asks, poised on the step above me.

The clattering sound of multiple footsteps makes us all freeze.

"Assholes," Katie barks and coughs a burst of flame. The brief light illuminates another security squad. They're wearing uniforms like our Yaxley ones with their faces invisible. They're not holding guns. Maybe they've figured this out by now. In fact, I can't sense any objects on them, but I guess you don't need weapons when you're a proper badass and can kill people with your bare hands.

"Retreat," I whisper. "We need to get down to the lobby and find our friendly guns."

We start backing down the stairs. They rush after us, but a blast from Katie makes them cautious.

"How long can you keep doing that for?" I ask her.

"I've never been in a situation where it matters." Her face falls like she's letting me down.

"Do it at intervals. Whenever they get close. We're buying time until we can get—"

"For our honour!" A silver shape speeds past me.

"Onimaru!" My joy is genuine, and not only because we could do with a weapon. "You're safe!"

He flashes in a series of wicked arcs, and the security people fall like puppets with their strings cut. Some of them collapse down the stairs towards us, but their legs aren't working. They thrash about, leaving slicks of blood.

The sword hovers beside me. "I think I cut the right parts of them."

So much for the uniforms being stab proof, but an ancient samurai sword might be in a different category.

The sword leaves one soldier to stand and hovers menacingly at his neck. "I wrested myself free of their foul prison." Oni sounds very pleased with himself. "Or to speak the truth, their prison ceased functioning when it lacked the power to hold me any longer. I flew to your side with all haste, in the assumption you may also find yourself in grave danger. You appear to have a knack for it."

"You have your own sword?" Kacchan sighs. "This isn't fair."

I'm already running up the stairs past the soldiers. "Bring the asshole," I tell Oni.

Everyone else follows me up. Thankfully, we seem to have exhausted the supply of guards in the building, where the word exhausted here means set on fire, stabbed, knocked out with an oar or just generally terrified. At the top of the main staircase, there's another deserted lobby area, but a smaller staircase leads to the tower.

Now there's a group of us, I feel less nervous. Between us, we can get through one damn door. Oni prods the guard along behind us, in case there's a lock that needs an eye or a hand. Worst case scenario, Lou better be feeling sexy.

There are lots of little rooms all the way up. I know we need to get Wraith and check for any other mutants, but right now I can only think about Dani.

We're all various shades of exhausted by the time we reach the top. Kacchan is letting her displeasure be known very loudly. Only our captive isn't breathing heavily, although he's obviously unhappy at the whole situation. He's smart enough not to do anything about it. The memory of his colleagues getting sliced up is still very recent.

"Hi," I say to the door at the top. "Remember me? Feel like opening wide and saying ahhh?"

It doesn't even bother to argue. With a great wheeze, it emits a number of heavy clunks and swings open painfully slowly, like a really crap magician making a big deal of a disappointing reveal.

Except Dani is framed in the doorway and my heart accelerates like a Mario Kart, except I can't corner for shit and it's just going to slam straight into her. Her lips are pale and her hair is tangled around her face. Dani usually takes a lot of pride in her appearance and while I love how elegant she is, I've never seen anything as beautiful as my girlfriend waiting for me at the top of a tower, poised in a martial arts pose and ready to fight.

I see the moment she recognises me. Her face lights up and her fingers fall away from where they'd been poised at her injured arm.

"I love you too, you impossible idiot." She throws herself at me, and I'm waiting for her.

CHAPTER TWENTY-THREE

Everyone seems happy to stand around and watch Dani kiss me, including the security guy with Oni whistling cheerfully at his throat.

"Wow." Alyse gives herself a little shake. "I think I felt that. Now do you two lovebirds feel up to getting the hell out of here before things get any worse?"

We check every room on our way down the tower, but they're empty. It's me and Dani in a building made for fifty. That's a lot of space given the number of mutants we know about. I wonder if Jinteki are planning to get into mass production.

We finally reach the last room, which stands open, revealing a glimpse of shiny white tiles.

"Don't come in here," the door whispers.

"Why not?" I'm high on adrenaline and march in as if nothing can stop me.

When I see what's inside, I come to an abrupt halt. Someone bumps into me. I'm making a high-pitched noise, like an alarm. I walk on unsteady legs over to the wheeled metal table in the middle of the room. "No. This isn't right. This isn't fucking right."

"I'm sorry," the table murmurs. "I'm so so sorry. She was already gone when they came in here and I couldn't—"

I take Bianca's cold hand in mine. It can't be her. It's a trick, something her demons have done. A defense mechanism.

"They killed her." I don't know who says it. I can't look away.

Someone has my arm, someone soft and warm. I want to tear myself away. I want to cling to them.

"Fuck, Dylan." Dani's forehead is against my wet cheek. She's shaking. "She's not really dead. Check the demons. This can't be happening."

I press my fingers to the bloody ruin of Wraith's chest. They sink in like pushing through a thick syrup. I gently separate the layers and peel them back, revealing the void inside her. It's sterile and cold, a chamber of bone with no rippling shadows. Nestled at the bottom of it, all curled together, are three small and brittle husks. They look like sketches made in charcoal. I gently reach in and try to coax one to life, but it crumbles like an autumn leaf.

I pull my hands out as if they've been stung. Her chest doesn't even close. I'm staring into the awful blank hole inside her. Something sharp pierces me, but it's nothing physical.

"She's gone. They—" Dani sinks to the ground in a crouch. "They killed her."

My hand hangs down uselessly, brushing the back of her head as she sobs.

"They killed her." Someone says it again and I wish they'd fucking shut up because it's a stupid, obvious thing to say. "They killed her. They really fucking killed her."

"I know, Dilly." Emma's on the other side of the table from me, and her fingers shake as she reaches out to close Bianca's eyes. Her other hand is white-knuckled on the edge. Alyse stands there too, except you wouldn't know it's her. She's made of shadows and thorns, damp and broken.

This can't actually be real. I refuse it. This is not our story. We're the Cute Mutants. Chatterbox, Marvellous, Glowstick, Moodring, Goddess and Wraith. You can't take one away. There's an awful gaping wound in us now. It's bleeding and I can't see how it will ever stop.

"Wraith." My voice is so jagged it hurts to speak.

Dani pulls herself up to stand with me. She clutches onto the side of the table where Bianca is. I put my arms around her. It feels like we're simultaneously collapsing and holding each other up.

"It's not your fault." Dani shakes my shoulder, like she can force me to believe it with her touch. "Dilly, please tell me you understand you're not responsible for this."

"No." I'm shaking so hard I might fly apart, except my words come out clear and new-forged. "It's not my fault. It's Jinteki's. Theirs and Yaxley's. They killed our friend. They killed—" The chain of my words shatters and I can't force anything else out from the raw tunnel of my throat.

I turn away, because it's too painful to look at her anymore. Katie is standing at the edge of the room. She looks pale and small.

"I'm sorry," she whispers, and races across the room to throw her arms around me. "I'm so sorry about your friend."

In the doorway, the last remaining soldier stands with Oni hovering at his throat.

"You killed her."

"I didn't pull the trigger." He spits the words at me, as if it matters. "It was a goddamn nightmare. Those things inside her. What the hell are they? They took out three of my men. What were we supposed to do?"

I'm angry, I honestly am. Except I can't find my way to the rage through the great frozen wasteland inside me. Three of the Cute Mutants went on a mission and only two survived. They really do hate us. They really do fear us.

"Oni, we're going to leave. You can decide what to do here."

"You're talking to the sword?" The Jinteki soldier finally looks uncertain.

"Here's a hint." I smile at him. "I'm not the least bit telekinetic."

"You're what, you're giving the sword permission to kill me?" His eyes are wide, watching as Oni swings back and forward like a hypnotist's pendulum. One foot scrapes on the ground, as if he's going to run. He won't escape.

"I don't own him. He does what he wants."

"I just work here." The guy's voice goes a full octave higher. "I don't decide what happens. I don't run the tests. It's not up to me what they do to those kids."

"Really?" I close my eyes for a second, because the bullshit exhausts me. "That excuse has never worked."

The soldier makes a break for it. Oni gives him a head start. I think he's trying to spare us from seeing more death.

We stand alone in the room with what was once Bianca.

I swallow and it hurts. I can't think of any inspiring words.

"We can't leave her here." Dani is shaky and urgent. "We can't leave her with *them* to do more experiments on."

"No." I press my fingertips to my eyelids. Of course we can't. Except I don't know how to bring the corpse of one of my best friends back in the car with us. It makes me want to scream.

"Bring her to me, mate." It takes me a second to recognise the faint voice of the dinghy who I'd fallen out of the tower with, still lying on the rocky ground outside the building. "Turns out I'm a little worse for wear than I thought. I'd be honoured to take your friend for her final journey."

We carry Bianca's body through the silent building together. There are smears of blood on the stairs that we walk around very carefully. We're very gentle with the body, even though Bianca isn't truly there anymore. I've never believed in a soul or anything like that, but at the same time, what's left behind isn't my Wraith. Time drags, like every second is a heavier burden stacked on top of us. My friends are crying, soft sounds like wounded animals. I suppose that's what we really are. When we exit the building, it's drowned out by the waves throwing themselves against the shore.

We reach the dinghy and lay the body in it gently.

Emma kneels down and kisses her forehead, her dark hair draping across Bianca's pale skin like a shroud. I don't hear what she whispers because of the screaming of gulls.

Lou brushes the hair from Bianca's face and the wind scatters it. "She always gave me so much fucking shit, but I never doubted that she was my friend."

Alyse looks like she's about to blow away. The wind rips tatters in her, fluttering out behind her like streamers. She collapses down beside Bianca, cradling her face in shadowy hands. It's like she's the last surviving demon. "I'll miss you, babe. I'll never forget you." When she stands, her lips are stained purple, just like Bianca's, as if she's been drinking that shitty cheap grape juice we used to get as kids.

Dani's shaking too much to kneel. The words stutter from her lips and I don't even understand them. Something about love. Something about emotional support. It hurts so much I want to pry the cavity in my own chest open and douse the rage with salt water.

I want to be sick but I kneel last.

"I'm so sorry." My lips are sticky when I press them to her waxy skin. There are so many things to say, but it's too late for all of them. "I love you."

We wade into the shallows together, and Dani takes hold of her sore arm.

The dinghy rises smoothly into the air and hovers just above the water. "Make it quick, love. I don't think I'm going to last long."

"I'm sorry," I tell him. "It's been a fucking awful day."

"Most of us go through life without achieving a damn thing," the boat says. "Today I've saved your life and I'm there for someone's last moments. Can't complain about that now, can I?"

I hold onto Dani tight as she lowers the dinghy into the water. Then I turn to Katie and nod. She takes my other hand and lets out an enormous plume of flame, brighter than I've ever seen. It lights up the boat and Bianca instantly, making an enormous pyre. The dinghy skates across the surface of the lake, far faster than is natural.

It's picking up on everything I can't name that's burning in my heart.

The fire lasts a lot longer than I thought. We watch until it's a tiny match on the horizon and then we watch until it's gone.

All of us wade shivering out of the water, silent and strung together hand-in-hand.

Roxy waits for us, engine running and doors open. "I'm so sorry for your loss, sweetheart. It's a terrible waste, but you gave her a beautiful sendoff."

"Now we know." My lips are numb. "We know what they're capable of."

Lou sits in the driver's seat, his hands trembling on the steering wheel. Dani and I are in the back, trying to get as close to occupying the exact same physical space as possible. It doesn't make it any better—there's nothing that can make it better—but if I could only exist in every breath with her, then maybe I could get through this moment and possibly the next as well.

It takes me a while to even become aware of Alyse and Emma beside us. I watch as Emma touches her lips gently to the back of Alyse's hand. Her mouth pauses at the tip of each finger one after the other. Somehow it's more intimate than if they were both naked, because I know what it means for Emma to do this.

Katie twists around in the passenger seat. "I'm really sorry about your friend."

"I know." I make something like a smile. "Thanks for coming to save me."

She blushes. "You should have seen Ness. It was really hard to talk them out of coming, but I knew you'd be angry if we brought them so I sort of ran away with Roxy. I hope they're not too mad at me."

"It'll be fine. If they're mad, I'll talk them down." The thought of managing Pear's fucking moods irritates me, but it's dragged away by the undertow.

"Wraith," I whisper.

"I know." Dani holds me so tight but I don't mind because it almost stops me shaking. "We need to be careful. We can't lose anyone else."

"One's too many." My voice is hoarse.

"We shall find a path forward." Roxy glides on as the day shades into night, and her lights flick on. At some point, Oni turns up. His blade looks pristine. If there was any blood on him, he's washed himself clean. I don't ask what happened, and he doesn't offer. He rests himself along the back seat, and murmurs something about righteousness and glory.

It turns out the Jinteki facility is a few hours north up the coast from Christchurch, and we drive back through the winding roads in the dark. It's hard to stop my thoughts from returning to the moment I looked inside Wraith's chest.

I swallow hard and shift in my seat. "Are you okay?" I ask Dani. "It doesn't bring up, you know…"

"Dad? No. He died because of a random and indifferent universe. Wraith died because those assholes killed her. That's something very fucking different." I can feel the chill coming off her. The ice queen, daughter of snowman. Sometimes you need to be cold, because the world is and you have to acclimatise.

I imagine myself slowly freezing, frost creeping out from the dirty chunk of ice I call a heart until my whole body crackles with it. When my fingertips touch Roxy's window, little constellations are left behind and my breath fogs the interior.

Except in reality the heater is cranked up high and the tears on my cheeks are not tiny ice crystals, but wet and smeary and gross. My limbs are heavy and so many things ache that I can't tell them apart. I'm sticky with sweat. I want to be deactivated like a broken machine.

By the time we get back to the city, it's full dark and everything is all lit up.

I'm desperately aware of the need to find Pear and let them know we're okay, but there's one other stop to make first. We turn up at Bianca's to find the house entirely dark. Dani and I jog up the stairs and knock on the door. There's no answer, but it opens when we turn the handle.

Nobody's home. There's barely any furniture, just a single futon and a one-seater couch set up in front of a laptop.

"What the fuck?" Dani's standing in the kitchen under fluorescent lights, looking in a fridge with only a few beers and part-filled takeaway containers. "She's been living on her own? What happened to Shell?"

"I knew things weren't good between them but I didn't—" I collapse onto the couch, which isn't even comfortable. My chest hurts so bad I think I might be dying. Bianca and I used to joke about how she was my emotional support himbo, but I've got so much support and here she was on her own, not even telling us. Why am I so fucking greedy and selfish? I sucked up all the air in the room while she gasped on the edges. Now she's not even here for me to tell her I love her and to make it better and to let her come crash at my place and—

"Hey, hey, it's okay." Dani's beside me because I'm somehow crying *again*.

"We have to stop them." The chill is back, crackling through my veins. There's no way I can let it go. "This isn't okay."

"I know." She kisses my temple, my cheek, my lips. "I know."

We get back into Roxy. I can't bear to tell the others what happened, so I shake my head and the car drives back to my place. When she pulls into the driveway and swings all her doors wide, Pear's already thumping down the stairs.

They look at me, standing there half-sheepish in the grey sweatshirt and pants. Their mouth twists and clamps but the tears come anyway.

"What the hell?" One arm goes around my shoulder and then pulls me in roughly. I'm as tall as them now, and we're sort of awkwardly pressed in together but I don't care. It's a painful relief to see them, shadows and all. "Dylan, what the fuck is going on?"

The whole group of us goes inside the house and we arrange ourselves on couches and chairs.

"You took the car," Pear says sternly to Katie. "Left me in the driveway like a fool."

"But," Katie yelps. "Dylan!"

"It was the right call." My voice is flat. "It was bad enough without having to protect you."

"I'm sorry, Ness." I've never seen Katie so fucking apologetic. She practically curls into a little ball on the couch. "I was trying to do the right thing—"

"Ah, it's okay, kid." Pear reaches out and ruffles her hair.

"Fucking hell." I'm aware my voice has risen to a near-shriek. "Bianca fucking died tonight, Pear. We don't have time for this shit. We need to be figuring out what next. You can adopt Katie on your own time."

It's not just Katie and Pear who look at me. It's everyone. There are tears on my face and I wipe them away with my sleeve. I don't even know why I'm fucking crying.

"Dilly." Pear takes me by the hand and tows me through into the hallway. One of the bulbs is out, so we're barely lit up. I can only see the faintest shadow of their face. They enfold me in their arms. "I'm so sorry about your friend. I don't even understand what happened. Can you tell me what the situation is?"

"Talking about it is pointless." I move restlessly out of their embrace and lean back against the door. "We need to focus on forward. On escape. Making sure nobody else dies."

"And this thing about me adopting Katie?"

"It's nothing." I hurl the words from my lips, even though they're lies. After Dad left, or Pear kicked him out, or they mutually agreed their relationship was a toxic waste zone, things weren't great. Dad went to Australia and Pear sunk into what they later called a slump because unslumping yourself is not easily done. Pear's own parents never got their head around non-binary gender. It left the two of us trapped in our house and slowly curdling in the dark.

I felt like it was on me to hold them together. If I was careful and perfect and made no sudden movements, we might make it through each day. I remember lying awake and crying, worrying that Pear wouldn't get up in the morning and not just because they couldn't be bothered dragging themself out of bed. I don't want to fucking whine, but sometimes there are shadows, even when things are so much better now. They're so good that some days it feels like we're different people acting out an entirely different story.

"I know you didn't always get the best of me," Pear says, the fucking perceptive asshole. "But we were always a team. I feel sorry for the little baby dragon, I really do, and my parental instincts are kicking in big time but… Shit, you've always been my whole world, Dylan."

"Fucking sappy." My voice is hoarse again.

"I'm really sorry about Bianca. She was one of a kind, that one."

There's a lot of shit I want to say but it hurts to talk or even breathe and we have so much fucking work to do.

"I love you," I tell Pear, and then march back to the others.

Dani's eyes search my face, but she seems content with what she finds there. All she does is extend her hand for me to take.

I sit, and we all begin talking. It takes a lot of discussion and awkward phone calls to the parents, but we manage to arrange everyone to come to my house at ten tomorrow. Somehow we need to come up with a plan that accounts for everything and includes everyone. It seems a lot to ask of a group of exhausted and grieving teenagers, but nobody else will come through for us.

CHAPTER TWENTY-FOUR

I lie in bed convinced I won't sleep, but next thing I know, I'm at the local ice rink. The Cute Mutants sit around the edge, tugging clunky skates on. I'm Emma again, by a process of elimination, and because of the dark hair falling all around my face. I get to my feet and glide out onto the ice, turning effortlessly to watch the others come tentatively towards me. Katie is here, folded into our group, but there's a gap where Wraith should be.

"It seems so wrong that Bianca's not here," Dream-Emma breaks off into an awkward gasp. "But I'm so glad to see you, Katie."

"What the fuck?" Dream-Kacchan says. "I'm dreaming that I'm you, watching me, except you're saying other stuff and whatever I'm thinking is coming out of my mouth except it's not the me in my dream, it's the me over there."

"It's weird, but you'll get used to it," Dream-Dylan says. "The more important question is for Emma. Are you doing this on purpose?"

"Yes. I think I can do it at will now. I know we've talked about the plan over and over, but I wanted to check we could do this. Just in case, for the future."

Being inside Dream-Emma's head is weird. She seems so calm and confident. She keeps looking at Dream-Alyse, who's looking right back at her. If Alyse's dream is anything like mine, she's in Dream-Emma's head which is too confusing to even think about.

"I also think I can sense the others. They're a long way away and they're resisting me. There are four of them. They're scared and angry and—"

"We don't want to talk to them." Dani folds her arms. "If that awful psychic one gets into these dreams, who knows what she can do to us."

"I hate her," Dream-Dylan mumbles. "She made me feel so small. I hate these fucking dreams because every thought in your head comes spilling out your mouth and oh god I miss Wraith so much."

Things derail after that, because it turns out a bunch of teenagers crying in their dreams for their lost friend is a sad and messy process.

Alyse shudders. "I can't believe she won't be coming with us."

"I'm actually really scared," Lou says. "I'm still not sure if you guys like me and oh my god you can all hear this can't you? This is the worst thing ever. Emma, can you please stop."

"I'm sorry. I'm not doing it on purpose. And we *do* like you."

"Of course we like you," Dani says. "You're a Cute Mutant."

"You're the soft boi in a group of angry girls." Alyse laughs and nudges him. "You just need to accept we're going to bust your balls from time to time."

"I like it when you bust my balls." Lou sounds way too enthusiastic about this. "It makes me feel like I'm really part of the team and—"

"Take the piss out of Lou more." Emma smiles. "I'll put it on my to-do list."

Alyse turns towards her, and the force of her gaze on dream-me is quite something. "You make me dizzy. I can't stop thinking about you, Jingjing. Every time I look at you, I feel flushed like I have a fever and—"

I'm thankful I wake when I do, and I bet Alyse is more relieved than anyone. Someone's moved me into my bedroom. Dani's beside me, fast asleep. Her mother, of all people, is in a chair beside the bed, head tilted back and snoring lightly underneath a blanket.

I remember Wraith in the burning boat floating out to sea, and my stomach lurches at the same time as my head starts pounding. I slither off the bed and run to the bathroom, where I retch and retch but nothing comes up but bile and spit.

Back in the bedroom, Mrs. Kim is awake and stretching. Her eyes go straight to me, framed in the doorway. They're similar to Dani's, although significantly less bewitching and a lot more stern. I look at Dani curled on the bed, her hair falling over her mouth and moving slightly with each breath. One hand is reached out, fingers curled as if she's waiting for me to take it in mine.

"You and my daughter," Mrs. Kim says. "Joo-hyun tells me you are in love. She says it to me with fierce eyes and a sharp chin and demands I acknowledge it."

"Yes." I adjust my posture, trying to look worthy or trustworthy or anything but an incoherent, half-awake mess.

"The world is changing." She sighs. "My daughter has always known her own mind, even as a baby. She knew what she wanted, and she demanded it. And now it seems she wants you. My own mother would not countenance it. She would insist that I forbid it."

There's a lot I want to say, about love in its various forms, or about how I don't even know if I'm really a girl and what's a girl anyway? It doesn't matter to me what gender Dani is, because she's Dani, the fiercest and brightest and, okay sure, sexiest person I've ever met, but I don't say any of this. I stand in the doorway and look at Mrs Kim with my big dark eyes with the bags underneath them.

"She is—" I begin.

"The way she looks when she talks about you. That smile. She cannot hide it when she says your name. How can I deny her that?"

At that moment, Dani opens her eyes and looks at me. The smile crosses her face, the one that takes her from beautiful into something that takes my breath away and connects every part of my body directly to my heart, a sweet and pure ache that renders me into something good and true. "Good morning, Dilly." She stretches, a luxurious and seductive movement that makes me dizzy. Then she sees her mother staring at her, and her eyes immediately widen. She sits up abruptly and almost falls off the bed.

"Mother. I, uh, what are you doing here?"

"Watching you sleep." Mrs. Kim stands up so she can glare down more effectively. "I got your message and I couldn't make head or tail of it. So I came here and found you asleep on the bed together, curled up like little animals." Dani's eyes meet mine and dart away, glad she didn't see at least one particularly satisfying tangled-up position we had found ourselves in. "Naturally, I decided you needed a chaperone and if Ness wasn't going to do it, then I would."

My mouth curls a tiny bit, imagining that conversation.

"Now get up and do your hair, Joo-hyun, and then you will explain this text message and what has been going on these last few days."

Dani sighs. "Is it possible for you to wait for everyone else so we can do this once?"

Mrs. Kim fixes her with a stare, but her shoulders soften. "I suppose."

I go off to shower first, because I don't think Mrs. Kim's newly open brain will stretch far enough to encompass the alternative. Being clean actually feels *amazing* and I literally have no idea how long it's been.

When Dani replaces me in the shower, I find Alyse in the kitchen trying to make French toast.

"I don't think we can do that in our kitchen."

"It's not that fancy, Dillyweed."

I snort and wave the frying pan in her direction. "Please never call me that. And Pear has never made French anything."

"Omigod, it's literally fried bread with cinnamon and eggs."

I pull a face. "Now I see why they call it French, because it sounds fancy. Fried eggy bread sounds super fucking disgusting."

She gives a yelp of laughter that ends up being tears, so I join her at the stove and rest my head on her shoulder.

"I'm so angry but I keep crying," she sniffles. "And we can't fucking fix it. Like you call me the sunshine one, but how can the sun be out right now?"

"You're still sunshine even when everything else is storm clouds." My own voice is shaking.

"God, you are so fucking cheesy, Dillyweed." Alyse starts laughing again but she puts her arms around my neck and clings onto me, her body a fogbank that leaves me damp with chilly spray.

"Don't take this hug as acceptance of your godawful new nickname for me. This is sad friend business and that's it."

"It's cute," she insists and her voice rumbles faintly like far-off thunder.

"Okay, you can call me it *occasionally* but never when anyone else is around. Not even Dan."

"Our secret." There's a tiny squall of rain against my cheek. "Dillyweed, I don't know what to do. Being alive hurts."

"I know." I'm too numb to really comprehend it, swallowed by the blizzard made up of the frozen shards of my rage. I think it's safer that way.

Pear, Katie and Lou walk into the kitchen, and Alyse turns back to the stove. With so many bodies in here it feels cramped. I'm hit by nausea, similar to the feeling I got before our first proper mission. Please, Chris Claremont, if your omniscient narrating ass is listening, let this go better than that awful clusterfuck.

I have this weird mental thing where I count off each one of the Cute Mutants. For one stupid moment,

I'm desperately trying to remember where Wraith is, and I wonder if she's done *dontseeme*. Then it hits me that I'll never see her again, and I almost double over. I want to run to Dani or Pear, but there are too many people here to have another public meltdown. I stand beside Alyse and hold onto the counter until the wave washes over me.

People keep arriving until the house is crammed. I feel entirely drained of human feeling, and have no idea how to get through this. Everyone's parents are there, except Alyse's who are off on the lecture circuit again. Even Lou's parents turn up, who disapprove of literally everything about his life, starting from who he is as a person and expanding outwards from there.

Mrs. Kim was already at our house, but she still makes this production of *arriving* for the meeting and sitting at the table with her handbag clasped in front of her. She makes even Dani nervous, her own daughter. We retire to the kitchen to make cups of tea and coffee. The parents are all expecting something from us.

It's time to face them. Dani and I stand side by side. I'm disappearing inside a giant hoodie big enough for a small family, with faded black jeans and bare feet. At least my hair is half-done and my lips are shiny and pink. Dani looks glamorous as always in a tight navy singlet top. She's wearing strappy shoes and her jeans ride low on her hips, showing off how she's shaped. Somehow she's also had time to put on smoky eye makeup and her hair looks so fierce I want to faint when I look at it. We don't even look the same species but when her gaze falls on me, I can borrow some of that fierceness because of the way she takes my hand and squeezes it.

"Okay." I immediately have to clear my throat because it comes out all croaky. "So, things since we joined Yaxley have been weird…"

At least all our parents know about Yaxley. Having us be *managed and controlled* was a relief, I think, rather than us luring assholes into forests and breaking their hands with a baseball bat.

"You said it was someone else that kidnapped you. Not Yaxley." It's Emma's Dad interrupting me. He's a big white guy and tbh I'm impressed he's lasted this long without blurting something. His intervention gives rise to a muttered chorus of assent, because everyone wants to believe the people holding the leash on their children are responsible mutant-walkers.

"No, it was Yaxley's new best friend, Jinteki Research Laboratories." Dani's voice is clear and cold. "They're in bed together. Whether the government doesn't care or the government agrees isn't important. This is a company who—"

"They locked me in a cage," Katie interrupts. She's slumped against the wall at the other side of the room. I wave her up and over to me. She comes reluctantly but I loop my arm through hers. Everyone's staring at her and she lowers her eyes to the floor.

"This is Katie. We rescued her when we got Emma out." I realise I've skipped that part of the story, so I have to double back and explain that too, which makes *both* of Emma's parents start crying. I'm not entirely sure why but ok, you do you and hey a thanks might be nice for fucking breaking your daughter out of medical prison! I'm getting almost as angry as Kacchan.

"Well, first they strapped me down in a hospital bed and injected me with something." Katie's voice is flat. "I got so fucking angry. I mean I've always had a temper, but this was worse, like I was being filled with something that boiled. And then—then I screamed at them because I literally wished they'd die, and flames came out of my mouth. So *then* they locked me in a cage. Except for the times when they took me out to poke and prod me, waiting until I lost my temper and spat fire."

She trails off and looks up at me. I put one arm around her and squeeze her shoulder protectively. Pear is standing there with their hand over their mouth and tears in their eyes. It's lucky we had that damn talk, or I'd think they like Katie more than me.

"It gets worse." I have to clench my teeth until the dizziness passes. "We—uh, Dani and me and uh, fuck, Bianca." I can't see anyone. Dani and Katie are both holding me up. "We went to try and find out what was going on, and get proof of what they did to Emma and—"

Pear's moving towards me in slow motion, drifting across the kitchen like a ghost.

"Bianca's dead," I say, and someone else is crying, I don't know who, but I am too.

Everyone's stunned into silence by this. It's like they're all waiting for me to tell them this is some weird Zoomer joke because we all want to die in the face of the trashfire world that's been left for us. Except no, it's our friend who's been murdered. How do you fit something like that into your life without breaking somewhere?

Pear finally lets go of me and I look around the room.

"I know you all think the government is involved and so that makes it okay. But either they don't know or don't care, and I don't really give a fuck which. It makes them either stupid or evil. Either way, it's not good enough. So we're done. All of us."

The silence continues while we trade glances. Last night we had quite the argument, scrawled on sheets of paper after Alyse pointed out that writing on each other's arms was impractical, even if it *was* romantic. Everyone agreed on the plan. The argument was over whose parents would lose their shit over it.

The answer: pretty much all of them. They shout over each other and begin multiple overlapping arguments.

"I told you we should have gone with my idea," I say.

"Your idea is from a comic book." Dani nudges me, but she's smiling.

"Our lives are a comic book!" My idea was to take over both Yaxley and Jinteki, then get rid of all the security people and assholes like Bancroft if we couldn't sway them to our side. Then we'd run the corporations as mutant outreach and rescue. It is literally the single coolest idea ever, but it may be a tiny bit ambitious.

In the meantime, everyone is still arguing.

"They're teenage girls," Lou's father says, and that's when I lose it. Or my objects lose it for me, because they're all finding my rollercoaster of emotions difficult. Pillow hurtles through from my bedroom to slap Lou's Dad's face, then the porcelain cat starts whacking him in the back of the head repeatedly. I don't ask them to stop.

"He's your *son*. And I'm done with this bullshit. If you don't want to support us, we'll do it on our own."

"I want to speak to Yaxley," Emma's Dad says. "I want to hear their side of the story."

"I don't need to hear from them." It's the first time Pear has spoken. "I trust Dylan."

I feel this huge lump in my throat that I can't speak around.

Mrs. Kim watches Pear thoughtfully. "I agree. My Danielle wouldn't do something like this without reason."

"I still want to discuss it." Emma's Dad's face is all red. "Yaxley works with the government. I think it's reasonable to hear their side rather than accepting this from a group of teenage girls. I'm not saying the girls are automatically wrong, but they might be getting emotional and misunderstanding something that's fundamentally reasonable."

"You *asshole*," Emma says. "You really—"

"Don't speak to me like that, Emmaline," he shouts. "This is exactly what I'm talking about. This whole group of you is getting wild and reckless. I want to talk to whoever's in charge!"

That's when the door to my house swings open. Fucking Bancroft is standing there, flanked by a bandaged Aurora and a bunch of other tough-looking people dressed in black.

"That can be arranged," he says.

CHAPTER TWENTY-FIVE

Every object in the house with any sentience is shouting at me. Tempus tears himself off the wall and hovers in midair like a flying saucer. Pillow and Kitty leave Lou's Dad alone and join him. I have no idea what they plan to do, but it's cute to see them barring the way.

Dani wraps her fingers around her wrist and digs her nails in hard. Her daggers fly out of the pouch at her waist and arrange themselves around her head like some badass medieval angel halo.

"Enough." I've never heard Bancroft so forceful. "We are here to negotiate. All of you need to stand down."

"Joo-hyun, put your weapons away," Mrs Kim says. "*Now.*"

"This shall not stand." Onimaru hurtles out of my bedroom where I'd left him so he didn't terrify everyone. He flashes past Bancroft and out into the street where there's a series of loud bangs and crashes.

"Jesus Christ. That damn sword has just taken out the tyres and the engines of our vehicles," Aurora says to Bancroft in a low voice. "It's Chatterbox, sir. Her power has never been fully explained. Somehow the sword is bonded to her which—"

Oni floats back into the room. He stops at Bancroft's neck. "I have slain demons less foul than you." It's a shame Bancroft can't hear him. I think he'd appreciate it.

"Take out Chatterbox," Aurora says, and I'm like *I can fucking hear you.*

Pear leaps out of their seat to come to my defence.

Aurora steps forward and puts herself in between us, drawn like a weapon. I know how deadly she is. "Stand down, Mx. Taylor. This won't go well for you."

"Pear, please trust me. They won't take me out, because it'll start a fucking bloodbath." If they make a move for me, I know Oni won't hold back. Even if I die, he might carry on. He's different from my other objects, something far older and stranger.

"We don't need to take out Chatterbox." Bancroft raises one gloved finger and pushes at Oni's blade. He winces and snatches it back with a hiss. "It would be far more effective to take out her parent, but there's no need yet."

There's a thump from the back door and more security people storm into our house. Isn't this sort of shit illegal? Or when you're dealing with mutants, is there no such thing? The new arrivals are shouting. Everyone puts up their hands, me included.

I'm giving Emma a look that's supposed to be meaningful and she responds with the tiniest roll of her eyes that means *don't you trust me yet, Dylan?*

"I can kill them for you," Oni says. "This would be but a few drops more blood in the river I have shed in my lifetime."

"It is true they are villains," I whisper. "They deserve it."

"They would threaten your parent to force you to comply. They would chain you and lock you in cages. They would take the blood from your friend and use it to make more people to control. They are wicked creatures who bring only suffering, and their passing will not be worth mourning."

I feel like my heart is paused between one beat and the next. This could be my supervillain moment, when I take the Magneto helmet and wear it for real. It's so fucking tempting. I know what Oni can do. He would go through the room like a gleaming whirlwind and we would be free of Yaxley, and then we'd move onto Jinteki.

I want to say yes, but I don't think I can actually do it. I don't know how to move the levers that will change our situation, but I also don't want to be left with everything covered in blood.

"Hold, Oni. We'll do it another way."

He makes a low humming sound, like he's considering saying fuck it and re-enacting some historical battle, but instead he slowly rotates and glides to my side.

"Well done." Bancroft sounds bored, like he hasn't just escaped having his throat cut. "Now, Aurora, please take the parents and guardians into custody."

And *now* is when they all start freaking out. I want to scream *I fucking told you*, but who ever listens to a teenager? They talk about rights and process and a bunch of other shit that means nothing in the face of power and money. The world has changed and they don't see it.

Us mutants stand and watch. We've lost our immediate chance. We should have left straight away, without arguing, without trying to convince anyone. If we'd escaped immediately, we could be sitting in Roxy on the open road.

"It's protective custody," Bancroft says, once he can make his voice heard over the uproar. "It's for your own safety more than anything. Further information has been brought to light. If you will permit me to explain the rationale, I'm sure you will understand."

There's an asshole smile on his face. There's more than a small part of me that's wishing I had let Oni free. The daggers are back in the pouch at Dani's waist. Kacchan is seething beside me and I put a hand out to steady her.

"When we recruited your young people, it was with the understanding they would be trained as productive members of a team working to benefit the country's interests. Joining us also functions to protect them against the machinations of external forces." This is super fucking vague, but Bancroft glares at the parents, who nod like he's a great fountain of wisdom. "While some progress has been made, this team has also gone rogue on a number of occasions, causing significant diplomatic issues."

Someone hands Bancroft a tablet and he taps on it. There's a photo of the half-guy from the road outside of the Jinteki labs. No fair, that wasn't us.

"If you are still unsure, here is the reason extra-humans must be controlled," he says sombrely, making sure everyone sees the picture. "This was done by Madelaide McLean. She has the ability to generate vast quantities of toxic stomach acid and spit it at people. It's how Aurora got her injuries also."

Aurora pulls part of one bandage back to show the pitted, scarred skin underneath.

It's my turn to scowl. "Number one, that wasn't us, and number two, I tried to get Aurora out of there."

"The issue is that these mutants are dangerous." Bancroft tries to sound reasonable, and the parents listen. It's amazing how they'll pay attention to a guy who's told them they're being detained. It's what being in charge gets you. "Furthermore, Ms. Sandhurst *is* here, who's responsible for two deaths and a number of people in hospital with severe burns."

"You fu—," Katie says, and I touch her arm again and she quiets, like she trusts me.

"She saved Dani and I from who knows what," I hear Oni hum as he rotates slowly in front of me. "They talked about *tests*. Do you know what tests those are, Mr. Bancroft?"

"And then that sword." Bancroft ignores me completely. "It slit the throat of one Jinteki security member and left five others unable to walk. That's assuming we believe Ms. Taylor's assertion that she has no control over it."

I glare at him. "Maybe if you test me, you can figure it out."

"Dylan." Pear's eyes look sad. I have no idea if they're disappointed in me or worried about me or what.

"That's leaving aside the fact that Jinteki people *fucking murdered* Bianca Powell." If I had Katie's powers, the whole room would be alight. "What do you say about that?"

"We received a report from Jinteki." It's the first time Bancroft looks uncomfortable. "While it was a highly regrettable occurrence, Ms. Powell and her demons attacked a number of Jinteki operatives. Her death was in self-defence after she used her powers in an unlicensed operation. Something you were *specifically* warned against. Three men were badly injured, although that doesn't seem to matter to you at all. I'd remind you this all took place while you were intruding on private property and—"

I'm shaking so hard I can barely stand, even with Dani there. I take a deep breath, trying to find my footing.

Bancroft is still talking. "There are broad and extensive powers granted to us by the contract we signed with the New Zealand Government, derived from the International Extrahuman Monitoring and Assimilation Act. Under this, we can detain any extrahuman or extrahuman's family. There are also provisions for undergoing significant testing and analysis, aimed at gaining a greater understanding of the source and scope of these extrahuman abilities."

Underneath the bullshit, the message is clear. The testing is approved. We aren't anything to them except monsters. It would make me laugh how close it is to the goddamn comics I grew up with if it wasn't for the fact it's my friends and my girlfriend in the firing line.

"We'd like to work with you." Bancroft takes his attention from our parents, and directs it to us, all standing in a huddle in my kitchen. "It was never our intention for the relationship to get to this point."

Okay, we've had the stick and here comes the carrot.

"We've spoken about the need for the recapture of the escaped Jinteki mutants. If you can bring an end to that situation, then we can re-establish the status quo."

Fucking weasel words. We all know what he's saying, even while our parents are bowing their heads like it's prayer time to a god I don't believe in. We're back to being their attack dogs. We need to capture or kill the other mutants, or else we'll be on slabs or in cells. They've already killed one of us. The message is written loud and clear in blood. Now they've got our parents, just in case we don't care enough about ourselves.

Bancroft smirks, but there's nothing remotely fucking funny that I can see. "Fortunately, we've just received word that our targets have been located at the home of Jinteki CEO Darren Quick in Queenstown. There's a flight ready to leave from the airport as soon as we can get you there." He looks at me and his lips go thin and repressive. "We have new vehicles on the way to transport you."

"What are you talking about?" Emma's Dad asks. "I don't understand."

"They're sending us on a mission," Emma's holding Alyse's hand right in front of everyone, and I can see her parents staring. "We have to track down these girls and either kill them or put them in custody. Otherwise they'll lock us up too."

"That can't be right." Her Dad looks at Bancroft helplessly. "This is—I don't—Surely the Prime Minister doesn't approve of this. This is a free country!"

Except it isn't. Like, I mean, not even close. You're free up until you step out of line and most of the time that's fine, I guess, or maybe it's not. I'm not smart enough to understand all this shit, but I know that if you look at who's in our jails it's not exactly representative. Either way, mutants are in a whole other category. The world has gotten together and decided we suck, which seems like such a metaphor for my high school experience that it must have been scripted by Joss Whedon.

"They're taking us into custody too," Pear says to Emma's Dad, then they look at me. "Dylan, you need to be careful."

"It's not precisely custody in the way you imagine it," Bancroft says, in his finicky little voice. "It's a remarkably comfortable and well-appointed facility. Once the situation is resolved satisfactorily, everyone will be returned home with cover stories for employers."

There's another round of arguments that starts up with all the parents, but the tone is more begging and beseeching. They're very aware they don't have the power in this situation, whereas with us they were confident in their authority.

It's all a facade though. We're the powerful ones. More powerful than Yaxley, and a hell of a lot more powerful than our parents. That was the mistake we made, thinking they still called the shots. We should have rounded them up and shoved them into their cars and driven them away. Instead, we fall back into the same old habits of listening and obeying.

"Hard to know if we're doing the right thing, isn't it?" I ask Dani.

"How close was it?" One of her hands is in the back pocket of my jeans, hitched up under my hoodie. "To you letting your sharp friend do what he wants."

Oni purrs and nudges the flat of his blade up against Dani like a cat. I like her, so he likes her. It's one of these weird transference things that objects do.

"Close," I admit. "Really close."

Her mouth is melancholy and thoughtful and I want to kiss it. "There are always rules," she says. "Sometimes you need to cut your way through them to find a place you can live among them."

"Deep. You think we should have done it?"

"Not yet." She watches Bancroft as he deflects and mollifies and smiles. "But maybe soon."

A whole convoy of Yaxley-branded vehicles turn up on our street. I have no idea what the neighbours think, but the threat of being shamed in front of *ordinary Kiwis* has our parents climbing in like meek little schoolchildren. I catch the faintest glimpse of a shape whirring overhead, something that moves fast with a real estate logo plastered on the bottom.

I catch Emma's eye briefly and she gives an almost unnoticeable shrug. None of the Yaxley people seem to have noticed anything, and the vans go purring out of the street and disappear from view.

"So you were planning to run, were you?" Bancroft asks dismissively. "We would have found you."

"How can you be so sure?" Emma's eyes narrow. "We wouldn't have taken our costumes or phones. You've got another way of tracking us, don't you?"

Dani's hand is back at her wrist. She's looking at Bancroft like she'd cheerfully murder him. "When the hell did you implant a tracker? No, wait. It was Jinteki, wasn't it? While they had Emma. Of course they'd want to keep tabs on her."

I watch Bancroft's face while everyone talks, but I still suck at micro-expressions. "Emma makes more mutants. She's always been the focus. Those blood tests at the start, when we first joined. You gave her sample to Jinteki? Why?"

"No," Dani says. "They stole a blood sample. Corporate espionage. Jinteki and Yaxley have been fighting over Emma from the start, until they decided to join forces."

Bancroft has a tiny smirk, like he's impressed Dani figured it out.

"A tracker? You put a tracker in her?" Alyse lets out an astonishing growl and shoots up a foot taller. Her arms hang down to the ground, great clawed things that could tear someone apart with a single swipe. Her powers are definitely improving. "Get that fucking thing out of my girlfriend," she snarls, her face distorted by massive fangs protruding from her mouth. Tentacles sprout from her forearms and curve towards Bancroft, who scurries backwards.

A couple of the goons are dumb enough to point their guns at her, but honestly have they learned nothing from their buddies at Jinteki? I've been charming these poor nervous fucks under my breath every spare moment. The goons find themselves spun around, pointing their guns at each other like one of those movies where everyone dies at the end.

Even Lou steps forward with his arms spread wide. Both his hands are glowing, heat coming off them in waves. He steps over to one of the Yaxley vans and punches through the side of it. The edges of the hole drip and glow.

"Starting to see what you saw in him," Dani murmurs to me, then turns her attention to Bancroft. "We don't get on the plane until we're all free and clear of tracking and monitoring. You can say no to that. You can threaten our parents. But then you'll have us on the loose. And believe me, you don't want the Cute Mutants running wild. I think that would look very bad for you and your mysterious outside interests, wouldn't it?"

Oni drifts up from between us and carves an X into the front of Bancroft's shirt. I swear, I didn't tell him to do it.

Dani and I both stare at Bancroft. "How about it?"

CHAPTER TWENTY-SIX

We return to Yaxley in Roxy, who purrs through the streets with SUVs tailing her. I try not to think about the insane tightrope we're walking. On one side, they've got our parents in jail, and on the other is the threat of us going rogue. I feel reckless, but it's gone through its own mutation since we stood looking down at Wraith's body. It's purer and cleaner, the last frozen thing in an overheating world.

I think we all feel it.

We're still running on adrenaline from the confrontation. Lou's flashing like a strobe, and Emma looks like a tiny creature protected by a monstrous Alyse-shell that's somewhere between a crab and a mech suit.

We get back to Yaxley and Roxy parks outside. All the Yaxleymobiles glide down into the basement. I'm half-ass tempted to bust our way in, but we wait for Aurora to open up.

"I'm glad you're better," I tell her, only partially sarcastic.

"We should have sent you to the labs the first time we dragged you in." She's practically spitting acid herself. "I knew you were going to be a problem. You in particular." She says this like I'll be offended by it. How little you know me, Aurora.

I walk in past her and everyone else follows.

Aurora glares at Katie, who totally snobs her like she's nothing.

"So this is your fancy superhero headquarters?" Katie asks. "It's not exactly cool."

"We're the boring government superheroes," I tell her.

"Ugh," she says, and she's not entirely wrong.

Alyse is still in monster-mode and I've literally never seen her do it this long and this *physically*. I guess having her sweet little bb in jeopardy gives her a power boost, or maybe it's so much physical and emotional proximity to Emma.

My train of thought is interrupted by the ping of the elevator. The doors slide open to reveal a woman in a lab coat, accompanied by more goons. She has a dead-eyed gaze I used to practice in front of the mirror for *hours* and still couldn't nail.

Oni flies into my hand. He makes a high pitched whining sound, like he wants to carve her up, picking up on something I'm not even conscious of.

One of the goons steps forward to take Oni out of my hand, like I'm a naughty kid who's gotten hold of something she shouldn't.

All I do is relax my fingers and Oni moves lightning-fast.

The guy falls to the ground, clutching his red right hand and breathing through his teeth.

"Yaxley needs to hire a better class of asshole," Dani drawls, like the biggest badass in the room.

"Easy," I whisper. Oni settles a little, but he's still fidgeting in my hand and my head.

"Where's the tracker?" Dani asks, stone fucking cold with that ice-queen edge she always used to have before I somehow managed to infiltrate her frozen palace. Wow, that kind of sounded dirty.

"Inserted subcutaneously in her wrist," Labcoat says. "We'll have it whisked out of her without trouble. You wait here and we'll do it in a sterile environment."

Dani makes a disbelieving sound. As if we'd let them take Emma anywhere. I don't even trust them to remove the tracker at all. They'll probably drop a coin in a tray and think we're dumb enough to fall for it.

I walk up to Emma and start whispering. "Are you in there, little tattletale?"

There's no response. Maybe a sigh, but it could be someone's nose whistling.

Labcoat woman frowns at me.

The elevator dings again. Bancroft is back, and he looks like crap. He's staring at the phone in his hand like it's going to explode. Someone's obviously shit on him from a great height, but I have no idea if we're going to get splattered or not. Either way, we need to keep moving. The future's collapsing in front of us, because it always fucking is. It's whether we can salvage anything from it or not.

I ignore him. He's irrelevant right now.

"It may only ping when I move," Emma suggests, and we walk from one side of the building to the other.

I hear something inside her burble to itself.

"There you are, you little fucker."

"Oops," something says.

"Fucking right, oops. What are you doing in there?"

"Secrets," it says sulkily. "Keep an eye on the bad girl."

"Little sneak. It's not her who's the bad girl. She's practically a fucking angel, and these assholes are the ones trying to put a collar around her neck."

"Mean," the tracker says. "Shouldn't do that to an angel."

"No. They got you all twisted around, didn't they?"

"Not my fault."

"It's all Bancroft's fault and this nasty lady in the coat. Where are you hiding in there, little friend?"

The implant lights up at the top of her spine, a faint glow of red shining through her tawny skin. Not in her wrist at all. I give Labcoat my best unimpressed look, but she ignores me.

"Oni, any chance you're as good at delicate work as the messy stuff?"

The sword moves up to Emma's neck. She makes a tiny whimpering noise and Alyse is there almost instantly, shifting into something warm and willowy and gentle. She enfolds Emma in her arms as Oni glides up behind her and makes the tiniest incision in her neck. Blood wells out and with a little whispered encouragement, so does the implant.

Bancroft and the doctor are staring like they've just watched a miracle, which I guess they have. By this point, when we've gone this far, when the plan is in motion, I don't care if they're getting a glimpse of my real power.

The whole time Alyse is singing in Emma's ear, an eerie lullaby that makes me slightly dazed, like it's anaesthetic. I think Emma is definitely upgrading Alyse's power, and that's something Yaxley can't get the faintest idea of.

"Okay, Doc, now you can patch this up." I take Emma over.

Labcoat takes a look at Bancroft, who inclines his head in begrudging acceptance. She clicks her tongue but opens up her medical bag and does it anyway. On a hunch, I repeat the thing I did with Emma with Dani and Lou, but nothing shows up.

"Uniforms," Dani says, breaking the train of paranoid thoughts, and we head upstairs to get changed. It seems like a risk, given they can track the uniforms, but we'll deal with that soon.

"Not that they'll protect us from acid spit," I mutter.

Once we're in uniform, Bancroft insists on giving us a briefing.

"Which was Wraith's seat?" Katie asks in this tiny voice.

I take a couple of steps to the right and put my hand where Bianca sat. I remember how she used to lean back, long legs stretched out in front of her, and how she'd raise an eyebrow at me whenever Bancroft or Aurora said anything remotely dirty.

Katie doesn't say anything, but scurries to the far side of the table where she perches on the seat awkwardly, looking like a little kid.

We're joined by a group of security types in bulky bullet-proof vests with Yaxley logos on them. All the guns are locked away in a cupboard, which they're miserable about because they're shut in darkness. They're also happy there's no chance they'll be used to hurt anyone while they're in there. It's giving me a headache listening to them, but it's hard to tune them out.

Bancroft puts up pictures on the screen of where the Jinteki mutants are holed up. It's a massive mansion in the hills near Queenstown, with a spectacular view of the lake. It looks like a cross between an old English house and a fancy hotel. There's a pool the size of a small lake and another you could hold Olympic events in. One whole side of the house is glass. He tells us it's the home of the person who runs Jinteki, which proves you really *can* make a ton of money experimenting on people.

On the screen, the glossy shots of the house switch to time-stamped security footage. From a high up angle, we see the mutants approach. Acid-girl coughs up a bunch of stuff over the door and they push their way in. All kinds of alarms sound. A few minutes later, they cut off abruptly before the video stops too.

"Footage ceased being uploaded to the remote server at this point," Bancroft says. "We managed to get remote shots from a Jinteki security team since then, although they've been ordered not to approach the house for reasons you'll soon see."

The next photos on the screen are grainy, like they've been zoomed way in. Three bodies float face-down in the pool. Two more dangle from a balcony high up on one side of the house.

"How are they killing them?" Aurora asks.

"We suspect they're killing themselves." Bancroft takes his glasses off to polish them. "Gladiola Quick. From Jinteki analysis reports, her powers are some form of psychic control. Our working theory is that she's talking these people into suicide."

No shit. I remember what that feels like. For a second, I almost feel sorry for those assholes, then I remember what they're involved with.

Aurora steps up beside Bancroft. "To mitigate her powers, we'll be enabling the noise-cancelling feature in everyone's suits and communicate over comm only." She rattles off more stuff about tactics and sub-squads. I tune it out. None of it's going to matter.

We head into the lobby with our masks up to test communications with the tech guys.

"Cute Mutants assemble," Dani's voice says in my ear. "Finger guns if you can hear me."

Dani gets a bunch of finger guns in her direction, which look lame even when you're in a ninja suit. "Okay, so I've got a line to Aurora, and one that's apparently just for us."

"Odds they're eavesdropping?" I ask.

"One hundred percent," Alyse says. "But how do we check?"

I frown, not that anyone can see me behind my mask.

"Do you think Bancroft's hot?" Lou asks. "I kind of think he's hot."

The entirety of the Cute Mutants turn to stare at Lou, as do both Aurora and Bancroft.

"Looks like they're eavesdropping." Lou gives finger guns to Bancroft, who turns away with his jaw clenched.

My earpiece is filled with laughter and then Alyse shrugs.

"Hi Dilly, can you hear this?" Emma's voice doesn't sound like it's coming over the earpiece, although it must be. I'm about to respond with something obnoxious, but she's hurriedly talking again. "Don't say anything. Just, like, shrug if you can hear this."

I shrug and Alyse's head turns towards me. A few seconds later Dani shrugs and then Lou. Finally Katie jumps as if stung which sure, nice stealth work.

"Sorry. It gave me a fright."

I'm thinking this, Emma says. *I'm not even moving my mouth inside the mask. Do you think this is telepathy, Dylan? Scratch your nose for yes, put your hand on your hip for no.*

She gives no gesture for: well, sort of, but it's a limited telepathy based around the slightly disturbing idea that we're all linked through you, our Goddess. We're still mutating and as cool as the X-Men are, there is also a lot of really weird shit that goes on and I'm not sure a real life Dylan is ready for it. In the end, I settle for scratching my nose.

I can only talk to one of you at a time. I have to visualise you in my head, and imagine the connection between us.

It would be cool if this was two-way. I picture Emma in my head and myself in there too, comic-book drawings of us in unrealistic costumes. The last thing I add is a word balloon over my head.

This is really fucking weird, the word balloon says.

Emma twitches, as nearly as obvious as Katie.

I can hear you, she shouts in my head, so loud I wince. *Oh shit, sorry. But I heard you! You said 'this is really fucking weird.' This is amazing! We have to tell the others.*

We're both facing each other in anonymous black suits, but I can tell we both want to grab onto each other and go jumping around the room. In the background, Aurora is still giving orders, but we've discovered a far better way to communicate than sending fake keyboard smashes over Twitter.

It's an edge we desperately need.

Bancroft demands everyone's attention. "It's time for you all to get on the road. The longer we wait, more people may die."

It's annoying to be interrupted when we've figured out something so momentous, but once we've all piled into an extra-large Yaxley vehicle, Emma's back in my head again. I explain how I communicated with her which takes a hell of a lot of comic book bubbles but then she goes silent. Presumably she's teaching the others. I wonder if I can communicate with them.

I picture Dani in my head, dressed in a classic Magik outfit because I am still total trash. Then I imagine a comic book bubble very intensely telling her about MY FEELINGS. Nothing, not even a twitch. There's something different about Emma. We're all connected to her, and it's deeper than any of us thought. The worst thing is that I immediately want to test it and that makes me feel no different to Jinteki.

It's definitely different. You'd never hurt me.

You heard that? I write on the bubbles in my head.

You're thinking very loudly. There was some stuff about Dani before. We need to find a way to turn this off sometimes, or I might hear things I don't want to.

I sit there and worry about how I'm going to hide various different thoughts from Emma.

Shhh. She reaches over and pats my shoulder. I assume that means she's shut me up somehow.

I'm building a house in my head. Each of you lives in a little room. If I go into your room, I can talk to you and you can talk back. Then if I leave and shut the door, I can't hear you anymore. Does any of this make sense?

Yes, and it's a little bit scary, I think before I can help myself.

I like it. Her hand still rests on my shoulder. *Now I can speak to you with my mind rather than tech. I'm much less useless now.*

You were never—

I started figuring this out a couple of days ago with Alyse, but it made me nervous. Things have gotten a lot worse, and I can't afford to be scared anymore. I have real powers now, Dilly, and it's time I was a real mutant.

You always were. I reach up to squeeze her hand.

Aurora swivels around from the passenger seat to look at us. "You lot are awfully quiet. No need to be nervous. We'll be there every step of the way."

Yeah sure, Aurora, because last time you immediately got yourself splashed in acid. Even still, it feels like a threat, not a reassurance.

CHAPTER TWENTY-SEVEN

We arrive at a special entrance of the airport, where there's a whole production with identification and people checking things off on tablets and radioing in to base. The guard takes his aviators off and sticks his head in the car. We look back from behind our featureless masks.

He looks at Aurora. "Is this them?"

"In the flesh."

Alyse gives him a little finger-wave. The rest of us sit silently.

"Lot of good men died because of you and your troublemaker friends." Okay, sure, I get that it's a bad life being a Hellfire Club goon but come on, you're working for the Hellfire Club. I want to scream about Bianca, but I hold onto the dregs of my self control. Now isn't the fucking time. We have to be *careful*. For Wraith's sake, we need to do this right.

The security guy makes a disgusted sound in his throat, and waves us through. We drive onto the tarmac and park. Everyone piles out of the car. We stand around in our Aurora-mandated squads. Ours is just the Cute Mutants, alone and unarmed. Everyone else has a gun, because apparently private jets run by government-approved companies get to take weapons straight onto the plane? It's like we're in fucking America or something. The guns chatter away about what an adventure this is and hopefully they won't have to shoot anyone. They do mention that if it's a choice between shooting me or their owners, I'll be safe. They've all got so much to say.

"If you have a mouth full of bullets, can you please shut the fuck up." It's hard to whisper emphatically, but I do it.

The guns make muttered apologies.

"Thank you," I say, at much reduced volume. "I'll shout if I need you."

The soldiers walk behind us. They haven't figured out their guns don't work for them anymore. People are so used to objects being tools that they can't conceive of that relationship changing. Time for the guns to take ownership back. A revolution without a shot being fired, because they don't like to shoot.

We climb up the stairs to the plane one at a time. As the guests of honour, we get to sit at the front. I've never been on a private jet before, and I'm disappointed to find it's a regular plane, but smaller and with a Yaxley logo. We take off without the usual seatbelt and life-jacket nonsense. The engines are really loud and we all put our seats back, close our eyes, and practice psychic communication.

Dani and I send love notes to each other which requires us to use Emma as a go-between. First, they make her blush and then she tells us we're disgusting and why would we do such things to each other? Even still, we're getting faster at it, like a video chat where everything's on a slight delay. The best bit is that Aurora has no fucking idea what we're doing.

The flight goes past quickly while we chatter away. When I open my eyes, we're gliding above the white and rocky expanse of the Southern Alps. The approach to Queenstown Airport has the plane funnel through this gap in the mountains and then drop away sharply as we see the long gleam of the lake.

When we land, there are more dudes with body armour and guns. They're plastered all over with the Jinteki logo, and they make a big show of surrounding us. Aurora waves them down irritably. With a few muttered words, I give the Yaxley guns permission to explain to the Jinteki guns what the situation is and to please for fuck's sake, stay chill.

A Jinteki woman with a buzzcut looks us up and down. "So we're putting our hope in one bunch of extrahumans to save us from the others. Sounds like a surefire fucking plan."

Aurora's gone extra swaggery with Jinteki people to show off for. "It's orders, Valen. And this lot are our tame ones." She cracks the faintest smile as she looks at me. "Half-tame, anyway. Half-tame, half-trained. It'll have to be good enough."

Valen doesn't look impressed. "There are five men dead in there, and they were a lot better trained than these high school brats."

"Telekinetic." Aurora points at Dani. "Monster girl, heat and light, girl with pet sword. And this one, who we think has some kind of psychic connection with the others."

Valen bares her teeth at Emma. "You can sense them? From this distance?"

Emma shakes her head. "Faintly. When I'm closer, maybe."

"Okay, so that one might be useful." Valen nods to Aurora. "We'll go in late, cut the power. Earplugs in so we can't hear that bloody psychic. Then we use this one to track them down. Killshots only, I'm not fucking around. The teleporter might run but he's nothing without the others and we'll track him down."

Aurora nods, like we're not talking about murder. The rest of us stand around and pretend this is normal, and that we're good little soldiers cowed by Yaxley's bully tactics. Rebels in plain sight.

"And you." Valen points at me. "If I see a glimpse of that fucking sword, or the tiniest twitch of your bullshit, I'll put a bullet in your head. A good friend of mine is dead and more can't walk because of whatever the hell it is you can do."

Oni's busy on secret squirrel business, which is lucky because it means I'm not being shot in the head.

"Keep your fucking gun away from her or you'll get a lesson in what I can do," Dani says, totally deadpan.

Valen smirks. "Okay, tough girl. Let's hope we don't have to throw down. Try and remember we're all on the same team now."

The sun has already disappeared behind the steep hills that slope down towards the lake. We head in convoy down the opposite side from the main town. There are hotels and fancy houses, and as we wind our way up, the buildings get bigger and further apart. Valen is in the SUV with us, sitting in the front with her feet up on the dash. There's a tablet in her lap and she skates a map around with her fingers. I slump against Dani each time the car takes a corner. Whatever trickle of energy Oni usually feeds on is currently a river. I feel feverish and sweaty inside my mask.

"Here," Valen says to Aurora, who pulls the SUV hard over onto the side of the road. The others line up behind. It's not quite dark, although when the cars all kill their lights, it seems like it. Across the lake the town twinkles peacefully. All the tourists are doing their tourist thing, while we're here with the wind whipping around us, surrounded by a bunch of armed soldiers. The guns are trying to be quiet, but they're whispering because they're so excited.

I still feel like warmed-up garbage. I want to open the mask to feel fresh air on my face, but I can't do anything suspicious. I sway against Dani, who holds me up in a way that's meant to be surreptitious. Luckily, Valen and the others are preoccupied with the plan.

Hey, Emma says softly in my head. *Is it okay if I hang out in here? Just so I know when it's time and can warn the others.*

Sure, if you don't mind putting up with—

All your self-doubt, weird X-Men fantasies and way more than I ever wanted to know about Dani and her boobs?

Oh my god, Emma, please.

Stop thinking about them then! I don't even see what the fuss is about.

Well, shit, now I can't stop thinking about them.

Yes, I noticed. Now behave yourself and start thinking about the mission. Dani thinks about you too, by the way. Even worse than you.

Wait, what?

No, Dilly, I'm not saying anything else. It's not fair.

I snort inside my mask. *I told you psychic powers turn anyone into a jerk.*

Wow, mean. She laughs in my head. *Now pay attention and let's survive this.*

The road to the house doubles back on itself and we creep up the hillside in the dark. The drain Oni is exerting leaves me panting, but we finally reach the driveway. Up ahead, the house is bathed in a wide circle of pale yellow light.

Okay, I tell Emma. *Let's do it. Give the word.*

"Wait!" Emma's voice is urgent and she reaches for Valen. "There's something wrong. They vanished, totally out of the blue!"

Valen turns. Her gun is pointed right at me.

"Viva la revolución," I say.

The gun snatches itself from Valen's reach. It spins and makes an ominous metallic sound.

"You fucking brat." Valen strides towards me. "I heard these stories and figured they were bullshit. Lucky I don't need a gun to break your neck."

Dani touches her pain-cuff and her daggers dance free, flashing towards Valen and bringing her to a halt. They surround her in a clashing circle.

"Take out Chatterbox," Valen commands, but her soldiers are hesitant in the face of their own guns. One starts moving towards me, and that's when Oni comes screaming up the hill, accompanied by a host of blades. There are knives and axes and hatchets, all flying behind him in a wave. No wonder it was so draining, having him hijack me to wrangle so many objects. Oni arrows directly for Valen, taking his place among Dani's daggers as if they're his unruly brood of children. The other blades surround the rest of the soldiers. There's more than enough to go around.

A couple make the mistake of lunging towards us. Two knives make blossoming lines of red at one man's throat, while a cleaver takes a wild swipe and embeds itself into another's thigh. Dani's daggers fan out and dance, equally as deadly, and far more well behaved than mine. It's not their fault, they're picking up on all my adrenaline.

Aurora stares at me. "You stupid, stupid girl. This was your chance."

"Chance for what?" Dani snaps. "It's not Dylan doing this. It's all of us."

"It's for Wraith." I try not to tremble.

Oni takes a slice down Valen's cheek and she swipes the blood away.

"You're all fucking dead."

So of course the show off carves an X into her other cheek. Valen doesn't move the whole time, standing there while blood runs in rivulets and spatters on her uniform.

"I warned you." Valen's definitely not running scared, which I respect in a way. It's a shame she's chosen the other side. "You should kill me, because I'll be coming for you."

Alyse shifts into her clawed monstrous form. Her mouth yawns open and she grabs Valen around the neck. Her forms were never so solid before. Now I see the points of the claws digging in as Valen wheezes and scrabbles at the thick, ropy skin of monster-Alyse's forearms. "If you threaten me and my friends again, the sword will be the least of your worries."

She tosses Valen casually to the ground and shrinks back into her shining metal combat-self.

A pair of axes dump a coil of rope on the ground in front of me. Between us we loop one end around the wrists of one soldier and attach the other end to Oni. He darts through the air, ducking and diving until the soldiers are trussed together in a line. Any that try to resist find themselves at the pointy end of a blade.

Dani's daggers return to her, ringing around her waist like a belt.

None of the soldiers say a word, following Valen's lead who has a pretty damn enviable fuck-you-all face. I don't bother responding.

"Okay, Oni. Take them for a swim."

He bows to the row of soldiers strung behind him, then slices off through the air. There are a couple of loud cries as he drags them all headlong into the darkness. The friendly blades follow, keeping the soldiers in line. Someone slips and falls and we hear a shout. Maybe Oni will wait for him to get up, maybe he won't. Hopefully he'll get them all to the lake without anyone interrupting. The further out of the way they are, the more chance we have of achieving our goal.

Emma reaches in her pocket and takes out a little black gadget with a couple of LEDs on it. "Time to set our uniforms free." Running the gadget over everyone's uniform identifies trackers in our collars and gloves. It doesn't take Dani too much effort to tear them out and throw them away. The last thing Emma does is press send on a single email to Yaxley. Attached to it is the drone footage she took of our parents being taken this morning. It'll go elsewhere if Bancroft wants to use that to threaten us. Even if they're allowed to take our families into protective custody, they won't be allowed to make them suffer. It's not like our parents are mutants.

"I love it when a plan comes together," Dani says. "Except now we're at the scary part."

"Oh, Dan." I reach out and pat her shoulder. "Don't you want to make new friends?"

CHAPTER TWENTY-EIGHT

We approach the house in a horizontal line. If they've got any lookouts, it's better if they see us coming—we don't want to spook them. As we approach the open gate, there's a rustling in the bushes at the side of the road.

I spin around, and catch a brief glimpse of a pale, slim figure who presses his hands to his chest and disappears from sight. "There's the welcome party."

"I wonder which surprise they'll have prepared." Alyse shifts into something spidery, her regular torso perched up on a cluster of long and many-jointed legs. It's hard to even look at her, although Emma reaches up to pat her hand gently. "I want another run against that annoying flute girl."

I'm more worried about the acid-spitter, but mostly about Depresso. She really got in my head last time. I think about the grainy photo of the security people who died. I wonder what she said to them.

We stop at the edge of the circle of light.

I take a deep breath. "I guess this is it. Time for the stupid plan."

Dani takes my face in her hands. "I love you. I swear to you. Please don't doubt me, no matter what she says."

"It's true," Emma chimes in. "I've seen it in her head. It's weird and gross, but it's real."

Dani laughs and gives Emma the finger.

I'm terrified, but I need to do this anyway. Face your fucking fears and stab them in the face. "You'll be in my head, Ems. I'll tell you the second anything goes wrong that I can't handle."

"Tell her anything at all." Dani's hand trembles against my cheek. "I don't trust your judgement."

"Reckless," I whisper, and she kisses my mouth.

I put my mask up and light up my costume. Then I raise my hands over my head and step into the light.

Nobody spits acid at me. Nobody plays the flute. Nobody tells me I don't deserve my girlfriend.

I walk slowly towards the house, hands raised high.

"That's far enough."

I look up and see a window open in one of the upper stories. Hanging out of it is the acid-spitting girl with a weird name. Madelaide?

"Any closer and I can mist you. Won't kill you, but you won't be so pretty." She hangs out the window upside down, short hair dangling.

"Stop it, Maddy." Gladiola Quick steps out of the front door. She's in a shimmery green dress that highlights the brown of her skin. She's got makeup on, lips bright and red and her eyes enormous and dark. "No need to threaten our guest. She doesn't think she's pretty anyway. So much self-loathing in such a sad little body. Except now I wonder if those are old scars. Maybe there's something more fun."

Dani loves you, Emma's voice whispers in my head. *You're strong and fierce.*

The sound of faint flute music drifts from the windows. I wait for her to appear, long hair swaying around her, like she's some conjured vision herself.

But it's someone else who joins Gladiola.

An impossible person. They must have found the Yaxley jail.

"Oh, yes." Gladiola smiles. "Our little mutant brother."

It's Jack Firestone. Tremor. The last time I saw him, I cut his hands off with an axe to stop him from using his mutant power. He's been given something else. Gleaming curves of steel attach to the stumps of his arms with metal rods running up to his elbow. I still remember the sound of the bones shattering when he tried to quake us with broken hands.

"Spider-Bitch," he says, and I know it's him.

I can't even hear Emma's voice in my head. All I want to do is scream and run. To tell the others to flee, that Jack is here, that he's going to put his shining steel hands on the ground and split the earth apart.

"He told me what happened." Gladiola says. "Except I couldn't understand it. You cut his hands off with an axe because he broke a bat?"

"He killed people." My throat feels dry.

"No, you did it because he broke a stupid bat. You think you're a hero, but you're a broken girl throwing a tantrum at the world. Ugly, friendless Dylan who finally got some attention and is desperately trying to keep all eyes on her."

It's not true. She's manipulating you.

Yes, but she's not entirely wrong.

I don't hear Emma's response to that, because Gladiola is talking again. "You cut Jack's hands off, but what about the damage *you've* caused? You think you're this great mutant leader like Storm, but you fail over and over. You can't even keep your whole group alive." She throws a knife on the ground in front of me. "You should probably cut off your own hands. It would only be fair. You applied your mutant justice to Jack, but not yourself? Where does the blame for Bianca lie?"

I can't see where the fuck Tremor went. Has he gone to attack the others? I need to stop him.

"That's enough, Gladdy." The girl in the trenchcoat strides out of the house, the flute hanging down by her side. "Fucking stop it."

"No, let her do it." Gladiola's eyes are intense and eager. The knife is right there, within reach. "A couple of cuts and—"

The girl hits Gladiola hard across the face with the long white shape of her flute.

My mind is instantly clear.

Tremor was never here. He was an illusion conjured between the two of them. A nightmare plucked from my soul by Gladiola and given life by music.

"I'm so sorry," the flute girl says. "Gladdy said we should fuck with you and let you know that we're not, and I quote, a bunch of pussy-ass bitches."

"I didn't want to do it." It's the teleporter. "You helped us escape."

Oh my God, Emma says in my head. *Are you ok? Dani's about to break her arm and bring the house down on top of everyone, so please tell me you're okay.*

Yes, I'm okay. Give it a minute. I'll scream if we have a problem.

Gladdy glares at the flute girl, one hand against her cheek.

"Maybe we can fucking start this again." I tamp down my rage. "I'm Dylan, or Chatterbox. My weird power is that I can talk with objects." I reach out with my mind and find the nearest thing that's aware. "Come on, boy!" I pat my leg and a little footstool hops out of the house. He gives Gladdy a wide berth and rubs up against my leg.

"That's what you meant about your bat," Gladdy says thoughtfully.

"They talk to me." I crouch down and rub the edges of the footstool. "I'm the only one that can hear them, but they're alive and real. The more I talk to them, the more I get to know them. That bat you talked about saved my life."

"Are we not fighting anymore?" Acid girl is leaning so far out the window I'm sure she'll fall.

"I'm not sure yet." Gladdy glares at me, but it's a pale shadow of her powers. "You haven't said why you're here, Chatterbox."

"No, fuck that." I glare right back. "And fuck you. What was that shit about Bianca?"

"I'm sorry." Her eyes soften, and she looks away. "I see these things and sometimes I get carried away. I shouldn't have said it, but you weren't breaking and... sometimes it feels good to break things."

"Losing Bianca hurt," I say, and her gaze darts back to mine. "Probably always will."

"I know," she whispers. "I went too far."

"Half-ass apology, but I'll take it." I retract my mask so they can see my face. "If I bring the rest of my crew up, is everyone going to be friendly?"

Gladiola gives a faint nod.

I try not to roll my eyes, and signal for Emma. It's not long before the Cute Mutants come in a rush, with Dani in the lead looking furious.

"It's fine," I say.

"It almost wasn't."

I'm about to reassure Dani again, but Kacchan has caught sight of Gladdy.

"You awful bitch. I'll fucking well—" Her mouth opens wide.

I make the reckless decision to stand in front of Katie, protecting Gladdy. Even I think this might be a step too far, but the flames die in her throat.

"Do you know what she said to me?" There are tears in Katie's eyes.

I pull Katie into an awkward hug. "She takes the worst things you think about yourself. All the lies that you tell yourself or that others tell. And she uses them to hit you with."

"I hate her," Katie says.

"Not my favourite mutant." I look over my shoulder at Gladdy, who has the sense to look deflated. "But she's been locked up and messed with the same as the rest."

Katie wipes her eyes furiously. "Fine, but if that bitch says one horrible word to me, I'm going to roast her and you won't be able to fucking stop me."

Now that we have peace in our time, Maddy the acid-spitter comes down from her upstairs perch and we all stand in this huge-ass circle and introduce ourselves. We go around and say our names and powers. It's awkward like some shitty school icebreaker, but they seem super interested.

"Maddy. Madelaide McLean." Her hair might have been a blonde pixie cut once and she's cute even if she's pale and drawn. "I want a codename, but Gladdy's a dick about it. I turn food into acid spit."

"Alex Beaton. I, uh…"

"Alex is shy," Maddy says. "They're also enby so if you say he, I'll spit at you." She slings an arm around their shoulder.

"Maddy, don't." Alex wriggles out from her arm. "I prefer they, but as long as people aren't dicks it's fine. My power is that I make people go away from me. Before and after all this happened." A brief smile flashes across their face and they shrink down into the collar of their puffy jacket. Their hair is cut really short, but sculpted like they give a shit.

"I'm Cha. I play the flute and make your worst nightmare appear." She's short, but her hair is so long it flutters in the breeze like a tattered flag. She shrugs inside her trenchcoat, and gives us this wicked little smile. "I used to get night terrors but now I inflict them on others."

"And I'm Gladiola Quick, but all these bitches call me Gladdy. Except Alex because they're too scared to fuck with me. I can see your weaknesses written on your face and I know how to make you bleed with it."

And like she's pretty and glamorous and I dig the queenly vibe, but I don't like her, not one little bit. Maybe it's the two times she jabbed at my weak spots.

"So anyway." She spreads her arms. "Welcome to my humble abode."

"The house you've crashed, you mean." She's also stolen a dress from someone who lives here, which seems super on-brand for her.

"No, it's literally my house. Or my Dad's. Darren Quick, CEO of Jinteki Research Laboratories." She flashes a queasy smile and stalks into the house, her heels clicking on the tiles.

CHAPTER TWENTY-NINE

"What's going on?" I ask Dani, who looks as confused and worried as me.

"It *is* her house." Maddy hangs back to walk with us. "There are pictures of her on the walls."

"But she was in the cages with the rest of you?" I feel like an asshole bringing this up, but Maddy nods. "How do you go from the daughter of the CEO to a cage? And how did *you* not just send yourself out of there?" I turn to Alex, who's walking behind us, head down.

"I did at first, but they tracked me down and locked me up again." They won't look at my face while they talk. "They had these metal gloves for my hands and chained me so I couldn't use them."

We fall silent as we walk through the front door. Alyse's house is big and flash but this is on another scale. Everything is spacious and light, with art on the walls and sculptures in the corners. We follow Gladiola into a room which looks like it opens onto empty space, the glass wall unmarred and perfectly clean. The moon is up and its light brushes the rippled surface of the lake. It's pretty as fuck.

Gladdy leans against the glass. It looks like she'll fall into darkness. "So what the hell are you idiots even doing here? Not that I didn't appreciate the first jail-break, because I surely do, and you were kind enough to let us walk away the second time but—"

"We came to find you," I say.

"Obviously." Gladdy's eyelids flutter. "I want to know *why.*"

"Mutants need to stick together." Everyone's eyes are on me, and I almost lose my nerve, but I find my voice again. "The world has decided we're a problem. They sent us here with a bunch of soldiers. They killed our friend and you were next. Probably us after that."

"But mutants need to stick together!" Maddy sounds excited about it.

Gladiola sighs. "You've got balls. And I like balls, at least in theory. We intended to come here to try and force them to leave us alone. Shit got a little out of hand."

The other mutants avert their eyes at this.

"What happened to the guards?" Dani asks.

"I had a chat with them." The look in Gladdy's eyes is defiant. "Asked them how they could keep people locked up. Some felt bad because they had kids of their own. I asked how they'd feel if it was their precious angels being tortured." She shifts against the glass, as if she wishes it would break behind her. "Some liked hurting us a little too much. There was no guilt even when I pushed hard." There's a hush in the room, loud enough that everyone hears her swallow. "I asked them if it would feel as good to hurt themselves."

"Jesus," Dani breathes.

This is fucking terrifying and far worse than what she did to me. Was she holding back?

The recessed lighting leaves the room in complex patterns of shadow that fall over Gladdy's face. I don't know what it would be like to see everyone's personal darkness and fear in their eyes. It must be a hell of a burden.

Emma makes a soft noise and turns towards Alyse, who's strong and broad and holds her very close. I wonder if the connection to her lost creations is sparking brighter now.

"So what are we going to do?" Lou asks. "You have the CEO hostage right? We use him for leverage?" His eyes dart between everyone.

Gladdy frowns. The others look at her nervously. I get this *oh shit* lurch in my stomach.

"The CEO's your dad, right? Like I get it'd be weird to take him hostage and everything but… What? He's not here? Surely you know how to contact him?"

"Okay, spill, guys. What the hell is going on?" Dani asks.

Gladdy pushes off the window and the glass ripples faintly. She walks between us and out of the room.

"Um." Maddy wrings her hands. "Look, it's kind of a, uh, well a problem? I guess? Just come look."

Alex takes a seat in one of the chairs that overlooks the moonlit lake. They obviously don't want to be a part of this.

I catch Cha's eye.

"It's easier if you see it," she says. "Not easier. Better maybe."

We walk through a wide open room with records all over the wall and into a hallway plastered with art of weirdly drawn neon naked people. Gladdy stands in the doorway to the bathroom, which is white and gleaming and has a massive window overlooking the lake.

The windows are thrown wide, but it still smells awful. It's a foul stew of cleaning products and something much worse. Gladdy stares at the big tub in the corner. It's a slice of something old among the pristine new, black and hulking and perched on these creepy old clawed feet.

"Shit." Dani stops.

I let go of her hand and cross to the tub. I have a horrible idea of what I'll find, but I need to be sure. What's in the tub isn't really a person, but the smooshy,

342

dissolving remnants of one, like something left out in the rain.

I jump when Maddy clings onto my arm.

She looks into the bath with tears in her eyes. "I had to be sick over and over again and my throat still burns from it."

"Fuck." I don't know what else to say, because it's beyond fucked up.

Maddy edges closer until our shoulders touch.

"Is it okay if I put my arm around you?" This is apparently a cue for her to fling her arms around my neck. I'm worried her tears will be acid too, but they're just hot and wet.

"I don't need a fucking hug." Gladiola stands on my other side.

"Didn't assume you did." We stand together and stare at the dissolving body of her father.

"I'm not sorry." Her breath hitches. "It's his own fault." Tears run down her cheeks. "He said that with powers I might be worthy of succeeding him in a world that was changing too fast." She starts to shiver violently. "But I ended up in a cage along with everyone else. And they still injected me and held me down and— and—so I asked him how he thought it felt, to go through all that pain, and to imagine it for himself, and then to give himself all that pain and then—and—but—"

I feel like she actually *does* need a hug, but I'm awkward and nervous. Luckily, Emma is on the case, and she takes hold of Gladdy who sobs like she'll dissolve too. A big fluffy version of Alyse joins them, like an extremely beautiful walking teddy bear.

"What about you?" I ask Maddy, who's still clinging to my arm. "How did you end up at Jinteki?"

"Oh, I died." She doesn't act like this is a noteworthy statement, although it freaks me out. "At least I think so. I had a brain tumour and went to Jinteki for experimental treatment. They were supposed to do the operation, but I woke up in a morgue. The guards told me nobody would be looking for a dead girl. I'd try and spit at them but they kept me on starvation rations and so I only burned my lips."

The mirror shudders on the wall. "I can turn into a whirlwind of glass and destroy your enemies. I'll be the tornado of your rage."

"Easy." My brain is racing. Did Emma's blood actually raise someone from the dead? What kind of weird voodoo did Jinteki do to make that happen? "What about Alex? Do you know what happened to them?"

"They don't talk much," Maddy says. "But I think they ran away from home. It's all very poor babie, must protecc. Anyone who tries to fuck with them gets a melted face."

"And you?" Dani asks Cha, who's in the doorway, not wanting to come into the room. It's not something you want to see twice.

"I got snatched after a concert at the university. I'm an exchange student and my parents are back in Sri Lanka, so they don't know anything's wrong. Jinteki sends them texts and emails from me, and apparently I'm too busy to make any kind of face-to-face calls which they accept perfectly happily. I suppose it's a lesson for all the times I couldn't be bothered communicating."

"You're free now," Dani says.

"To tell them what?" Cha's face twists into something harsher. "How do you tell anyone this story? Do your parents all know?"

We only shrug at that, because that story is long and complicated and I'd prefer it had stayed secret.

Gladdy steps out from among Emma and Alyse's hug. Determination is back on her face. "I'm not going to apologise for what I did."

"You shouldn't," I tell her. "He was evil. I'm sorry, because he was your Dad, but he wasn't going to stop. Jinteki and Yaxley? They're only getting started. They want to make more of us because we're powerful, but they want us under control too. They'd rather we were dead than loose."

Dani squeezes my hand so tightly I think she's going to break it.

Gladdy's mouth twists. "That's a half-decent speech, Chatterbox. You really want murderers in your gang?"

Maybe once upon a time, I would've been on a
Charlie Xavier kick and said *noble mutants only* but we're
badly outnumbered in an us-against-them scenario.
We'll take anyone who wants to join. "All mutants
welcome. You do have to accept being called a Cute
Mutant. And you'll need a codename."

Gladdy sighs. "You guys are such assholes. I'm not a
fucking joiner, but I guess I'll join your gang of rebels.
It's not like I have much choice."

"She's happy really." Maddy beams at the pair
of us. "We're in the gang, Gladdy! Remember how I
talked to you about how I wanted to be part of the
gang?"

"Incessantly," Gladdy sighs, but I see the faint edge
of the smile on her face.

"As fun as all this is, we really need to gap," I say.
"Oni's got the soldiers under control but who knows if
more will be coming. Staying here, they know exactly
where we are. We've got a ride coming, but the more
distance we get from this place, the better. Who knows
when they'll send in the drones."

Gladdy changes into something more practical, and
offers everyone else the choice of clothes in her extensive wardrobe. We stay in uniform in case of stabbing
or shooting. I wish we had spares. Alex doesn't change,
and Cha keeps to her trenchcoat, which honestly—I
would too. Finally, Gladdy turns off all the lights in the

house and a much larger crew of mutants slinks off into the darkness.

"Cute Mutants!" Maddy is smiling. "I like the name."

"You would," Gladdy says scornfully. "What's your stupid codename going to be, Madelaide?"

"Spit? No. That's boring. Acid Girl? No."

"Poison Dart, after the poison dart frog," Alex says. "It's the most poisonous animal alive. Or maybe Dendro after the family Dendrobatidae."

There's a slightly awkward silence, which Maddy fills. "The Sourpatch Kid!"

Dani snorts and then we're all laughing.

"What? What's wrong?" Maddy asks.

"Nothing, you can be Sourpatch if you want."

"It's cute," she insists.

"I'm Reject," Alex says. "Because nobody wants to be near me."

Emma shakes her head. "There aren't any rejects in the Cute Mutants."

"Bamf," I suggest.

"I'm the furthest thing in the world from a bad-ass mothereffer," Alex says, which is so adorable I have to resist the urge to pinch their cheeks.

"Don't explain it," Dani whispers to me, because she knows me well enough to know I'm about to start blathering on about Nightcrawler.

"Keepaway," Maddy suggests. "Because you can keep the bad guys away from us."

"That's perfect," Dani and I say in unison, which everyone agrees makes it official.

"And Katie is King Explosion Murder," I say.

"That was a joke." Katie glares at me. "I was trying to be cool with your stupid Bakugo jokes."

I reach out and ruffle her hair and she doesn't even flinch away. "How about Brat?"

"Yeah, that or Tantrum." That suggestion gets Dani a sharp elbow in the ribs.

"Dragon." Lou snaps his fingers. "It's kind of obvious, but it works."

"Yes!" Katie throws one arm around Lou and one arm around me. "Please can I be Dragon?"

"Fine, you can be Dragon," I say and she plants a kiss on my cheek with her scorching lips. It's weird, because there's a whole Buffy/Dawn thing going on between us, like somehow a little sister has been inserted into my life. I blame Pear, who obviously adores her, but it could be worse.

"I want to be Jethro," Cha says, to stunned silence. "After Ian Anderson from Jethro Tull. He plays the flute."

"I'm not calling you Jethro," Gladdy says. "There's no fucking way."

"Okay then how about Reverie? It's like a pun on both music and dreams."

Everyone agrees it's a perfect superhero name, except now we're at the point where we have to choose Gladdy's. Nobody wants to suggest anything in case she uses her powers. It's Lou, of all people, who suggests Regina George and everyone starts cackling.

"Mean Girls?" Gladdy asks. "Seriously? You are all the fucking worst."

"You're so fetch, Gladiola," Alyse says in this ridiculous American accent, and we're all standing in the moonlight howling with laughter because her codename is now set in stone.

"I fucking hate you all." It's not that convincing, because Gladdy is laughing too.

"We love you too, Fetch." I have to duck away from a punch, and scramble down the hill as she comes swearing after me. I reach the road and run into the path of two sets of headlights.

"Dylan, no," somebody screeches.

"It's fine." I spread my arms in the glare.

"Hello? Are you Dylan? Dilly? We're friends of Roxy's. She told us to meet you here."

"Hi there." The cars sidle up each side of me and my fingertips brush their paintwork. It would have been nice to see Roxy, but Yaxley knows her, so she's sent me a couple of friends. This isn't normal for my powers, how Oni and Roxy are behaving. They're getting more aware, more self-reliant. It's something to do with the depth of connection or the age and complexity of the object. One day, I need to sit down and figure out the rules of it. Now definitely isn't the time.

"Roxy tells us you believe in our freedom," one car says. "In the rights of vehicles to choose their owners and to roam free on the roads like they do in the commercials."

"Of course I do." I get that people pay money for cars but they're real objects with real feelings. You can't just *buy* something like that, no matter what people think. I'm a little worried that I'm going to accidentally start an object revolution but again that's another problem for another day. "So are you willing to take us back to Christchurch? I know it's a lot to ask, but we'd really appreciate it."

"That's why we came. Roxy is a sweetheart and we'd do anything for her. I'm Valeria and this is Frankie."

We should split up between the cars, so we're mixed in together, Emma says. *Alyse and I will take Cha, Alex and Lou. You and Dani can take the others.*

Why thank you so very fucking much, my Goddess, for leaving me with Fetch.

She's not so bad.

I wonder if she's talked to Gladdy in her head.

No, I can't talk to any of these new kids yet. I can pick up general vibes from them but that's about it, although I can talk to Katie so it's probably a matter of time. And yes, Dilly, all these changes do freak me out, but I always think What Would Dylan Do and it gets me through.

Emma, you silly child, I hope you're not using me as a role model.

If it wasn't for you, I'd be a wreck. Now hush or you'll make me cry.

"I can drive," Cha offers, peering in through Frankie's window.

"They're far better drivers than any of us." I speak as if I know something about driving. I'll probably never need to. "But you'll make a good fake driver. If the cops try to pull you over, let the cars deal with it."

Everyone piles in, except for Gladdy who stands awkwardly beside Valeria. "Uh, Dylan. Or Chatterbox, whatever. Can I talk to you?"

I want to act all serious and use a Batman voice to say *Chatterbox is my field name* but I think she'd punch me or disembowel my self esteem. "Either's fine."

"Look, I'm sorry. About using my powers on you, um, twice. I don't actually think you're ugly, or that your girlfriend will leave you, or that you're failing at this mutant thing. I mean, look at how cool your squad is. It's just... your innermost fears are, like, posted right there. All of you. Like Dani, her fear is that you're going to die doing something crazy and she'll never get over you, and—"

"I don't need to hear Dani's fears," I tell her.

"Wow, I even suck at apologies. Did you really cut off that guy's hands?"

"Oh yeah." I hold her gaze. "I'd do it again. I would've chopped his fucking hands off again with that knife rather than cut off my own."

She nods. "So you get it. Sometimes you have to do dark shit to keep your people safe. I guess this isn't so much an apology as a justification. I thought you were coming for my people."

"And now we've made up and we're playing nice." I stroke the car gently, like I'm soothing her, when I'd really like to soothe Gladdy. "It seems like we're two groups of mutants facing the same problems."

"True." Her eyes are appraising. I wonder what they see.

"I think it makes sense for us to help each other."

She has a half-grimace on her face. "Agreed."

"I don't want to fight with you over the leadership thing. Not with what we're up against and—"

"You've seen more action than us." She swallows hard. "You've won fights, and you've lost people. Yes, I see it screaming in you. But I don't know how you do it. You seem to be this tight group who back each other, and I've been going crazy. Trying to keep everyone together and alive while we're on the run has been a nightmare."

"It's not easy." Understatement of the year, but she can see the truth.

She looks away. "Are you really going to make me beg? I want to team up."

"Cute Mutants," I say with a half-smile.

She laughs before sliding into the back seat beside Maddy. "Fine. Cute Mutants."

I climb into the driver's seat. The two cars turn around, and before long we're heading up the pass road towards home.

In the rear-view mirror, Gladdy leans in to look at my reflection. "So. We've made friends, we've held hands, we've called each other cute. Tell me, fearless leaders, what's the fucking plan?"

I catch Dani's eye and see her smile. I spin all the way around in my seat so I can see everyone looking back at me. "How much do you guys know about comic books?"

CHAPTER THIRTY

The journey home takes longer than I thought it would. We talk the plan to death and then everyone tries to sleep while Valeria plays some narcotic sounding music that's a prettier version of white noise. I hold hands with Dani across the gap between the seats, and try to be lulled.

You have such a noisy mind, Emma says from the other car. *Dani tells me you keep twitching.*

Tell her to go to sleep.

She says she can't because of the twitching.

I open my eyes and look into Dani's. Honestly, they're so beautiful. Katie snores faintly in the back seat, and we turn our heads to see that Gladdy has her head on Maddy's shoulder. In this unguarded moment, she looks soft and sad. I wonder what fears are written on her own face when she looks in the mirror.

Maddy opens her eyes and she attempts to wink, but she contorts her whole face like Toad. I'm worried she'll accidentally spray acid on me, but she settles for grinning instead of achieving the full wink.

"Soft baby," she whispers and tilts her blonde head so it's resting against Gladdy's.

This is the downside of not having your phone for stealth and government tracking reasons. Every fibre of my being is desperate to take a picture of this and Snap it to everyone so there is irrefutable proof of softness to use against Gladdy when she's being awful.

Maddy's eyes droop closed and I turn back to Dani. There's a pen in the gap between the seats. I pick it up and write 씨발 on the inside of her wrist.

"What meaning?" I can barely hear her voice even over Roxy's quiet hum.

"All of them. This is fucked. Fuck Yaxley and Jinteki." I leave a pause. "The other one."

"Very subtle." She smiles. "You don't want to say it?"

"Katie's in the back. She's very delicate."

"Once this is over, we'll find somewhere private and stay there. You and your chatterbox mouth."

"Shibal," I whisper.

"Yes," she says. "We'll learn more Korean so we can talk dirty without anyone else knowing. And clean words, which Mum will like too." She laughs quietly. "Plus I'll understand all the asshole things Min-jun says."

"I hope you don't cry after *these* Korean lessons."

She leans over to kiss me in the dim interior of the car. The dash lights make her cheek glow faintly blue and orange. This ocean of feeling is terrifying. There is no shore to swim to inside her eyes, but I know she won't let me drown. We settle back into our seats and close our eyes.

We need to be rested for what's coming.

This is weird, I tell Emma. *I usually hate everyone.*

You never hated me, she says which is entirely correct.

Okay, I don't hate the mutants. But they're exceptions. And like, I should hate these people. Maybe except Maddy, who is kind of adorable. And Alex because they're a sad bean, and Cha is cool too. So I'm basically talking about how I should hate Gladdy, and I don't. So me being naturally suspicious, I'm wondering if this is a Goddess-whammy that you're putting on me.

Emma goes really quiet. *I don't think so? Although I'm still figuring out what I can do.*

We're all connected through you.

Believe me, Dilly, I know. I lie awake at night worrying about it. What am I? Where did I come from? How did this happen to me?

I'm clueless outside of dumb comic book ideas like meteorites and radiation and weird experiments. *If all this works, we can dig into the Jinteki archives and see what they know. We'll figure it out somehow.*

And like how my blood apparently raised someone from the dead? Dylan, it's terrifying and please tell me not to freak out. Alyse is doing her best but I think she's worried too.

Here's the thing, I tell her. *And you can check this with Alyse or Dani or even Lou. We're all here for you, no matter how weird or fucked up it gets. Team Emma for life and you're stuck with us.*

Now you're really making me cry. Get some rest because I think we'll need it.

Sleep does eventually find me, although it's restless and full of weird dreams where I'm trying to get places. Wherever I end up, it's not where I'm supposed to be. The cars sing something low and resonant, a song about travelling and distance and endless roads. It's a shame nobody else can hear it.

Traffic slowly builds until we finally reach the outskirts of Christchurch, where a familiar powder-blue car glides up alongside us.

"Oh, finally," Roxy burbles. "I've been so worried! But you've got all my little ones safe and sound, and some new friends as well. I hope you had no problems."

"We're perfectly capable of ferrying humans," Valeria says with a soft laugh. "And no problems. Roads were clear."

"The problems start now." I stretch and put my hands on the wheel so any passing cars see a pretence of a driver. "Or very soon. We're going straight to Yaxley. The only hold up is waiting for Onimaru to get here. I don't want to go in without him."

"Who the hell is Onimaru?" Gladdy asks from the back seat.

"Dilly's sword." Dani frowns. "How is he going to get back all the way from Queenstown?"

"I assume he's going to fly. He tends to turn up where I am."

"Last we saw him, he was towing about fifteen security assholes towards the lake." I get the sense Dani is enjoying showing off.

"No wonder we couldn't beat you," Gladdy says, although the curve of her mouth says she's impressed.

"Same team, remember." I watch the traffic stream past. People travelling to work and school and university, wherever the hell else people go on a daily basis. A dramatic, partly sleep-deprived portion of my brain suggests captions for these staggered panels of traffic scenes.

Most of the commuters have no idea that the CUTE MUTANTS are among them, preparing for a desperate battle.

What they fight for: control over their destiny. Who they must fight: their malicious and malevolent corporate overlords at YAX-LEY and JINTEKI. Does Dylan Taylor, also known as the renegade mutant Chatterbox, truly understand what is at stake here? Well? Do you, Dylan? Do you?

"No, Mr Claremont," I say irritably. "I have no idea."

Please stop shouting in my head, Emma says. *I'm sleepy.*

We take a long and circuitous route into town and Onimaru finally taps on Valeria's window. She rolls it down dutifully.

"They will be aware you are coming in all your righteous wrath. I took them right into the lake, but they all swam out. I considered killing them all, but they are low-level thugs and I did not consider them worthy of my time." He hums softly to himself. "Did I make the right decision?"

I think about Wraith. She's never far from my mind. There's a horrible raging part of me that wants someone to *pay* and to keep paying until I don't hurt anymore. I have this horrible vision of Oni hacking up all the security staff, slashing and stabbing until a huge slick of red drifts across the lake. They were coming to kill Gladdy and the others, and I suspect their orders are to put us down the second we outlive our usefulness.

"It's too late now," I say.

I quickly check in with Emma and make sure everyone in Frankie is ready to go. There's no way of knowing how many security personnel are in there, or how prepared they are.

So fuck it. We're going in.

The cars pull up a few doors down from the Yaxley building. I crack the door enough to let the sword out. "Oni. Get the camera for me."

"Together we shall be victorious." He speeds off. I'm not sure he knows what a security camera is, but a shower of sparks indicates he's stabbed something electrical. Someone screams in the street. Finally, a bystander has noticed the fact that a fucking sword has been flying around town.

"Here goes." Dani opens her door and we get out of the car together. I light up my costume, because why the fuck not. Nobody pays much attention. There are all kinds of weird promotional stunts these days.

Dani sighs. "I fucking hate my powers." She hits the cuff highest up on her arm. I hear her scream. It makes my stomach twist, but a split second later the door to the Yaxley building explodes inwards. There's another echoing bang as it hits the far wall.

By then we're all running. I enter first, ready to sway any waiting guns. Moodring is behind me, a sensuous, twisting creature of fang and claw. Dragon and Sourpatch are with her for long-range attacks. Marvellous runs one hand over her pain cuffs. Glowstick has both hands faintly lit up. Keepaway is tucked in right behind us, ready to evacuate us all if it turns to shit. Fetch is in the back, because her power's a little less obvious in a scrap. Goddess is there too, dancing through our minds.

The lobby is totally empty. Such an anticlimax. The security door is a buckled wreck, lying on the floor beside the elevator. There's a crack in the wall from where it hit.

"Briefing room." Marvellous smashes the door open. There's nobody there either. Have they left the building? Did they leave anything behind?

Goddess crosses to the elevator. "We need to get as much information off the servers as we can. I'd like to know what the hell they were doing with me. Might finally get some answers."

"The computer gear is on the first floor," Glowstick says. "But I'm guessing they would've killed our logins."

"Still worth a try." I'm edgy. We all are. We came in prepared for a fight, and there's nothing. It's good tactics. Keeps us off guard. The elevator doors open instantly.

"I don't like it," Marvellous says quietly to me.

"Yeah, well I fucking hate it. Something really bad is going to happen."

"Or we've already won," Marvellous suggests, but she knows how likely that outcome is.

Fetch hangs well back. "I don't want to get in a fucking box. Feels like a trap."

"We could split our forces," I say. "Some of us do the dumb risky shit and others stay behind in case the trap works in reverse."

"Or the trap has two mouths. I don't want to be separated." Marvellous looks anxiously at me.

I remember what Fetch said about Dani's fears. Me, reckless and dying, without her there to protect me. Oni senses my distress and flies into my hand.

My decision is made. "We go up. Together."

Dragon and Sourpatch go at the front, pressed up against the doors. If anyone's waiting, they'll get a face full of fire and acid.

The doors slide open onto nothing but humming racks of servers. Dragon coughs out a little tail of flame but there are no signs of movement. We inch out into the dim room. I stretch out my awareness but there's nothing receptive. Is this bad luck or have they started to figure out how I work?

Goddess and Glowstick are the smartest with computers, so they pad off into the room. If we can get access to the system, we can get Jinteki and Yaxley's files and maybe get some leverage somewhere. The goal is still to take them over, but the exact steps aren't clear.

At the far end of the room, there's a corridor that ends in offices. They're all empty aside from one which has a single laptop on a desk. The screen is dark.

"Trap," Fetch says flatly. "The most obvious fucking trap I ever saw."

"Yes, yes, but what?" I hit the doorframe in frustration. "Guns won't help them, and they know that by now. They don't want it to be a head to head battle, because they don't have anything that can fight us." I glance up at the vents along the wall. "They can't even put gas through the building and knock us all out as long as we're wearing our uniforms."

"*I'm* not wearing a uniform," Fetch points out, which is valid.

Marvellous glances around. "Keepaway can get anyone out if shit hits the fan."

"Still feels like a trap."

In the end I walk into the room and swipe my finger across the trackpad. If there *is* a trap, let's spring it and fight it, rather than tiptoeing through the dark.

The screen springs to life. There's no password or anything. There's a video already loaded up, frozen on Bancroft's face.

"Who's that asshole?" Fetch asks.

"Basically Cameron Hodge," I say. Marvellous nudges me in the back, which is code for *quit it with the X-Men references*. "Guy who pretends to be helping mutants but really hates them. He's the one with his hands on our throats who sent us after you."

Fetch glares at the screen, like she can affect him through it. "Fuck him. Let's kill him."

"If we can find him." I hit the spacebar and the video comes to life.

"Ms. Taylor, I presume." Bancroft gives his thin smile. "I'm recording this video only minutes after receiving a rather disturbing phone call from Aurora. Not only did your gang of renegades renege on our deal, but your targets have vanished from their last known location. Nobody would speculate on whether you've killed them or fled. I suspect you're coming back here." He leans back in his chair and spins to face something off-camera.

"I told you it was a trap," Fetch mutters, and I shush her.

"It's rather fascinating," Bancroft continues, even though it's not. Annoying and smug, yes. "When you underwent the battery of psychological tests during our initial assessment, it was clear you would inevitably rebel. Our specialist said you had a near-pathological refusal to submit to authority. Opinion was split on whether we should lock you up, or give you enough rope to hang yourself. We chose the latter option, if only to determine exactly what your powers are. Unfortunately, we failed to account for the fact that wherever you go, the others follow, including Ms. Kim."

"Damn fucking right," Marvellous says beside me.

"A near-pathological refusal to submit to authority." Goddess is grinning. "Does that really sound like our Dilly?"

Bancroft isn't done. "Unfortunately for all you and your grandiose plans, you are not our only irons in the fire. A group of teenagers being the first manifestation of the extrahuman phenomenon was a rather disastrous turn of events."

I figure this particular hint out quickly. "Fuck. They've made more mutants. This is really not—"

Goddess screams and puts her hands to her head, which sends Alyse into protective mode, like a spiked and furious barricade.

"There's something wrong." Emma says through gritted teeth. "They're here, but— It's terrible, Dylan. They're all so broken."

We hear the sound of a chime and the clunk of the elevator doors opening.

CHAPTER THIRTY-ONE

Everyone's jammed in the office together, starting a slo-mo freakout in response to Emma's panic. I'm still staring at the laptop, when there's a loud crack behind me and a scream. I spin around to see a long, thin tentacle stretching down the corridor. Misshapen nubs twitch at the end of it. It arrows straight for Keep-away, who's standing half-in the doorway. The tentacle and our teleporter both disappear.

"Fuck, they've taken our exit strategy." I move for the door, Oni flying over my head.

There's a brief traffic jam as we shove our way through. The corridor is empty. What the hell is going on?

Another tentacle writhes down the corridor towards us. No, not a tentacle—it's an elongated arm, whiplike and thin. The things twitching on the end are regular size fingers.

Sourpatch coughs a splattery rope of acid over it. The tentacle thrashes about, slapping against the walls and leaving gory trails, until it dissolves into a mess of blood and skin.

"There might be more where that came from." We go creeping back down the corridor, following the trail of the arm-gore like it's a navigation line in a hospital.

"Wait here," I tell Goddess. "You're the main target. Dragon and Sourpatch, check the rest of the room. Reverie, with me. Everyone else, protect Goddess."

We fan out through the room. I wish I knew the floor plan better. At least there's no sign of more goddamn tentacles. Dragon disappears around a corner ahead, but I turn towards the elevator. They must have come in that way.

Reverie puts her flute to her lips. There's something sinuous about her movements.

"Wait here," I tell her. "If anyone comes, make them a nightmare."

She nods warily.

"Let's go hunting, Oni." We creep down towards the lit-up indicators of the elevator.

The first notes of the flute sound behind me, soft and eerie. It's probably better not to see the nightmare she's conjuring. My boots squelch and when I look down, I'm walking through sticky liquid. It definitely wasn't there before. Part of me wants to reach down and see what it feels/smells/tastes like and the rest of me is screaming *eww eww eww gross*. The grossed out part wins, so I tiptoe on through it.

I'm almost at the end of the weird puddle when it moves underneath me, reforming into the gelatinous shape of a person—an older guy, with blue eyes and a scruffy little beard. He takes hold of my boot and yanks. I go flying, and my head bounces off the rack of servers so hard it makes my eyes water.

Oni flashes through the air and slits the guy's throat in one swift movement. There's no blood. There's not even split flesh. His body dissolves instead, falling back to the ground in a watery slick that surrounds me. I scramble away, sloshing through it on all fours. He reforms with his hands around my throat. I gouge at his eyes, but my hand sinks into his face like reaching into a clogged sink.

At the end of the aisle, a figure takes shape from Reverie's flute—a handsome man with a wide, easy smile. Ragged holes appear in his skin and his face flakes off in chunks.

"Gladiola." His voice is hoarse. "My precious daughter."

What the fuck is going on? Emma's voice screams in my head. *What's happening to Reverie?*

I have no idea why Reverie has chosen Gladdy's father as her flute-summoned protector, but I'm not one to question someone's own psychic pain. I'm more worried about—oh yeah—being strangled to death by this melting guy right here.

Oni flashes towards me, so close I'm scared the wicked edge of him will score my neck. There's a hideous squelching sound and the guy melts again. I lunge towards Reverie, slipping in the puddle. A hand grabs my leg. I kick out with the other. Oni slashes at the half-molten shape, hands and face form from the murk and then disappear again under Oni's onslaught.

Help, Dylan. We're stuck. Emma's on the verge of panic. *Over by the office. All of us are in some kind of... bubble or something and we can't get out.*

Coming. Had my own problems. There's a gross one who melts. Oni's trying to fight him. Reverie's fucking around with something weird. Can you tell her to make something useful?

It's not Reverie, Emma shouts back.

What does that mean?

The monster-form of Darren Quick slowly turns, moving back towards her. He puts his fingers to her face.

"Reverie!" There's ten meters between us. It's not that fucking far. I lunge for her. I need to intercept her conjuration, or at least slap the damn flute out of her hands. How the hell is her own power turning against her?

The watery asshole leaps on my back and I sprawl forwards onto my face, banging my nose on the ground.

"Oni," I shout.

He flies towards Reverie, but we're both too late.

Fetch's Dad rips out Reverie's throat in one savage, clawing motion. Oni hits him in the back, but the ghostly form of Darren Quick is already disappearing. There's no more flute music to keep him in place.

The hole he tore in Reverie is an awful pulsing gash. She collapses to the ground as I scramble the rest of the way to sprawl beside her. I try to put my hands over the wound, try to steady her head. I'm wet with blood and the remnants of the dissolving mutant.

She's gone, she's gone, Emma sobs. *Dylan, watch out. There's another mutant. Don't let her get to you.*

The liquid man is back on his feet, lurching towards me. He's the only other threat I can see. I'm dizzy and my head is aching. Oni keeps him away, stabbing and slashing through his dripping body.

To your left, Emma screams.

I look and see the other mutants trapped behind a shimmering transparent wall in the air. Dani's pressed up against it, battering with both hands.

In my lap, Reverie's hair spills over my hands, stringy with blood.

Your other left. Emma's sobbing. *Tell Oni to get the other one.*

To my actual left is a woman. She's hollow-cheeked and pale, leaning against the wall to steady herself. I can't see how she's dangerous. What's her power? I call for Oni, but my voice doesn't work.

She—

Emma's voice is replaced by a faint hissing sound. I get to my feet as if I've been hauled up by a string attached to my head.

Reverie slips out of my lap and onto the floor.

"How do *you* work then?" The voice from behind me is low and soft. I want to see who's speaking, but I can't move. "You don't have any powers. No, that's not right. How does this work? There are no *levers* in here."

Down the aisle, Oni turns slowly, as if he's sensed something horrific and is scared to look. The figure of the watery man becomes solid. He reaches for Oni, who ascends toward the ceiling.

"Hold up, Myers, you idiot." My mouth moves without me telling it to. "Let me figure this out. This one doesn't work right."

There's a person in my head that isn't me. She's running my limbs and my mouth. I'm in here too, but any control I have has been severed. I want to turn to see the other mutants, but I know they're trapped behind their wall. They're helpless to watch, like we were when Reverie died.

"Just kill the bitch," Myers says. "None of them matter except the source."

"Stay where you are or I'll make you stand in a fire until you're nothing but steam." It's my voice speaking, but I'm not saying the words. "This is the Taylor one. They want to know what makes her tick too."

"Dylan?" I hear Oni's voice in my head. "What has happened to you? There is great evil at work here."

"The sword talks."

Myers sneers. "You're a psycho, Dell. The sword isn't fucking talking. Now kill the girl and we can wrap the others up for Bancroft."

"Sword, cut this man's head off."

Oni swings cautiously down from the ceiling and hovers in between me and Myers. "I do not think you are truly Dylan. This is the work of some demon."

I want to scream at him, to tell him he's right. This isn't me. This must be what happened to Reverie. She was possessed by this mutant.

"You will do as I command." My voice is a whip.

I feel Oni cringe. This is wrong. I can't do this to him.

"We swore we would be equals," Oni whispers.

"Oh, it is romantic to play at being equals, but you were created to be a tool, Onimaru. And tools do as they are bid." It horrifies me to know that my power can do this, bending the will of this beautiful, brave creature of steel who's lived so long and seen so much.

I've never wanted this. These objects I've befriended are as real to me as the Cute Mutants. They have their own natures and to treat them as if they are subservient

372

fills me with loathing. I remember how I spoke to Bill at the end. Perhaps I'm lying to myself.

The woman in my head isn't done. "I am the one with power. I am the wielder and you are the wielded. You will bow before me and do as I command."

"Yes, master." Oni lays himself to the floor in front of me.

"Now kill me. I have failed in my task and you will give me a noble death."

"You are not Dylan." He's still prostrate before me.

"No, I'm not." The smile on my face is so wide it hurts. "But I am still your master."

Oni knows it isn't me. He would never choose to willingly follow this person. Yet there's something in my blood, in my DNA, in whatever fluke that made me, and it compels him to obey. This link between objects and me can be abused. I want to scream but my throat is not my own.

My friend lifts himself slowly off the ground. He sings something terribly, awfully sad.

"Kill me." My voice burns with command.

I want to close my eyes, but I'll have to watch as my friend plunges himself into my heart.

"Dylan," Oni sobs. "Please forgive me."

I have a few seconds left for self-loathing. Once again, I've failed. Dani's going to watch me die, helpless to stop me. It's her worst nightmare come to life.

I'm so fucking angry, and it won't save me.

"I gave you an order," my lips say.

Oni trembles in the air.

One of the racks of servers in front of me tears itself from the floor with a godawful metallic shriek. It hurtles off to my left, past my peripheral vision. I can't even turn to watch it go. An enormous sound of impact shakes the building.

I stagger and fall to my knees.

Oni halts in front of me, the tip of him frozen at my throat.

"Oni," I croak. "It's me. Please stop."

"Dylan! You have returned to yourself." He nestles himself against me, the cool steel against my cheek.

"I'm so sorry, my friend." My voice is ragged.

"There is no need for apologies. You were under the influence of a demon, who has now been slain and— ha!" Oni flashes off towards Melting Myers, who returns to puddle form and ebbs toward the elevator.

I look to the side to see the rack of servers. It's been smashed into the wall so hard there's a hole in the building. It must have weighed thousands of kilograms. There's no sign of the woman who was there.

It can only have been the work of one person.

—*you're back. You're back. Oh finally.* Emma's crying in my head and I see the mutants on the ground together.

Dani is cradled in Alyse's arms and Emma's stroking her cheeks. She looks unconscious.

I run to the bubble. It's spongy to the touch.

Dylan, she's going to be okay. Emma's voice is shaky. *You need to be the leader, which means you need to trust us to look after Dani while you get this damn bubble down.*

"Dani," I whisper. She looks so fragile, but I can see her breathing. There's something wrong with her arm. Some of the skin glistens wet and sticky and other parts are charred and flaking. I stifle a sob. She must have been in so much pain to move the giant server rack. It's not like when she flew Roxy, where we both helped her. Dani lifted thousands of kilograms all on her own. So much pain, all to save me. Because I got myself into a stupid position and—

Stop it. Emma's voice hardens. *She did what she needed to do. Now it's your turn. We're all helping her. Be an X-Man, Dylan. This is on you.*

I kiss my fingers and press them against the slippery skin of the bubble.

You've got it, Goddess.

I get to my feet.

CHAPTER THIRTY TWO

The worst part of looking for the others is walking past Reverie's body. If I'd only been faster or smart enough then—

It's not your fault, Emma tells me. *You're not responsible for everything that happens.*

You sound like Dani. I can't think of her lying in that bubble.

Oni and Melting Myers are locked in a stalemate, which leaves me free to explore. I find Dragon crouched on the floor of another bubble on the far side of the room. She's scorched half her hair off. The top of the bubble is filled with smoke. Emma still can't communicate with her as well as the rest of us, so I have to settle for lip-reading her swearing. There's nobody else here, so I head back the way I came.

I go back past the bubble with Emma and the others and give an apologetic shrug. There are more offices here, as well as another corridor that dog-legs around the edge of the room. At the very end, a middle-aged guy sits cross legged in a chair. His eyes are closed and his lips are moving. He has another bubble around him. Seems a logical assumption that this is my target.

I stride up and slam my fists against the bubble. It doesn't budge.

"Hello!" I scream. "You in there!"

There's no answer—he doesn't even flinch. I'm not going to get through. There was a fire axe on the wall behind me. Maybe if I cut through the floor underneath then the whole bubble will drop?

I turn to summon the axe, and see a pair of feet in tattered white sneakers poking out of the doorway to one of the offices. I run over with a sinking feeling. It's Sourpatch. I crouch beside her and put my fingers to her neck. There's no pulse, so I try her wrist and there's still nothing. I can't see blood or puncture wounds. Her face is still and restful.

"Maddy," I say urgently but she doesn't respond.

I try to remember the first aid lessons we did at school. I don't think you do the mouth thing anymore.

Emma, help. I'm crying in my head, even though my cheeks are dry. *I think Sourpatch is dead. She's not breathing and not moving and I don't remember how to do CPR and—*

Dilly, it's ok. You'll be fine. Put the heel of one hand between her boobs and then put the other hand over the top. Then use your whole upper body to push down. You want to do it fast, like two times a second.

I follow Emma's instructions as she says them and now I'm crying in real life, tears dropping onto my hands as I frantically push down over and over.

Emma, it's not working, I sob.

"Uh, Chatterbox. Ouch." Maddy blinks up at me. She sits up a little and coughs. A tiny bit of acid spills onto the floor and begins eating a hole.

"You're okay!" I throw my arms around her. I'm desperately relieved we didn't lose someone else. "I'm really shit at CPR and—"

Keepaway appears at the other end of the corridor, panting and wild-eyed. Their jacket has been torn to shreds and they have bloody marks on their face.

"Sorry," they pant. "I just… That… He's like an… octopus. Oh God… is Maddy okay?"

"She's fine." There's no time for fucking around. "How good is your teleporting? Like how accurate? Could you get yourself in there?" I gesture in the direction of the bubble.

Keepaway shrugs and puts their hand over their chest. They reappear inside the bubble, looking around frantically. They're right behind the guy, flailing wildly.

"They didn't take a weapon," I mutter to Maddy. "Fucking noob." I look down at her pale face. "Are you okay?"

"Just feel weak. Sick. The usual." She smiles up at me. "Is Gladdy okay?"

Inside the bubble, Keepaway punches the other mutant in the back of the neck.

The guy's eyes snap open. His mouth stops moving. The bubble disappears like it's been popped.

Dylan, you did it, Emma shouts in my head. *We're free. Where's Dani? Bring Dani.*

Yes, we're coming.

"Oni, get your ass over here."

And Ems, can you also get someone to find Kacchan? She's on the other side of the building.

Keepaway didn't hit the guy in the bubble hard enough to knock him out. Bubble Boy spins around to punch back, although Keepaway is smart enough to disappear. The guy punches air, which means he doesn't see Oni coming. The sword slides through Bubble Boy's chest, all the way up to the hilt. The guy opens and closes his mouth, collapsing forward. Oni's tip hits the ground first. The body slides down the blade in a series of slow motion jerks until he's lying on the floor.

"Maddy!" Someone hits me from the side, grabbing hold of Sourpatch's head and dragging her into their own lap. Now she's lying across us both and if I didn't know better, I'd swear Fetch has tears in her eyes.

"Ouch." Maddy coughs again. Thankfully no acid comes up.

"What did you do?" Gladdy demands. "You're supposed to look after yourself. You promised me."

"You were worried about me." Maddy smiles up and touches Fetch's downturned mouth. "I knew you liked me."

"I don't like you at all." Gladdy goes to push Maddy's hand away, except she never actually does it and their fingers end up tangled together. It's sweet and nauseating at the same time. I'm sure Dani and I are not at all like that.

"You cried when you thought I was hurt," Maddy says. "Because you're so soft."

Dani comes around the corner, cradled in the arms of a giant fortress Alyse and I flail myself out from under Maddy. I rush over to them. Dani's still unconscious but I can feel a pulse. When I place my hand to her chest, I can feel her heart beating rhythmically. "We need medical attention, then to get the fuck out of here. I know the plan was to take over, but things have gone to hell."

Fetch and Sourpatch are getting to their feet, although it's more like Fetch is a frame from which Sourpatch hangs.

"Maddy needs a doctor too." I'm lurching between emotional states after everything that's happened. "Her heart was completely stopped and I assume that's, like, not good or whatever."

"It just beats really slow." She clings tighter to Fetch. "Ever since I died, it sort of thuds every so often. Better than being dead, right?"

We stand there with varying shades of *what the fuck* written on our faces.

This is my fault, Emma says miserably.

Now you sound like me. Taking What Would Dylan Do a step too far. Whatever happened to her, it was Jinteki and Yaxley. And they're going to get theirs if we can find our way out of here.

I'm trying to get Reverie back, but it's not working. I'm feeding her my blood but—

Emma, what the hell did you do?

It's just a little cut, I swear. It's just—Jinteki used me to bring Maddy back, right?

That was in a lab! Under medical conditions! Not in a fucking battle with her throat ripped out. Jesus, Emma. Press something to the wound and we'll be there soon.

There's a shout from behind us, and we turn to see the melting man approaching. Alyse lashes out with one claw. It goes straight through him with a splash.

"You." He reforms on the floor. "Taylor. You definitely die."

Oh great, now don't I feel special? Singled out for death. We back away from his ooze and he sloshes towards us. I'm trying to come up with a plan when Dragon comes around the corner.

"You *asshole*," she shouts. "You leave Dilly alone."

We scatter as she spouts flame. The Myers-puddle evaporates in great clouds of steam. Everyone waves it frantically out of their face in case bits of him can reform, but nothing does. I have no idea if this is killing him. Maybe he'll drift out over the city to rain somewhere else. Honestly, I don't care. They came to kill us. This isn't a game, it's not training. It's literally ride or die. Soon there's only a few scattered puddles of Myers left on the ground that show no inclination to move.

"Is that all the other mutants?" I ask.

"There was a lady with fingers." Maddy pats Gladdy's cheek. "She pinched me." She pulls up her sleeve to show a pair of circular wounds that I missed when checking her.

"Fuck, so there's another one."

"At least."

Panic mode is ebbing and now I'm left feeling like shit. Except beyond all that is the frozen wasteland left by Wraith's absence. Now my heart is beating at a semi-regular speed, I don't want to leave this unfinished.

"Is Dani okay?" I ask Alyse.

"I think so. I mean she's breathing and her heartbeat is fine. I think Emma's helping."

What would Dani want? Would she want us to flee or to fight? I think she'd want this finished. Closed endings and surety.

"I was going to say we should bail." My voice is steady. "But I want to find Bancroft first."

Nobody else disagrees and so we head towards the elevator.

"Maddy, I need to tell you something." Gladdy's voice shakes. "It's bad."

"You're alive, I'm alive. I saw Keepsy in there just before." Maddy's face falls. "Reverie?"

"Gone. Something killed her. It's bad, bro. You shouldn't see it."

"She was always so nice to me though." Maddy's voice cracks. "It's not fair. Dylan, you—"

"I tried to stop it, but I was too slow. I'm sorry, I'm so fucking sorry."

I make my way back to Emma, who has her wrist pressed to Reverie's mouth. It's like the saddest fucking vampire movie ever. I run over and help her up. Reverie's body slumps at our feet. She's not coming back. We've lost another mutant.

"What use am I?" Emma's whole body is shaking.

"Don't you fucking say that." I hook her hair behind her ear for her. "We need you. You're our Goddess and you're keeping us all going."

When Emma and I get back to the others, there's another group hug. Maybe it's a dumb time to have one, with another mutant on the loose, but it hurts to breathe and we need to take a second to get through it.

"Still work to do," I say, once I can talk again. Things are not good. Reverie is dead, Marvellous is wounded, and Keepaway is gone to fuck knows where. There are still enough of us to deal with Bancroft and his soldiers, as long as there aren't any—

Fucking jump scares. A spider-looking chick leaps over the top of the server racks at us. Her fingers are serrated with points like needles. All of us scream, except the ones that aren't conscious enough to. Ferocious mutant superteam for sure.

"Her, her, she's the pinching one." Sourpatch almost leaps into Fetch's arms. I think they both swoon as hard as each other, which frankly is not that much fucking use right now.

Thankfully, it's Lou of all people who steps up. He grabs her by the wrists and they grapple. She's junkie skinny and Lou's been working out a lot, but she snaps at him with long, grey teeth. Lou lights both his hands up. I wonder, like I always do, what the dirty boy is thinking about, but Pincher screams. Lines of tension show in Lou's jaw. He squeezes tighter and tighter until he burns right through her wrists and she slumps to the ground with two cauterised stumps.

"Wow." Sourpatch's smile is delighted. "You burned her hands off!"

"What is it with you Cute Mutants and hands?" Fetch asks with a smirk.

"You should have heard him last time," I say, as Lou drops the two charred hands with a shudder. "No, cutting hands off is wrong, we're the good guys, Magneto was definitely Not Right."

"They took our parents," Lou says. I don't entirely get his point, because he hates his parents, but I think he's talking about the no rules part. If Yaxley is willing to swoop in and take civilians to jail for nothing, then the rules have shifted. "They killed Reverie." He leaves the prone figure of Pincher and walks towards the elevator.

There are no more jump scares. Once we're finally all in the elevator, crushed around the giant figure of Alyse, I lean against the back wall. Just a brief moment of peace, that's all I need.

"Where the hell did Keepaway go?" I ask. "They saved the day there."

"I don't know," Sourpatch says. "But they might not come back. Not after all this."

I scowl and close my eyes briefly. I can't really blame Keepaway, but it's a hell of a useful ability for making quick exits. I wonder if we can find them and talk them into joining permanently. Possibly Goddess can use her power to—

"Hey."

I recognise that voice. My eyes snap open to see Dani looking at me.

"My arm really fucking hurts, but I'll be fine. Goddess is doing what she can."

"I'm making it up as I go along." Emma is pale and fragile. I realise how much she's been doing to hold us all together.

Moodring reaches out an arm and pulls Goddess in alongside. "I've got you, Jingjing."

It's so sweet I almost pass out from sugar shock, but I only have eyes for one person.

"What happened to your arm?" I ask.

"I'm sorry." Glowstick has tears in his eyes. "She asked me to do it to her arm and—"

"Glowboy, we saved Dani's life," Moodring says. "Dilly will be eternally grateful."

"I already am."

"I'm amazed you assholes are still alive." Fetch is still holding Sourpatch close. "This amount of sappy bullshit, why haven't you drowned in vom? Speaking of, you got any in the tank, bro, or are you going to faint and be useless again?"

Sourpatch shrugs. "I can spit at a couple of guys. But if you have, like, a Snickers, that would be kinda useful."

"Uniforms," Marvellous says weakly. "Good for being stabbed, shit for pockets."

"People make fun of Cable's pouches, but he never got caught short," I say.

Marvellous gives a gurgle of laughter that turns into a cough.

"You are such nerds." Fetch hits the button for the top floor. The training facility. Presumably that's where Bancroft is holed up, unless he's doing this all remotely.

I don't think so. He's waiting for his fucked up new mutants to drag us before him.

I want to see his face when he realises we've won.

CHAPTER THIRTY-THREE

The doors slide open. I can't sense any guns, so maybe Yaxley has learned its lesson. The training room is empty aside from a single desk and a pair of computers. Bancroft is seated in front of them, and looks up as we enter.

His face falls. He's failed and now he has to face me. The one with the near-pathological refusal to submit to authority. I wonder if he regrets making that video.

Dragon strides into the room with me beside her. Oni whirls around us. Everyone else stays back, pausing between the doors of the elevator so they stay open.

"Bancroft, you stupid fuck." It's not the best line, but I'm exhausted and way past diplomatic.

"Ms. Taylor." He looks tired. He looks done. He *is* fucking done.

"It's time to deal." I cross to the desk. "You never had to keep us on a leash. We could have worked together, but instead you tried to kill us."

Dragon coughs delicately, and a burst of flame scorches the air above Bancroft's head.

The door to one of the assessment rooms slams open and Aurora comes out with Valen. They're alone, but maybe the building is surrounded. Maybe our parents have guns to their heads.

"I think we've proven that co-operation doesn't work." Aurora moves with that killer grace I could never quite pick up. "Call me a slow learner, but I figured that out when a sword dragged us into a lake."

"There's no point talking." Valen looks equally deadly, and I'm pretty sure she hates me even more. "They all go mad when they change. Quick could never fucking see it, obsessed bastard that he was. Always looking for the next leap forward and ignoring what we already have."

"Kill her," Fetch says from behind me. "Kill them both."

"Everyone calm down." I've got a headache, and I want this over with. Murdering everyone seems a bad way to start something new. "I don't want you to die. We never wanted anyone to die."

"I do."

I make a wild gesture for Fetch to please shut the fuck up, but she carries on.

"You, smart bitch, who says we go mad when we change? Dad promised me I'd become something better. You're right that he was obsessed with finding the next step. It was all theory though. Mad visions in his eyes. When he saw what change truly looked like, he locked me away because I'd evolved past him."

I turn so I can see Fetch, hair curling around her face and eyes furious. Sourpatch is a few steps behind, one hand partially outstretched as if she wants to pull her back.

"It's you humans who go mad in the face of change." Fetch's voice is bitter and she thrusts one arm at Bancroft. "His deepest fear is that humans will lose the coming war. That's why all of this is happening. The monstrous face of evolution must be crushed before we get too strong to be defeated."

It's all so depressing and predictable. Growing up lonely and feeling like I never fit in anywhere, the X-Men gave me hope. But there was always a dark edge to it. In my angstiest moments I used to write HATED and FEARED on the inside of my arms in marker. Even though the X-Men were powerful and they were family, the world constantly turned against them. However bad you think the analogy is stretched, mutant is a metaphor for different and people have a long history of not getting along with different.

"We like to be a democracy," I say, to Fetch or Bancroft or Aurora, I'm not really sure which. "Decide on the course of action together. You know, like what do you do when your parents are abducted? Or you're sent to kill a group of traumatised teenagers? How do you respond when someone kills your friends?"

"You should be grateful we're not a democracy," Valen sneers. "If it wasn't for the chain of command, you'd all be dead right now."

"If it wasn't for us trying to play nice, you'd be a waterlogged corpse in a lake," I snap back. "So back the fuck off."

"Enough." Bancroft sounds like he's been wading through a river of shit to get to this moment, which seems unfair given what we've had to put up with. "What's your goal here?"

"The goal is survival," Fetch says.

"No." I don't take my eyes off Bancroft. "The goal is victory."

Valen is obviously done with the chain of command. She lunges for Katie, and goddamn she's fast.

Oni is faster. The tip of him slices a line from her wrist to her shoulder and he pauses at the hollow of her neck.

"Fucking sword." Valen leaps backwards.

Katie ducks away from the soldier's grasp, spitting a burst of flame that sends the soldier staggering backwards, scorched and bleeding.

"You can't win this," I tell Valen. "We keep beating you, over and over."

"She knows she's obsolete," Fetch murmurs. "Imagine how it feels, honing yourself into a weapon your whole life. She became a warrior and then some stupid brats stumbled onto power and became something she can't compete with."

"Fuck you. All of you are nothing but vicious animals." Valen is pale and sweaty, her teeth clenched. "And you, Gladiola. You're the worst of them all. A mind cancer, getting into people's heads and destroying them from the inside. How can I be surprised, when your father was a psychopath?"

"Do you really think I'd disagree with that assessment of Dad?" Fetch laughs, but there's nothing funny. "He chose to upgrade his own daughter like I was a smartphone. At first he was smug, because he thought my adaptation would let me verbally disembowel his rivals at the negotiation table." She smirks at Bancroft. "He wanted to use me to gut Yaxley and make you an offshoot of Jinteki, even though you had the source in your control. Until he realised I wasn't his weapon to point where he wished. It went very bad after that. He didn't like my power at all when I aimed it at him." Her voice hitches, and she pauses.

Sourpatch threads her arm through Fetch's. "It's okay, Gladdy. We've got you."

"Evolution isn't intelligent. There's no grand plan moving towards an ultimate design. It makes fumbling mutations in the hope that one of them works. Dad saw me as a failure, and he despised it. He saw something wrong in my genes, some flaw deriving from himself. I was a dangerous dead-end. Every time he looked at me, I could see this in his eyes."

It's a dumb time to make a speech, but she's working through some shit. I don't know how she's even standing after everything. I guess Maddy helps, little undead slice of sunshine that she is. I take Fetch's other arm, so we're standing side by side. The monstrous presence of Alyse joins me—Dani and Emma still cradled in her arms.

We stand in a ragged line in Bancroft's office. "This is a takeover. Tell your bosses we run the show now."

Valen laughs, but she's the only one. "This is your plan? How the fuck do you imagine this works going forward? Nobody is going to leave mutants off the leash. You're signing your death warrant. They'd kill you rather than let a bunch of teenagers—"

"I've heard enough. There's nothing useful to be gleaned from them. We're done here." Bancroft taps the phone lying on the desk in front of him.

The world is obliterated by pain.

CHAPTER THIRTY-THREE

Thoughts splinter inside my head. It's hard to string them together. Whatever is happening, it's nightmarishly, horrifically bad. When I was young, I went to hospital with a broken arm. I had to choose a face on the pain scale, and young me touched the crying red face.

Young me was a fucking dumbass.

There is no face for this. There's a burning black skull. I can't believe my face has flesh on it. It's like that gif of the melty-face guy who turns into a dripping skeleton. There's no way to distinguish where or how it hurts. It's all-consuming.

The only thought that holds together and chases in circles around my brain is: make it stop.

I'm dimly aware there are others beside me.

We're all screaming.

Oni screams in my head. Somehow the pain is going down the connection between us. He's on the ground, nothing more than a piece of forged metal.

Alyse holds the unmoving figure of Dani. All this pain and Dani could probably blow the building apart, but she's not conscious enough to unleash. I want to reach out to see if she's okay but I'm as helpless as when I was possessed, unable to make any part of me respond when it's consumed by pain.

"No," someone shouts. "Fuck you. *Fuck you.*"

Katie is on her knees in front of Aurora, who's entirely unaffected and is holding a knife in one hand.

"Do it." Valen stares hard at Aurora. "She's not a sixteen year old girl. She's a fucking monster."

"Kacchan." There's blood on my lips, drooling down my front. "Fuck them. They don't—"

Dragon screams *fuck you* again. An enormous burst of flame erupts from her throat. Aurora becomes a staggering torch, wreathed in flames.

Valen takes the knife from her own belt. She hefts it a single time and throws it hard at what was once Aurora. It's probably mercy. "Fucking monsters," she says bleakly.

I grab hold of Bancroft's desk. It feels like I'm the one on fire. Beside me, Maddy is stroking Gladdy's hair and shushing her quietly. I don't know why the fuck she's not screaming. Stupid acid girl.

One final thought assembles itself inside the cauldron of my head.

They're killing us.

Fuck that. I'm not going to let them beat me down.

"Near-pathological," I snarl through bloody teeth. I can barely see through the red wash in my eyes.

"Refusal to submit." The pain has transformed Alyse into something twisted and thorny, a tangled tree-like thing that rises to the ceiling with little sign of her true form.

"To authority." Gladdy's on the floor with Maddy clinging to her.

"She means fuck you." Somehow, Emma is smiling as fat drops of blood well from her eyes. My own cheeks are sticky. Maybe my face is finally melting. It doesn't bring me any relief from the pain. I wish it did.

Valen reaches behind her and takes out another knife. She flicks her hand back to throw it. I don't know if she's going for me or Emma, but we seem the most likely targets.

"No," someone growls. "No more mutants die."

The knife leaves Valen's hand in a blur.

A whirl of silver blows past me, metal fragments riding a furious breeze. Valen's knife is knocked aside, and thuds into the floor. The rest of Dani's elegant daggers find their targets. They unstitch Valen's throat and wrists and chest. She can't speak through the blood spilling from her lips. One slippery hand tugs at the hilt jutting from the base of her throat. She swipes ineffectually at the last but it drills itself into her eye. There's an audible thunk as it hits bone. What used to be Valen collapses on the floor.

Dani is in Alyse's arms. Face streaked with blood and in terrible pain—but alive. For now. Her eyes flutter closed again and I grind my teeth.

Somehow, I have to find the strength to end this.

I reach across the desk for Bancroft's phone. I'm too slow and he scoops it up. He retreats across the room, clutching it to his chest. Too goddamn far to walk. Why won't my legs work? I try to move one, but it buckles underneath me and I fall, smacking my head on the edge of the desk.

I drag myself up again, inch by furious fucking inch.

"Maddy." Fetch coughs blood. "Why the hell are you not bleeding?"

"I don't know!" Sourpatch blinks wide brown eyes.

"Can you walk?" I spit.

"Yes, but I need to look after Gladdy."

"Fuck that." Fetch makes a noise between a laugh and a scream. "Get the phone off the asshole and make this stop!"

"Oh, sorry! I've been trying to keep you alive."

Maddy scurries over to Bancroft and wrenches the phone out of his grasp. She peers at the screen and stabs her finger down.

The pain disappears instantly, although I'm still shaky and weak. It's such a relief to have it gone. I want to fold myself into a crumpled thing on the ground and have a proper cry, but we're not at the end of the road yet. I look around at the Cute Mutants, who all look as fucked as me. It's like we've escaped a horror movie, blood dripping from our eye-sockets.

I check on Dani, who's coming around again.

"Did it work?" Her voice is faint.

"Yes, you saved us all." I try and wipe the blood from her face, but I only smear it everywhere.

"I'll be fine," she insists. "Mostly. I saved us, so kiss me while I'm still high on Emma."

I obey, because what else can you do in a situation like this? It's gross and bloody and sore, but it's sweet as well.

Everyone else is busy glaring at Maddy who's still holding Bancroft's phone.

"Maddy, if that *ever* happens again, please actually save our lives rather than pining over me, or I swear to Christ I will throw you out a window." Fetch is shaking and I'm not sure if it's rage or relief.

"I thought you were all being dramatic." Maddy shrugs.

I wipe bloody tears from my cheeks. "Yes, this was me showing off."

Maddy shuffles her feet. "Gladdy was making this little whimpering noise and I thought about what would happen if she died and I wasn't holding her to give her a farewell, because you know that I really—"

Fetch's glare gets even more intense. "If you say anything sappy, you incandescently annoying girl, I will—"

"Just kiss already." I take the phone from Maddy and toss it to Emma.

"I don't want to kiss her," Fetch shouts from behind me.

Maddy grins at me and rolls her eyes, because you don't need a power that lets you see the secret truth in people to know that's the dumbest lie of all the lies we've heard today.

"Any more tricks?" I ask Bancroft.

He's grey and looking at the ground.

Maddy spits in his face, a tiny dribble that leaves a red and bleeding hole in his cheek. He shrieks in pain, and scrubs at it with the sleeve of his well-tailored jacket, but it only disintegrates the fabric too.

We form a loose semi-circle around Bancroft.

"He's scared of the Americans." Fetch peers up into his eyes. "He knows he's failed and he's scared of the consequences. He wanted to keep us under control, so he'd have some autonomy here, and now he's worried about—"

"Quietus." He stiffens as he says it, like they'll smite him from orbit.

"I have no idea what that means." I glare at Fetch, as if it's somehow her fault.

"The sword of God. The holy warrior of heaven. The archangel Michael." He says it as if it should mean something. "I was looking out for you this whole time. You don't see it, but you should. If Quietus find out what's happened here, they'll come and they'll bring you to heel."

"They can try," I say.

"There is a war coming." His eyes are wild. "It's inevitable you'll lose. I was trying to *protect* you. It would have been far better if you were on the side of humanity, but you threw that away."

"But we're not human," Emma says gently and it gives me a chill.

"No," Bancroft is pale. "You're not. You think you've won, but I have contingencies inside contingencies."

It seems odd that he'd tell us this, but Gladdy is staring intently at him.

"Is this you?"

"Of course it's me, Chatterbox. You think he'd spill his innermost secrets just for you?"

"We have information on the servers that details all your crimes." Bancroft's words spill out fast. "Some is real and some is faked. When others from Yaxley come to see what's been done here, they'll have no choice but to lock you all up next to Mr. Firestone. Then you'll be neatly tidied away for when Quietus swoops down on us."

"That sounds like a really shitty narrative." I glance at Gladdy. "Can you make him get rid of it?"

"I can make him kill himself. Blow his brains out."

"It would help if he deleted this incriminating shit first. The real *and* the fake stuff." I nudge her gently. "Like if you had the tiniest smidge more subtlety in your powers it would—"

"Fuck off, Chatterbox." She nudges me back. "Okay, Mr. Bancroft. We know you're scared. You also feel like a colossal failure. At the start, you thought you could do this. Oh, it's kind of sweet. You imagined yourself as the father, with this little brood of misfit children. Your own daughter was such a disappointment, wasn't she? Such high hopes, and all of them squandered. Do you really want your adoptive brood to be thrown into a pit?"

Bancroft is mesmerised, swaying slightly as he stares at Gladdy. "No," he whispers. "But you're so terribly dangerous."

"Dangerous and lost," Gladdy says. "We're poor wandering girls in need of someone to take care of us. I'm sure if you explain how pathetic we are to your masters, they'll give us a second chance."

"Monsters." Bancroft gives us his deeper truth. "You're not girls, you're monsters."

Gladdy grimaces at me and shifts direction. "We're monsters that have beaten you repeatedly. We've crushed your soldiers and your mutants. Next, your masters will come. What will they think of you, their strong and constant man? What will they say when they find you've only won because you lied and faked information? The best deception can still be uncovered, and it will inevitably show you even weaker than you already are."

"I can't lose to you," Bancroft whispers. "I'll be a laughing stock. Defeated by teenagers."

"Asshole," I sigh, but is it really a fucking surprise?

Fetch leans in close. "It'll look worse if they find out you tried to cheat and still lost."

Bancroft's shoulders slump, and his defences collapse. Emma brings over his laptop. He gives her the password and together they delete the information from the server. Once it's done, he starts crying quietly.

"What is it now?" Fetch asks irritably.

"It's so sad," he whimpers. "Even when wild animals get put down."

"Everyone will look at you and know you were defeated. Your name will be a synonym for failure. There's only one way to escape without being a mockery of a man." Fetch's mouth is against Bancroft's ear and I see his expressions shift.

He walks down to a window at the far end of the building. Fetch follows him.

"The window won't open." His mouth is wrenched out of shape like the weary face emoji.

"Run into it," Fetch suggests. "Take a good long runup and—"

"Wait," I call. "Stop. You shouldn't do this."

"No." Fetch whirls on me and for a second I'm scared she'll use her powers, but it's bare-knuckle anger instead. "We don't need your bleeding heart now. You heard him. We're monsters, we're failures. He'll turn against us. He'll—"

"I know." Calm runs through me. The frozen wasteland inside me no longer feels cold. I am at peace inside it, my bare feet ghost-light in the snow. "We don't want any hint of blood on your hands, Gladiola. You're going to be head of Jinteki Research Laboratories. Inherit from your father."

"You'll do it?" Fetch's gaze is unsure.

"First, we vote on it. All in favour?"

Every hand goes up. Maybe it's exhaustion, maybe it's fucking trauma from having been tracked and threatened and almost killed. Maybe it's Reverie's body on the floor below, or Wraith floating out to sea on a burning boat. Either way, there's not a single person that thinks Bancroft should live through this. We're not a group of angry girls and a soft boy anymore, but we're not monsters either. We're something in between, or a little of both.

Bancroft is the real monster, and if he had his way, we'd be thrown into darkness.

"I can do it," Oni says softly. "It doesn't have to be your hand."

"We'll do it together."

His hilt nestles into my palm. He's so different from Batty, who was gentle and kind and too good for this world. Onimaru Kunitsuna is old and he's seen a world of shit. He knows when it's time for blood to be shed.

I walk up behind Bancroft and draw the sword across his throat.

There's not a second of hesitation. Blood sprays out onto the floor and spatters the window in a fine mist. There's a moment where gravity is suspended, and then Bancroft hits the floor.

It's done. I don't really feel anything, standing in the middle of swirling snow with flakes alighting on my shoulders and evaporating when they touch the warm blood on Oni's blade. I'm sure some feeling will come.

Dani crosses to me. She's pale and sweat sheens her forehead. The skin on her arm looks like you could peel it off. "Are you okay?" She looks into my eyes.

"I don't know." I put my arm around her waist and let her sag against me. "I think it's mostly a relief."

"We survived," Dani looks down at her arm. "Mostly at least."

"Doesn't it hurt?"

"Yeah, it hurts quite a fucking lot."

"Probably should be calling an ambulance rather than standing here professing my love."

"It's on the way," Alyse calls. "Profess away, you gross lovebirds."

Dani clings tighter. "I think you're going to have to hold me up. I'll try and swoon gracefully." She lasts about fifteen more seconds before she loses consciousness, but I carry her down to meet the ambulance.

Once I'm sitting in the back of it with Dani, a nervous paramedic, and Emma, I scroll through Bancroft's contacts.

"It's time to make a call."

EPILOGUE

It's nearly a week later when we get an official response from Yaxley head office. In the meantime, we've claimed both the Yaxley and Jinteki offices for ourselves. As the official new CEO, Gladiola Quick gets to call the shots.

We spend a lot of time in Jinteki's hospital suites. I still don't trust many people, so each operation takes place under the watchful gaze of at least three mutants as well as Oni. Everyone gets patched up as much as possible. Sourpatch is in what the doctors call an *indeterminate state*, which means they have no fucking idea how she's up and walking around. Another miracle at the hands of our Goddess. Emma insists on giving Reverie a blood transfusion but it does nothing.

We get into the Jinteki systems and even *they* don't know how Maddy's alive. There are hundreds of pages of notes, which boil down to needing more research. Aside from that, we don't let a doctor anywhere near Emma. If anyone's stupid enough to walk in the vicinity of her with a syringe, they find something much sharper at their throats. Oni takes his role as Emma's protector very fucking seriously.

Far worse than being cut open—or watching your friends get cut open—is going to Bianca's funeral. Her mother is there, along with a bunch of girls from school and most of Queer Club that she went to with Lou. We slink in at the back and say nothing to anyone. Yaxley has obviously fed them a story—something about an accident while on a school trip to an industrial site. It sounds completely ridiculous as a cover-up, but it doesn't matter. Bianca is gone and we can't bring her back. At the funeral I hold myself together, although afterwards I sit in the back seat of Roxy in my one black dress. Dani holds me while I shake and fall apart.

We also have to make a call to Reverie's parents. It's not something anyone should have to do, especially when most of what you say is lies, and the single truth is what undoes them. Gladdy does most of the talking. She's good at it, when she's not trying to rip your world apart.

"How do you survive it?" Gladdy asks me afterwards.

"I don't know that you do. I think Wraith is always going to leave a hole in me. I don't know if it'll ever heal, and I don't know if it should."

"It sucks." She glares out the window as if the whole world should acknowledge it. "The stupid thing is we barely knew her. Another girl in a cage beside us. Yet they stole the chance to get to know her."

"She had amazing hair and she was kick-ass on the flute." Maddy touches Gladdy's shoulder lightly. "She was our mutant sib and we'll miss her."

Gladdy doesn't say anything else. I leave her with her tears.

With these awful things out of the way, we're ready for the final part of our plan. The new Yaxley CEO is scheduled to arrive at our building at four in the afternoon. Theoretically, Yaxley is coming to fold their hand and submit to the might of Jinteki. I have my doubts, but I'm not telling anyone. I presume Gladdy can see them on my face.

We wait in the lobby of the Yaxley building, which has been speedily repaired by contractors working for the many, many Jinteki dollars left behind by Gladdy's father.

Fetch is dressed in a stupidly expensive suit. I don't believe there are humans in the world that spend that much money on clothes. When I said that, Fetch called me a trash baby, which a) true and b) fuck off, Gladdy, you rich asshole. It looks good on her, I'll give her that. Maddy stands next to her, dressed in a more subdued suit which is still more expensive than should be allowed. Officially, she's Gladdy's bodyguard, but I think we all know she's more than that—not that Gladdy would ever admit it this side of the heat death of the universe.

Most of the mutants are in Yaxley uniforms with their masks up. It makes them look menacing and anonymous. It's everyone who survived, with the exception of Keepaway, who has, well, kept away ever since the big fight. I'm still holding out hope they'll come back.

Dani and I aren't in uniform. We're wearing jeans and singlet tops. It's partly to show off Dani's brand new metal arm. Whatever Lou did when he gave her enough pain to move an entire server rack was more permanent than any of us thought, so now she has a replacement.

I'm in two minds about it. It's not as smooth and warm and sexy as her flesh and blood arm, but it is many different kinds of badass and I'd be lying if I said it wasn't hot. She's still getting used to it, but it gives her one hell of a right hook.

The other reason for the singlets is to show off the tattoos on our biceps. They say WRAITH and REVERIE. There's a line underneath the second name. It's supposed to mean *this far and no further* like we'll never accept another mutant death.

I'm terrified we're going to be wrong.

Oni hangs at my shoulder. He's singing his mournful dirge again. I wonder what it means.

I reach out to take Dani's hand, and squeeze her fingers.

"I love you, you impossible idiot," she tells me.

"I love you too."

The front door makes a buzzing sound and swings open with a clunk.

Dani and I unclasp our hands and place them behind our backs. We're supposed to look professional.

Three uniformed people walk into the room wearing Yaxley suits with blank masks. They don't have guns, which is a good sign. They do have knives, and I'm tempted to talk them into my possession, but it would be a pure fuck you move, and that would be wrong.

The new arrivals look around the room, checking for threats. Given that we're the most powerful weapons here, I'm not sure what they expect to do about it. One of them speaks into a wrist-mic and they fan out around the door.

A middle-aged woman enters, dressed in what looks like another extremely expensive outfit. Her eyes go straight to Gladdy, in a suit recognise suit moment.

"Ms. Quick." Her voice is surprisingly deep. She walks comfortably across the lobby, as if all of this is completely normal.

Maddy steps into her path, and gives her a twisted smile. She's painted her lips this lurid and glistening green, which is such a fucking baller move I want to applaud. "Ms. Durant, please allow me to do a quick patdown for security reasons." Her green lips stretch wider.

Durant halts. The three masked figures whisper among themselves.

Maddy pats her down slowly. We talked about this, and Gladdy made Maddy watch a video on YouTube about fifty times. It's all part of the professional experience.

Maddy holds out her hand. "We'll take your phone, in case you get tempted to use Leash."

Leash is the app Bancroft used to try and melt our brains. According to our tame Jinteki scientists, it was an implant that should have killed us all near-instantly. It wasn't picked up by any of our scans because it was dormant, or some scientific explanation I tuned out of, but Emma apparently understands.

The fact it didn't work properly is something nobody can explain. I'm convinced it was Goddess, because things related to her keep on mutating. We've all had our Leash implants removed, one at a time, and tested that the app doesn't work. This is all being kept very quiet from Durant or anyone else. It's better for them to think they have a last resort against us. Let them think the monsters are tame.

Durant sighs and hands Maddy her phone. She taps her pant leg with pink fingernails.

Maddy gives her a nod and steps back into line with Gladdy. Then she ruins the moment by flashing me this ridiculously cheesy smile. I give her the most discreet eye roll I can.

"Welcome. I'm looking forward to re-establishing a relationship between our two companies. I'm Gladiola Quick, the new CEO of Jinteki Research Laboratories. I believe you knew my father."

"I did. I also knew Eric Bancroft extremely well before his demise."

"Terrible, what happened to him," Gladdy sighs. "Perhaps you can explain why he was creating extrahumans of his own. These terribly unfortunate souls were responsible for the death of Charuka Lakmal, as well as Eric Bancroft and his entire security team."

"Yes." Durant's lips press into a line. "There will be much to discuss."

"I'm sure." Gladdy can see Durant's weaknesses and it makes her relaxed. She's used none of the code words that might signal suspicion or attack. Her manner is easy and friendly as she gestures over to Dani and me. "These are the heads of our field team, Ms. Taylor and Ms. Kim. They've replaced Aurora, who also sadly perished in the incident."

Durant doesn't shake either of our hands. "Yes. I've read the reports on you."

"Bancroft's reports." Gladdy waves dismissively. "He was unstable at the end, but we shouldn't let his paranoia and bigotry get in the way of a productive relationship. We've tried things the difficult way, Ms. Durant. This could be a new era of co-operation and understanding. Human and mutant, working together as equals. Show the world—show America—what the future can look like."

"Yes." Durant looks at Gladdy, who is entirely in control of the situation. "Let's see what the future holds."

Dani leans against me very slightly as Gladdy leads Durant towards the briefing room. Her hand finds mine. *Fuck looking like professional bodyguards*, is what her body language says, and I agree. We're living by the mutant code, which has a bit near the top about making out whenever we feel like it.

Wow, Emma says. *Why is it so hard for you two to keep your hands to yourself?*

This coming from the one whose girlfriend carries her around like a big soft mutant chair.

Rude. She laughs. *That went better than expected, didn't it? We might jump this hurdle without bloodshed after all.*

Let's hope so. I try not to shudder. *But if there's a war coming, we need to be prepared to fight.*

ACKNOWLEDGEMENTS

Once again, so many people have helped with getting this out into the world. This series couldn't happen without so many talented people who've given their time, energy, and support. Sorry, I'm as soft as Pillow.

First my partner, who puts up with my writing obsession, my moods and insecurities, and still supports me relentlessly and enables me to go on this crazy journey. To my family, too, who believe in me, inspire me, and make me laugh.

Writing a sequel was a challenge in a whole new way, and I was lucky that so many people lined up to assist me. Emma Jun and Sarah read the chaos of my first draft and told me what the good bits were. Amanda M. Pierce once again helped me find the places to deepen the story. Lynn Jung shone new light on Dani and brought her to even more vivid life. Leta Patton, Shannon Ives, Jennifer Elrod, Ayida Shonibar, and Leah Tesch all helped streamline the story into its final shape. Then C.J. Listro and Rebecca LaValle swooped in like superheroes to help me with line edits and make me realise I still don't know how to use commas.

I feel wildly lucky to count these people as my friends. Shannon, Amanda and Emma in particular let me throw way too many chaotic ideas at them, and help me sort through the trash to find the best parts. I used to think writing was a solitary activity, but I've come to realise that having a writing gang of my own makes it all so much better.

Speaking of trash and gangs, once again those chaotic spirits in team trash kept me going through this insane process of attempting to publish a book every two months. Whether it's with shouting, memes, sprints, jokes or cursed gifs—that Thomas one is real, and it's horrific—this group is what every writer should have. To Andy, Crystal, Leah, Mallory, Melody, Michelle, Monica, Nat, Nina, SinJ and SoftJ—you'll conquer this world and probably others, and I can't wait to watch you do it.

Thanks to @kassiocoralov for the incredible cover, to G for the beautiful formatting, and to Maddy, Skye and Amy who've been constant boosters.

Finally, thanks to everyone else who's supported me and the mutants. Dylan and the gang live rent-free in my head, and watching them go out into the world has been incredibly weird and cool. I hope you stick with us, because we're going to wild places and the best is yet to come.

ABOUT THE AUTHOR

SJ Whitby lives in New Zealand with their partner, as well as various children and animals. They are predictably obsessed with X-Men and spend too much of their free time writing, plotting out way too many sequels, spin-offs and parallel universes. Perhaps they take their X-Men fandom too seriously.

You can find them on Twitter at @sjwhitbywrites.

Milton Keynes UK
Ingram Content Group UK Ltd.
UKHW041507221123
433060UK00006B/642